BALTIMORE NOIR

BALTIMORE NOIR

EDITED BY LAURA LIPPMAN

AKASHIC BOOKS
NEW YORK

Series concept by Tim McLoughlin and Johnny Temple

Published by Akashic Books
©2006 Laura Lippman

Baltimore map by Sohrab Habibion

ISBN-13: 978-1-888451-96-2
ISBN-10: 1-888451-96-3
Library of Congress Control Number: 2005934820
All rights reserved

Fourth printing
Printed in Canada

Akashic Books
PO Box 1456
New York, NY 10009
Akashic7@aol.com
www.akashicbooks.com

Also in the Akashic Noir Series:

Forthcoming:

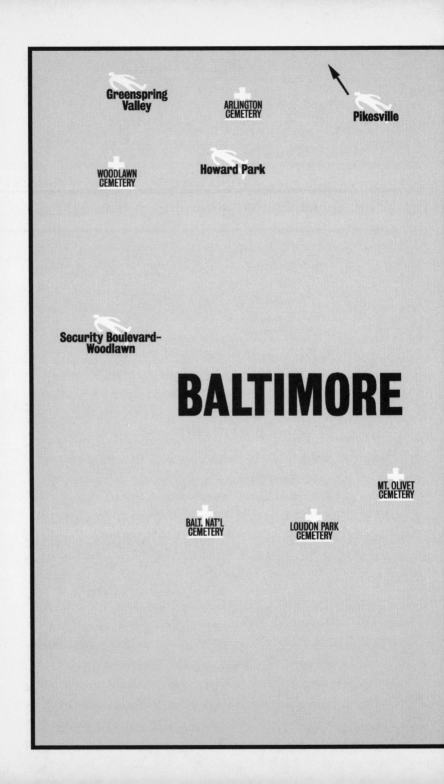

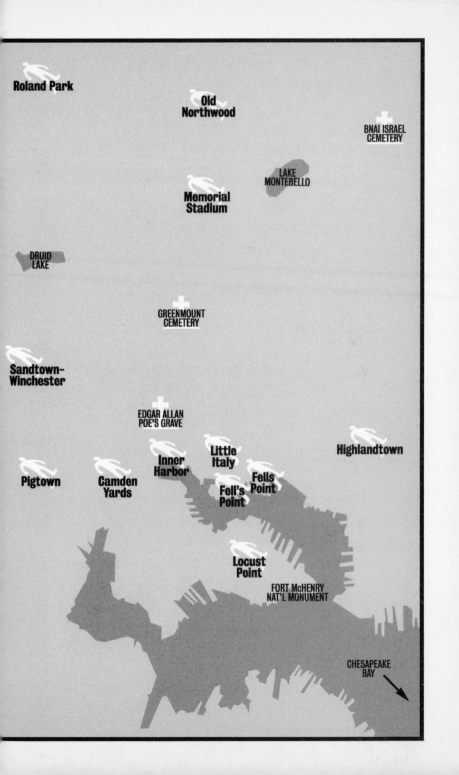

TABLE OF CONTENTS

PART III: THE WAY THINGS NEVER WERE

INTRODUCTION
GREETINGS FROM CHARM CITY

I belong here," F. Scott Fitzgerald wrote of Baltimore, "where everything is civilized and gay and rotted and polite. And I wouldn't mind a bit if in a few years Zelda and I could snuggle up together under a stone in some old graveyard here. That is a really happy thought and not melancholy at all."

Fitzgerald was far from the first or last writer to feel a kinship with this mid-Atlantic city, although not all would have worded their sentiments as he did. Given that it was his wife's psychiatric problems that drew him here, Fitzgerald, who belongs more to St. Paul than to Baltimore, can be forgiven his cynical view.

As it happened, the couple ended up buried in suburban Rockville, Maryland, but Fitzgerald's Baltimore roots went deeper than Zelda's consultations with the city's best psychiatrists. He was a descendant of Francis Scott Key, who penned our unsingable national anthem, a song that Baltimoreans defend only out of civic loyalty. We can't sing it either, but we love to shout the "OHHHHHHHHHH" at baseball games, in celebration of our beloved Orioles. Which is odd because a *true* Baltimorean, one who speaks in the local accent known as Bawlmerese, refers to the team as the Erioles, as surely as he calls a blaze a "far" and "warshes dishes in the zink." (Baltimore joke: Why were the three wise men covered with ashes when they came to visit the Baby

Jesus? Because they came from a *far*. Guess you had to be there. Correction: Guess you have to be *here*.)

Edgar Allan Poe lived here, got a boost to his literary ambitions by winning a prize here, and, far more famously, died here, creating twin mysteries—the truth of what happened to him in October 1849, and the identity of the "Poe Toaster," who visits the original Poe gravesite on the writer's birthday, January 19, leaving behind three red roses and a half-bottle of cognac.

John Dos Passos passed time on the North Side, as did Gertrude Stein. (With Alice B. Toklas, of course.) Ogden Nash punned and rhymed here. Dorothy Parker's ashes were kept in a file drawer here, but only because Baltimore is the national headquarters of the NAACP, which was willed her remains.

H.L. Mencken avowed that he knew of no better place to live. Across Union Square from Mencken's house, a boy named Russell Baker grew up. On nearby Stricker Street, Dashiell Hammett lived for a while as well, a trifecta of talent that should put Southwest Baltimore on any map of literary landmarks.

As for Baltimore's noir pedigree—it was here that Hammett worked as a Pinkerton agent, reporting to an office in the Continental building, a downtown high-rise that happened to feature a decorative motif of carved falcons. Painted gold now, but thought to be black in Hammett's time. Am I claiming that the Maltese Falcon was born here? Prove that it wasn't.

Today, Baltimore is home to award-winning writers such as Anne Tyler, Madison Smartt Bell, Stephen Dixon, and Taylor Branch. But perhaps one of the more interesting developments in Baltimore's recent literary history is the large number of crime writers that have emerged—many of them from the daily newspaper, the *Sun*, and most of them represented in this volume. No one is sure why *Sun* writers so often turn to homicide, fictional and factual; the theories are speculative at best, if not downright libelous. But it happens that *Sun* reporters have won the Edgar, Anthony, Agatha, Nero Wolfe, Macavity, Shamus, Barry, John Creasey, and Steel Dagger awards for their novels and short stories. Very fitting for a newspaper where James M. Cain once worked.

But then, to live in Baltimore—Bulletmore, Murderland, according to one famous piece of graffiti—is to be aware of killing; we have not enjoyed the sharp declines in homicide rates achieved by cities such as Boston and New York. We remain steadfastly in the top five, per capita, year in and year out. Statistically, two people died while I was working on this foreword.

Baltimore also has an odd geographic distinction. It is one of only two major U.S. cities that lies in no county. (St. Louis is the other.) Landlocked on every side but one, which is water, it cannot expand or annex. Squeezed this way, it is a perfect setting for noir, which depends on an almost Darwinian desperation among its players.

The Centers for Disease Control will tell you that Baltimore is the off-and-on capital of syphilis, but the true local malady is nostalgia, a romanticizing of our past that depends on much glossing and buffing, as if our history was just another set of marble steps to be cleaned. I have never forgotten listening to two colleagues at the *Sun* discuss the racism inherent in our celebration of the habits and attitudes of the Eastern European immigrants who helped to make Baltimore a great city. "Ask Thurgood Marshall how fondly he remembers Baltimore," one said of the late African-American Supreme Court justice, who grew up here. "Ask him if any waitresses every called him *hon.*"

The writers in this collection eschew nostalgia without sacrificing affection. They confront the full irony that is Charm City, a place where you can go from the leafy beauty of the North Side neighborhoods to the gutted ghettos of the West Side in less than twenty minutes, then find your way to the revamped Inner Harbor in another ten. Homegrown Baltimore philosopher Virginia Baker once said: "If it ain't right and it ain't decent, stay the hell away from it." Alas, Virginia. Baltimore's *not* right. Fitzgerald's claim aside, it's hardly even polite anymore. But for a Baltimore writer, escape is the one concept where the imagination steadfastly fails. We belong here.

Laura Lippman
February 2006
Baltimore, Maryland

PART I

THE WAY THINGS USED TO BE

EASY AS A-B-C

BY LAURA LIPPMAN

Locust Point

Another house collapsed today. It happens more and more, especially with all the wetback crews out there. Don't get me wrong. I use guys from Mexico and Central America, too, and they're great workers, especially when it comes to landscaping. But some other contractors aren't as particular as I am. They hire the cheapest help they can get and the cheapest comes pretty high, especially when you're excavating a basement, which has become one of the hot fixes around here. It's not enough, I guess, to get the three-story rowhouse with four bedrooms, gut it from top to bottom, creating open, airy kitchens where grandmothers once smoked the wallpaper with bacon grease and sour beef. It's not enough to carve master bath suites from the tiny middle rooms that the youngest kids always got stuck with. No, these people have to have the full family room, too, which means digging down into the old dirt basements, sending a river of mud into the alley, then putting in new floors and walls. But if you miscalculate by even an inch—*boom.* You destroy the foundation of the house. Nothing to do but bring the fucker down and start carting away the bricks.

It's odd, going into these houses I knew as a kid, learning what people have paid for sound structures that they consider mere shells, all because they might get a sliver of a water view from a top-floor window or the ubiquitous rooftop deck.

Yeah, I know words like ubiquitous. Don't act so surprised. The stuff in books—anyone can learn that. All you need is time and curiosity and a library card, and you can fake your way through a conversation with anyone. The work I do, the crews I supervise, that's what you can't fake because it could kill people, literally kill them. I feel bad for the men who hire me, soft types who apologize for their feebleness, whining: *I wish I had the time.* Give those guys a thousand years and they couldn't rewire a single fixture or install a gas dryer. You know the first thing I recommend when I see a place where the "man of the house" has done some work? A carbon monoxide detector. I couldn't close my eyes in my brother-in-law's place until I installed one, especially when my sister kept bragging about how handy he was.

The boom in South Baltimore started in Federal Hill twenty-five years ago, before my time, flattened out for a while in the '90s, but now it's roaring again, spreading through south Federal Hill and into Riverside Park and all the way up Fort Avenue into Locust Point, where my family lived until I was ten and my grandparents stayed until the day they died, the two of them, side by side. My grandmother had been ailing for years and my grandfather, as it turned out, had been squirreling away various painkillers she had been given along the way, preparing himself. She died in her sleep and, technically, he did, too. A self-induced, pharmaceutical sleep, but sleep nonetheless. We found them on their narrow double bed, and the pronounced rigor made it almost impossible to separate their entwined hands. He literally couldn't live without her. Hard on my mom, losing them that way, but I couldn't help feeling it was pure and honest. Pop-pop didn't want to live alone and he didn't want to come stay with us in the house out in Linthicum. He didn't really have friends.

Mee-maw was his whole life and he had been content to care for her through all her pain and illness. He would have done that forever. But once that job was done, he was done, too.

My mother sold the house for $75,000. That was a dozen years ago and boy did we think we had put one over on the buyers. Seventy-five thousand! For a house on Decatur Street in Locust Point. And all cash for my mom, because it had been paid off forever. We went to Hausner's the night of the closing, toasted our good fortune. The old German restaurant was still open then, crammed with all that art and junk. We had veal and strawberry pie and top-shelf liquor and toasted grandfather for leaving us such a windfall.

So imagine how I felt when I got a referral for a complete redo at my grandparents' old address and the real estate guy tells me: "She got it for only $225,000, so she's willing to put another hundred thousand in it and I bet she won't bat an eyelash if the work goes up to $150,000."

"Huh," was all I managed. Money-wise, the job wasn't in my top tier, but then, my grandparents' house was small even by the neighborhood's standards, just two stories. It had a nice-size backyard, though, for a rowhouse. My grandmother had grown tomatoes and herbs and summer squash on that little patch of land.

"The first thing I want to do is get a parking pad back here," my client said, sweeping a hand over what was now an overgrown patch of weeds, the chain-link fence sagging around it. "I've been told that will increase the value of the property ten, twenty thousand."

"You a flipper?" I asked. More and more amateurs were getting into real estate, feeling that the stock market wasn't for them. They were the worst of all possible worlds, panicking at every penny over the original estimate, riding my ass.

You want to flip property for profit, you need to be able to do the work yourself. Or buy and hold. This woman didn't look like the patient type. She was young, dressed to the nines, picking her way through the weeds in the most impractical boots I'd ever seen.

"No, I plan to live here. In fact, I hope to move in as quickly as possible, so time is more important to me than money. I was told you're fast."

"I don't waste time, but I don't cut corners," I said. "Mainly, I just try to make my customers happy."

She tilted her head, gazing at me through naturally thick and black eyelashes. It was the practiced look of a woman who had been looking at men from under her eyelashes for much of her life, sure they would be charmed. And, okay, I was. Dark hair, cut in one of those casual, disarrayed styles, darker eyes that made me think of kalamata olives, which isn't particularly romantic, I guess. But I really like kalamata olives. With her fair skin, it was a terrific contrast.

"I'm sure you'll make me very happy," was all she said.

I guess here is where I should mention that I'm married, going on eighteen years and pretty happily, too. I realize it's a hard concept to grasp, especially for a lot of women, that you can be perfectly happy, still in love with your wife, maybe more in love with your wife than you've ever been, but it's been eighteen years and a young, firm-fleshed woman looks up at you through her eyelashes and it's not a crime to think: *I like that.* Not: *I'd like to hit that,* which I hear the young guys on my crews say. Just: *I like that, that's nice, if life were different I'd make time for that.* But I had two kids and a sweet wife, Angeline, who'd only put on a few pounds and still kept her hair blond and long, and was pretty appreciative of the life my work had built for the two of us. So I had no agenda, no scheme going in. I was just weak.

But part of Deirdre's allure was how much she professed to love the very things whose destruction she was presiding over, even before I told her that the house had belonged to my grandparents. She exclaimed over the wallpaper in their bedroom, a pattern of tiny yellow roses, even as it was steamed off the walls. She ran a hand lovingly over the banister, worn smooth by my younger hands, not to mention my butt a time or two. The next day it was gone, yanked from its moorings by my workers. She all but composed an ode to the black-and-white tile in the single full bath, but that didn't stop her from meeting with Charles Tile Co. and choosing a Tuscany-themed medley for what was to become the master bath suite. (Medley was their word, not mine. I just put the stuff in.)

She had said she wanted the job fast, which made me ache a little, because the faster it went, the sooner I would be out of her world. But it turned out she didn't care about speed so much once we got the house to the point where she could live among the ongoing work—and once her end-of-the-day inspections culminated with the two of us in her raw, unfinished bedroom. She was wilder than I had expected, pushing to do things that Angeline would never have tolerated, much less asked for. In some part of my mind, I knew her abandon came from the fact that she never lost sight of the endpoint. The work would be concluded and this would conclude, too. Which was what I wanted as well, I guess. I had no desire to leave Angeline or cause my kids any grief. Deirdre and I were scrupulous about keeping our secret, and not even my longtime guys, the ones who knew me best, guessed anything was up. To them, I bitched about her as much as I did any client, maybe a little more.

"Moldings?" my carpenter would ask. "Now she wants moldings?" And I would roll my eyes and shrug, say: "Women."

"Moldings?" she asked when I proposed them.

"Don't worry," I told her. "No charge. But I saw you look at them."

And so it was with the appliances, the countertops, the triple-pane windows. I bought what she wanted, billed for what she could afford. Somehow, in my mind, it was as if I had sold the house for $225,000, as if all that profit had gone to me, instead of the speculator who had bought the house from my mother and then just left it alone to ripen. Over time, I probably put ten thousand of my own money into those improvements, even accounting for my discounts on material and my time, which was free. Some men give women roses and jewelry. I gave Deirdre a marble bathroom and a beautiful old mantle for the living room fireplace, which I restored to the wood-burning hearth it had never been. My grandparents had one of those old gas-fired logs, but Deirdre said they were tacky and I suppose she was right.

Go figure—I've never had a job with fewer complications. The weather held, there were no surprises buried within the old house, which was sound as a dollar. "A deck," I said. "You'll want a rooftop deck to watch the fireworks." And not just any deck, of course. I built it myself, using teak and copper accents, helped her shop for the proper furniture, outdoor hardy but still feminine, with curvy lines and that *verdi gris* patina she loved so much. I showed her how to cultivate herbs and perennials in pots, but not the usual wooden casks. No, these were iron, to match the décor. If I had to put a name to her style, I guess I'd say Nouvelle New Orleans—

flowery, but not overly so, with genuine nineteenth-century pieces balanced by contemporary ones. I guess her taste was good. She certainly thought so and told me often enough.

"If only I had the pocketbook to keep up with my taste," she would say with a sigh and another one of those sidelong glances, and the next thing I knew I'd be installing some wall sconce she simply had to have.

One twilight—we almost always met at last light, the earliest she could leave work, the latest I could stay away from home—she brought a bottle of wine to bed after we had finished. She was taking a wine-tasting course over at this restaurant in the old foundry. A brick foundry, a place where men like my dad had once earned decent wages, and now it housed this chichi restaurant, a gallery, a health club, and a spa. It's happening all over Locust Point. The old P&G plant is now something called Tide Point, which was supposed to be some high-tech mecca, and they're building condos on the old grain piers. The only real jobs left in Locust Point are at Domino and Phillips, where the red neon crab still clambers up and down the smokestack.

"Nice," I said, although in truth I don't care much for white wine and this was too sweet for my taste.

"Vigonier," she said. "Twenty-six dollars a bottle."

"You can buy top-shelf bourbon for that and it lasts a lot longer."

"You can't drink bourbon with dinner," she said with a laugh, as if I had told a joke. "Besides, wine can be an investment. And it's cheaper by the case. I'd like to get into that, but if you're going to do it, you have to do it right, have a special kind of refrigerator, keep it climate controlled."

"Your basement would work."

And that's how I came to build her a wine cellar, at cost.

It didn't require excavating the basement, luckily, although I was forever bumping my head on the ceiling when I straightened up to my full height. But I'm 6'3" and she was just a little thing, no more than 5'2", barely one hundred pounds. I used to carry her to bed and, well, show her other ways I could manipulate her weight. She liked me to sit her on the marble counter in her master bath, far forward on the edge, so I was supporting most of her weight. Because of the way the mirrors were positioned, we could both watch, and it was a dizzying infinity, our eyes locked into our own eyes and into each other's. I know guys who call a sink fuck the old American Standard, but I never thought of it that way. For one thing, there wasn't a single American Standard piece in the bathroom. And the toilet was a Canadian model, smuggled in so she could have the bigger tank that had been outlawed in interest of water conservation. Her shower was powerful, too, a stinging force that I came to know well, scrubbing up afterwards so Angeline couldn't smell where I had been.

The wine cellar gave me another month—putting down a floor, smoothing and painting the old plaster walls. My grandparents had used the basement for storage and us cousins had played hide-and-seek in the dark, a made-up version that was particularly thrilling, one where you moved silently, trying to get close enough to grab the others in hiding, then rushing back to the stairs, which were the home-free base. As it sometimes happens, the basement seemed larger when it was full of my grandparents' junk. Painted and pared down, it was so small. But it was big enough to hold the requisite refrigeration unit and the custom-made shelves, a beautiful burled walnut, for the wines she bought on the advice of the guy teaching the course.

* * *

I was done. There was not another improvement I could make to the house, so changed now it was as if my family and its history had been erased. Deirdre and I had been hurtling toward this day for months and now it was here. I had to move on to other projects, ones where I would make money. Besides, people were beginning to wonder. I wasn't around the other jobs as much, and I also wasn't pulling in the kind of money that would help placate Angeline over the crazy hours I was working. Time to end it.

Our last night, I stopped at the foundry, spent almost forty bucks on a bottle of wine that the young girl in the store swore by. Cakebread, the guy's real name. White, too, because I knew Deirdre loved white wines.

"Chardonnay," she said, wrinkling her nose.

"I noticed you liked whites."

"But not Chardonnay so much. I'm an ABC girl—Anything But Chardonnay. Dennis says Chardonnay is banal."

"Dennis?"

She didn't answer. And she was supposed to answer, supposed to say: *Oh, you know, that faggot from my wine-tasting class, the one who smells like he wears strawberry perfume.* Or: *That irritating guy in my office.* Or even: *A neighbor, a creep. He scares me. Would you still come around, from time to time, just to check up on me?* She didn't say any of those things.

She said: "We were never going to be a regular thing, my love."

Right. I knew that. I was the one with the wife and the house and the two kids. I was the one who had everything to lose. I was the one who was glad to be getting out, before it could all catch up with me. I was the one who was careful not to use the word love, not even in the lighthearted way she had just used it. Sarcastic, almost. It made me think that it wasn't my marital status so much that had closed off that possibility for us, but something even more entrenched. I was no different from the wallpaper, the banister, the garden. I had to be removed for the house to be truly hers.

My grandmother's parents had thought she was too good for my grandfather. They were Irish, shipworkers who had gotten the hell out of Locust Point and moved uptown, to Charles Village, where the houses were much bigger. They looked down on my grandfather just because he was where they once were. It killed them, the idea that their precious youngest daughter might move back to the neighborhood and live with an Italian, to boot. Everybody's got to look down on somebody. If there's not somebody below you, how do you know you've traveled any distance at all in your life? For my dad's generation, it was all about the blacks. I'm not saying it was right, just that it was, and it hung on because it was such a stark, visible difference. And now the rules have changed again, and it's the young people with money and ambition who are buying the houses in Locust Point, and the people in places like Linthicum and Catonsville and Arbutus are the ones to be pitied and condescended to. It's hard to keep up.

My hand curled tight around the neck of the wine bottle. But I placed it in its berth in the special refrigerator, gently, as if I were putting a newborn back in its bed.

"One last time?" I asked her.

"Of course," she said.

She clearly was thinking it would be the bed, romantic and final, but I opted for the bathroom, wanting to see her from all angles. Wanting her to see me, to witness, to remember how broad my shoulders are, how white and small she looked when I was holding her against my chest.

When I moved my hands from her hips to her head, she thought I was trying to position her mouth on mine. It took her a second to realize that my hands were on her throat, not her head, squeezing, squeezing, squeezing. She fought back, if you could call it that, but all her hands could find was marble, smooth and immutable. Yeah, that's another word I know. Immutable. She may have landed a few scratches, but a man in my work gets banged up all the time. No one would notice a beaded scab on the back of my hand, or even on my cheek.

I put her body in a trash bag, covering it with lime leftover from a landscaping job. Luckily, she hadn't been so crazed that she wanted a fireplace in the basement, so all I had to do was pull down the fake front I had placed over the old hearth, then brick her in, replace the fake front. It wasn't planned, not a moment of it, but when it happened, I knew what to do, as surely as I know what to do when a floor isn't level or a soffit needs to be closed up so birds can't get in.

Her computer was on, as always, her e-mail account open because she used cable for her Internet, a system I had installed. I read a few of her sent messages, just to make sure I aped her style, then typed one to an office address, explaining the family emergency that would take me out of town for a few days. Then I sent one to "Dennis," angry and hate-filled, accusing him of all kinds of things, telling him not to call or write. Finally, I cleaned the house best I could, especially the bathroom, although I didn't feel I had to be too conscientious. I was the contractor. Of course my fingerprints would be around. The last thing I did was grab that bottle of Chardonnay, took it home to Angeline, who liked it just fine, although she would have fainted if she knew what it cost.

Weeks later, when Deirdre was officially missing and increasingly presumed dead according to the articles I read in the *Sunpapers*, I sent a bill for the projects that I had done at cost, marked it "Third and Final Notice" in large red letters, as if I didn't know what was going on. She was just an address to me, one of a half-dozen open accounts. Her parents paid it, even apologized for their daughter being so irresponsible, buying all this stuff she couldn't afford. I told them I understood, having kids of my own, Joseph Jr. getting ready for college next year. I said I was so sorry for what had happened and that I hoped they found her soon. I do feel sorry for them. They can't begin to cover the monthly payments on the place, so it's headed toward foreclosure. The bank will make a nice profit, as long as the agents gloss over the reason for the sale; people don't like a house with even the hint of a sordid history.

And I'm glad now that I put in the wine cellar. Makes it less likely that the new owner will want to dig out the basement. Which means there's less chance of a collapse, and less likelihood that they'll ever find that little bag of bones in the hearth.

FAT CHANCE

BY ROBERT WARD

Old Northwood

Thomas Weeks, a screenwriter of some renown, had last been to his hometown, Baltimore, Maryland, two years ago, for his father's burial. Now he was back again, to visit his ailing and cantankerous mother, Flo, a resident of Pinecrest Retirement Community. The visit had not gone well. His mother had once been a complex and interesting person but had in the past ten years committed herself to being a cartoon version of herself. Now she played a fat, bitter, and foul-mouthed woman, the kind of person who scuttled all friendships and lived in a sordid fantasy of her own violated innocence. As Weeks presented her with an assortment of new mystery novels he thought she might enjoy, she screamed obscenities at her only son, craning her neck out of her pink terry cloth bathrobe, like a puffed-up cobra on Animal Planet.

"Don't try to bribe me with your shitass books," she hissed. "You left me here to die while you went out 'ere . . . to Hollywood, sucking up to all the producers and them other whores."

For his part, Weeks said nothing. Armed with years of psychotherapy, and the latest SSRIs, he merely gave her a weak smile and laid the books on the edge of a table, which held her collection of porcelain cats.

His mother stared at him through her small darting eyes

and shook her head as she launched into her next soliloquy.

"Yeah, you think I don't know what's up, but I do, Mister Hollywood. You come back when I'm half-dead to appease your conscience. And to keep yourself in line for my money when I'm gone. Well, buddy boy, I have amassed over $400,000, but you might not get a cent of it. Yeah, you think you can lord it over me alla time and then show up and do your Prince Charming routine for a couple of days and I'll forgive you for leaving me here to die. Well, you just might have another thing coming, mister!"

There was a voice inside of Weeks that screamed, *"Fuck you, you horrible old bitch!"* but he managed to put it down. His shrink, Dr. Jerry Leamer, had drilled him in healthy avoidance tactics.

"Don't let her get to you," tan and cool Doc Jerry said. "Take her to public places, movies, restaurants, where she can't open up on you."

"Would you like to go to the movies, Mother?" Weeks asked. He thought for a second that his voice sounded remarkably similar to Tony Perkins's in *Psycho.*

She looked at him and made an animal sound of disgust—*Errrrahhhhgh*—but then nodded her head. "Yeah, all right. Anything to get the fuck out of here."

Though it was far from fun, Weeks silently congratulated himself on managing his mother's terrifying mood swings. Maybe he was even getting good at this coming-home stuff. Once he had helped her into his rented car, he popped another half a Paxil, and by the time they had arrived at the White Marsh Mall his head was as pleasantly empty as a Kenny G. solo.

The movie was a Richard Gere vehicle called *Shall We Dance?* Gere pranced through it, romancing Jennifer Lopez, blinking his eyes to convey emotional growth. Flo loved it. Her furious face turned soft and her wrinkles smoothed out. Watching her in the dark, Weeks suddenly felt a secret child- ish love for her. He impulsively wished he could chuck his Hollywood career and move home. After all, some of what she'd said was true . . . he *had* turned his back on his homeys and gone for the brass ring, and many of the producers and actors he knew in Los Angeles *were* blowhards and frauds. Maybe he could buy a small house here and come back more often, help her to calm down. That was what a good son should do, he thought, staring at Gere's perfect hair. Then, only seconds later, he ripped the notion from his mind. What the fuck was he thinking? She was insane, and the old hard- assed town would crush him, as it had crushed the hopes of most of his boyhood pals.

Halfway through the insipid movie, Weeks felt a wave of nausea overtake him. The smell of burned popcorn, the stale air in the theater, his mother's cheap drugstore perfume . . . all conspired to turn his stomach, and a flash of bile came up in the back of his throat. Christ, he thought, Baltimore was a crab cake filled with poison.

He wasn't used to so many emotions anymore. In Los Angeles he faked his way through both meetings and friend- ships, pretending to have passion for things he had no inter- est in, pretending to be intimate with people he barely knew. The City of Angels was famously superficial, of course, but there was charm to living without the baggage of tortured involvements. Indeed, coming back to his hometown, with its solid brick rowhouses and old-school loyalties, made Weeks feel that the weight of history had pinned him to the mat, like a dead insect.

He slid by his mother in the row and headed out to the men's room, his head awash in psychotropic drugs and sentiment, his insides tied up in an old familiar guilt. He walked down the wide hallway and staggered into the bathroom, suddenly feeling faint.

As he stood in front of the urinal taking a piss, he saw visions of himself at Orioles games, rooting for the Ravens, maybe playing cocktail piano in some little bar. This was his hometown, after all, and though he had run from it like a man escaping the death house, he had never quite forgotten it. Never forgotten the neighborhoods where people actually knew each other, going to Thanksgiving dinner with your grandparents on both sides of the family, loving all of them. And the friendships, the fierceness of them, the loyalty and dearness of old friends, came storming back to him.

While he pissed, he lay his head against the cool tile wall and felt a great mass of confusion swing through him.

"Holy shit," said a rough voice behind him.

Weeks zipped up his pants and turned around. There, standing and smiling at him, was none other than Tyler Edwards, a guy he'd grown up with thirty years ago. A sandy-haired, freckle-faced kid, Tyler had been a minor devil in Tom's personal history. They'd both grown up in rough old Govans, gone all through school together. Tyler was a brilliant but maniacal child . . . a boy who once broke off every aerial on every car as they walked ten blocks from their homes to the Guilford Bowling Alley.

In the '70s Tyler had become a serious drug dealer for a while, then a golf pro at the Maryland Country Club. Sometime in the '80s Tyler had gone to prison down the Cut at Jessups. Word came back that he had killed a man in self-defense down there but bribed his way out of being prosecuted for it. Weeks tended to believe the story. If anybody could get away with murder, it was charming, demented Tyler.

"Tommy Weeks," Tyler said. "The kid who conquered Hollywood."

"Hey Ty," Weeks said. Though he had always felt a mixture of excitement and dread around Tyler, he now felt a rush of affection for the sick old hustler.

Tyler's left eyebrow moved up and down like a puppet's, and his smile revealed a map of wrinkles on his face. But even so there was the same impish mischief in his large, buggy eyes, a promise of malevolent fun.

"Out here to see your dear old mom, hey?"

"Yeah," Tom replied. "And she's dearer than ever."

"Yes indeed," Tyler said. "Nothing like the old homestead. The smell of fresh hard crabs, snowballs in the alley, and Mommy's tender kisses."

"Stop before I puke," Tommy said, laughing.

"Well, I suppose you're tied up, which is a shame and a pity, because I'm heading downtown to the fabulous Bertha's Mussels and I'd love to carry you along with me."

"Sorry," Tom said, "but I'm not free for another few hours."

Tyler smiled and put his hand under his chin, a real-life parody of *The Thinker*. "Tell you what. I have a few morbid duties to perform. Why don't I do them now and meet you down there at say, 8 o clock?"

"I don't know," Tom said. "I'm really tired and I've got to get my mother to bed."

"Come on, it'll be fun to get out and about. You really need to make this trip, Tom. Get in touch with your old hometown-self, so to speak."

Weeks could feel something inside of himself pulling him

toward Tyler. Unlike Tom's fake bad-boy friends in Hollywood, Tyler was always an inspired imp. A night with him might be terrifying but at least it would be real. And wasn't that the reason he came back to Baltimore now and again? To experience something he couldn't buy or fake his way out of?

"Fuck it," Tom said. "I'm on. See you at 8, Ty."

"Attaboy," Tyler said. "I promise you something special. You'll see."

After the movie, Tom took Flo out for a drink at a mall bar called The Firehouse. It was loud and brash and filled with obese guys with scraggly facial hair and plaid shirts, which they wore hanging outside of their pants. Their girlfriends and wives wore bright red lipstick and dyed their beehive hair in primary colors.

"I hate it here," his mother said. "I always hated this side of town anyway. Parkville, the Belair Road. Buncha hairhoppers and rednecks. Christ, I'd rather live over in the Northwest with the Jews. 'Cept the Jews don't live there no more. Now it's all the so-called black nations."

Weeks liked to think he was up on the latest demographics in Baltimore, but he was shocked when he heard the Jews had moved away from Northwest.

"Where *do* the Jews live these days, Mom?"

"Further out, hon," his mother said. "I heard from Harvene that the Jews have just about taken over Pennsylvania. They nearly run the Amish out. Of course, as soon as they left Pikesville, the jungle bunnies moved right in and had about ten million kids, and started killing each other over drugs at the drop of a hat."

Weeks shut his eyes and imagined blacks all over

Baltimore, dropping their funky baseball hats and firing 9's at each other. The hats floated down like leaves, followed by their wiry, blood-soaked bodies.

"What kind of drink do you want, Mother?"

"Vodka," she shot back. "And not that cheap well shit either. I want Grey fucking Goose."

"Good for you," Weeks said, as he watched three fat men in Ravens T-shirts roll by. They were all singing along with George Thorogood's version of "Bad to the Bone." Weeks felt an intense jealousy for their innocent belligerence. When was the last time he had sung anything with his pals? That was easy, 1968. The year the singing stopped.

"Yeah, I know what you're thinking," Flo said, with a mischievous grin on her face. "I get good and drunk, then you can drop me off back at the goddamned prison camp and go see one of your old girlfriends."

"I haven't got any girlfriends, old or otherwise, in Baltimore anymore."

"Bullshit," his mother said as the waitress approached. "You've always had girlfriends everywhere you go. Girls made fools of themselves for you, because they don't know what a rotten bastard you really are."

She laughed and looked up at the waitress, who wore two-inch false eyelashes and enough rouge to make her look like a clown in drag.

"Gimme the Goose," Flo said. "A double. And keep 'em coming. My big shot son is here and he can afford it."

The waitress looked at Weeks, and when she smiled she showed about a half-inch of gum.

"Your mother is soooo cute," she said.

"Yeah," Weeks said. "Mom's a living doll."

* * *

By the time Weeks carried the drunken, cursing Flo up to her apartment, he had a screaming headache and a pain in his chest. He thought about popping another blood pressure pill, but they tended to wear him out and he still had to drive all the way downtown to see Ty.

Fuck it, he thought, as he gently lay his mother down in her bed and kissed her sweating forehead. Maybe he didn't really need to see Ty after all.

And yet there was something about meeting the old convict that was impossible to resist.

He was about to leave his mother's side when she reached out a bony hand and grabbed his wrist. "Hey," she said. "You can fool those pinheads out in California but you can't fool me. You know what you did the first two months of your life?"

"No," Tom said, feeling dizzy again. "What?"

"You wet the bed every night. Every damned night. And it wasn't your father who came in and cleaned you up and walked you around when you were screaming. It was me, your horrible old mother. The one you hate so much."

Weeks felt something cracking inside of him. Like his bones, his heart. All of it cracking and falling into splinters.

"I gotta go, Mom."

"Well, you have a good time," she said as she shut her eyes. "Have a few laughs with your girlfriend. Tell her what an old fool your mom is, asshole."

Weeks pulled his wrist out of her grasp and made his way out of her apartment. When he got outside it was snowing and he stood there for a minute, letting the flakes come down on him, hoping somehow they might make him feel light and white and clean. Like when he was a kid.

But the snow-magic didn't work anymore. All he felt was soggy, middle-aged, and cold.

* * *

When he'd been a student at Calvert College, Tom rented an apartment on Thames Street, right across from the pier on which he'd once been in Sea Scouts. Back then, he thought, as he parked his car on Aliceanna Street, Fell's Point had symbolized freedom, sex, drugs (black hashish right off the ship and carried in a seaman's trunk right into his apartment), and an endless party. Even the names of the bars had seemed so quaint and cool. Besides Bertha's, there was The Horse You Came in On, and The Admiral's Cup, and The Brass Monkey . . . The cobblestone streets, the arty girls from Maryland Institute, the student filmmakers, the folksingers, the occasional Goucher Girl in rebellion against her rich parents . . . God, it had been great back then . . . a place where every day seemed to have an unlimited possibility for surprise and romance.

Now, however, as Weeks walked the few blocks toward the bar, he was stunned by how small and seedy everything appeared. The ramshackle little bars with their neon lights looked tawdry and trashy. Dead End Ville. Drunken students wandered from bar to bar looking for girls and drugs, just as Weeks himself had years ago—but now, to his jaundiced eye, they seemed hapless and lame.

He walked by a man sitting in the gutter with a torn shirt and a bloody nose. Behind him a woman screamed, "If you weren't such a pussy you'd go back in 'ere and kick his ass, Terry!" The beat man looked up wearily and said, "Fuck you, babe. Don't try and promote that Who Struck John shit wif me." Weeks looked down at the guy and realized he was only in his early twenties. He felt that he could already see the downward trajectory of the boy's life . . . a few years of stumbling about in Fell's Point, perhaps pretending to be some kind of artist, then either jail, addiction, or worse.

That's what had happened to most of his old pals. So many of them gone the way of drugs, like Mike who died from a hot shot in The Bottom, and Brad who had been killed by a head-on collision while driving on pills down to Ocean City.

It had been a mistake to come back here, Weeks thought. What could he possibly find but sadness? The old story of the middle-aged man who tries in vain to find the lost spirit of his youth in a place that's forever changed. It was pathetic, ridiculous. What he should do is just turn around now, go back to his car, and forget this absurd quest. Head back out the 95 and dive into the safety of his king-sized bed at the Quality Inn. That's exactly what he should do.

And yet, he found himself opening the thick wooden door at Bertha's and going inside, looking for something he knew he could never find, but drawn on in spite of that. Or perhaps because of it. Weeks had always had a weakness for lost causes.

Ty sat at the bar drinking Wild Turkey and a pint of amber beer back. He wore a white scarf and a camel's hair coat. He looked, Tommy thought, a little like Richard Widmark in *Kiss of Death*.

As Weeks sat down, Ty put his bony arm around his shoulders and smiled. "I'm glad you made it, Tommy. I thought you might blow me off."

"No way," Weeks said. "But I can't stay too long. Gotta fly out tomorrow."

"Whoa," Ty said. "Got a big meeting in Hollyweird?"

"No, nothing like that. But I do have a couple of deadlines."

"Good old Tommy," Ty said. "You always were an ace student. First kid in the class with his hand up."

Weeks wanted to protest that this wasn't so. He hated being thought of as a good little academic. After all, he was as much a hipster as any of them, wasn't he? But perhaps it wasn't true. Perhaps he'd only given the appearance of being a rebel, while being careful not to burn too many bridges. The thought that he was playacting a badass used to torture him as a kid. He suddenly hated Ty for reminding him of his youthful cowardice, but his old friend was smiling at him with what seemed like real affection.

"What are you drinking?" Ty asked.

"Jack Daniel's," Tommy said. In Los Angeles these days he mostly drank juices or fizzy water. But here in Charm City a man still had to drink hard whiskey.

"Jack it is," Ty said. "You look good for your age, Tommy. California must agree with you."

"It's all right. I've been doing fine."

"Oh, come on," Ty said. "I've read all about you in the *Sun*, and I've seen your movies. You specialize in action stuff. Tough guys."

Tom felt his face redden. "Yeah, well . . . that's how I got pigeonholed. Just *The Business*."

"Sure," Ty said. "I understand. But some of the old crowd might not get that. I've talked to guys who . . . actually think you're representing *yourself* as a tough guy."

Tommy winced. This was getting to be a drag. "Not me. I'm just a humble scribe doing a job of work." He took his shot of Jack from the barmaid and downed it. It burned his throat and he had to repress a cough.

"Yeah, well that's what I told them," Ty said, looking at his watch. "Funny thing, out there you're pigeonholed as a tough guy, and back here as an academic kind of dude. The many lives of Tommy Weeks."

Tom signaled to order a second drink. "Who's been saying that kind of lame shit about me?"

"Just some jerks," Ty said. "Mouse Wiskowski and Bobby Hamm."

Tom felt a sudden rush of sadness. Though he hadn't seen either of them in twenty years, he hated the fact that they thought him a phony. In a weird way it mattered more to him what they thought about him than anyone he'd met in Los Angeles.

Now Ty reached over and massaged his stiff neck muscles. "You're getting all tense back there," he said. "I should never have mentioned it. Those guys don't matter at all. I can tell you one person who's said nothing but nice things about you. Ruth Anne. Those guys start in with their 'He's gone Hollywood' crap, Ruth Anne takes up for you every time."

"Is that right?" Tom said, taking another hit of the Jack Daniel's. He tried to keep his voice level, as if this information was of no more interest than an Orioles score, but his breathlessness betrayed him.

As as kid, Ruth Anne had lived around the corner from him on Craig Avenue. Black-haired and green-eyed, she'd been the neighborhood darling before she became the homecoming queen at the University of Maryland. Every boy who ever met her fell madly in love with her, and Tom was no exception. But he had never gotten beyond "friend" status before. Now, even after all these years, the thought that she might actually think of him at all, much less argue among the old timers that he was still a true blue Baltimore guy (even if it wasn't really true), cheered him up immeasurably.

"You still see her?" he asked now, not even trying to keep the surprise out of his voice.

"Sure I do," Ty said. "She just recently came back to the old neighborhood. Lives only a few blocks away from me over on Chateau Avenue."

"You're kidding."

"I am not," Ty said. "Been through a lot of tough stuff, kiddo. Got divorced and ended up limping back to town. But she still looks great."

"She does?" He knew that he sounded like the hopelessly smitten teenager he'd once been, but after his third Jack Daniel's he didn't care.

Ty smiled and rubbed his shoulders again.

"I promised you a surprise, old buddy, and that's it. Ruth Anne's having a party tonight and she absolutely insisted you come."

"Hey, that's great," Tommy said. His head was spinning and he suddenly felt another rush of pure affection for Ty. Why had he been so worried about meeting Ty? It was crazy, really, his old paranoia still informing his life. Why, Ty was an adult now, and so was he. They could be friends, without all the old one-upsman bullshit.

Ty looked at his Cartier watch and squeezed the back of Tom's neck again.

"Hey, the party's already started. Let's get over there before all the food's gone."

"Great," Tom said, feeling about fifteen years old. "That's just great, Ty. Wow, Ruth Anne. I can't believe it."

They drove across Kirk Avenue, past City, Tommy's old high school. He remembered hanging out there on the stone wall outside the school, listening to the black guys singing acappella harmonies, and knowing even then that nothing would sound purer or better than that, no matter where he went or how long he lived. And he'd been right, nothing ever had. They drove by a hair salon at Kirk and 33rd Street, the place that had once been Doc's Drugstore where he'd hung out with the City guys, eyeing the Eastern girls, of which Ruth Anne was number one. If he could have talked to her, he felt now, maybe his whole life would have been different. Maybe he would have married her and stayed in town and had four or five kids, and been happy and satisfied with a normal job and taking care of his family. Maybe his mother wouldn't be so angry with him for leaving her behind.

They drove down Loch Raven Boulevard, then down the Alameda, and he suddenly felt that maybe it wasn't too late. Maybe he and Ruth Anne would see one another and they would instantly understand that they were meant to be together. Maybe he'd invite her out to Los Angeles, and after a few visits she'd move out there with him but they'd keep a place here in town, too.

That was crazy, but why not? It happened all the time, didn't it? Old acquaintances meet and fall head over heels in love, and after all he wasn't the scared little kid from Govans anymore. No, he was a successful screenwriter, knew all the stars, all the directors. God, a guy like him was a catch for her . . . and yet it didn't feel that way. Thinking of her, he still felt scared, breathless, unsure of himself. He didn't want to come off like a Hollywood phony, dropping names, but he didn't want to miss the chance to impress her either.

Let her know that he was the new Tommy Weeks now, not some goof who mumbled into his SpaghettiOs, like he used to back in junior high school whenever she came around . . .

He looked up and noticed that they were heading right down Winston Avenue, his old street. The single Victorian houses flashed by, old man Greengrass's place, the balding old coot who never let them come into his yard to retrieve their pinkies, and there was the little store that Pop Ikehorn used to own. Right there on the corner at Craig and Winston, where he used to buy sodas and horror comics, and hang out with his little friends, Danny and David Snyder, and Eddie Richardson . . . and . . . then Ty was pulling over, parking his Mercedes.

There was someone huge standing on the corner, a guy at least six-foot-five, but he was cloaked in shadow.

"What's up?" Tom said, looking across the seat at Ty. "I thought we were going around the corner to Chateau."

"We are," Ty said. "But I'd be a poor host dragging you out for just one surprise. Hop out. There's an old pal of yours standing right there. He wants to welcome you back."

Ty raised his left eyebrow and looked exactly like a demon, Tom thought. In spite of his best efforts to hop gamely out and face this unexpected visitor, Tom found his stomach jumping with butterflies. Who the hell could it be standing there on *that* corner at 10:30 in the cold?

He took a step toward the huge hulking figure, and then, even before the guy lit a cigarette revealing his long, haggard face, he knew.

The man was none other than Crazy Louis Wetzel, and the shock of seeing him here, right here where it had happened so long ago, made Tom break out in an icy sweat.

"Hey, look who it ain't," Wetzel said, spraying some spittle in Tom's direction.

He smiled a weird, gap-toothed grin at Tom, and reached

out to shake hands. Tom hesitated. He didn't want to shake this jerk's hand. He had spent years in therapy because of him, and now the guy was offering him his hand in a gesture of friendship? Fuck that.

And yet, if he refused to shake hands with him, then Wetzel would know how much pain he'd caused Tom, which would make him happy, the sadistic son of a bitch. More than anything he didn't want to make Louis Wetzel happy.

So he reached out and took the big man's hand.

"Good to see you, Tommyboy," Wetzel said, taking it and holding on.

"Yeah," Tom replied. "How you doing, Louie?" Why the fuck wouldn't he let go?

"Great. 'Cept for my back. Had an accident downa Point . . . I worked at Bethlehem for years. Was working inna rod factory and shit got overheated and jumped on me. Got third-degree burns on my legs, and when I fell down I fucked up my back."

"That's too bad," Tom said. Good, he thought, may it hurt you every day for the rest of your sick fucking life, you piece of shit. He finally managed to extricate himself from Wetzel's grasp.

"That must seriously limit your mobility," Ty said, leaning on the hood of someone's '76 Caddy.

"Nah," Louis said, glaring at Ty, as though he'd been cursed out. "Not that bad at all. I could still take you, buddy."

"Don't doubt it at all, Lou," Ty said.

"'Course, if I had a way wif words, like Tommyboy here, I could write me some movies and make a ton of money. 'Cause you guys know I got the fucking stories."

"No doubt," Ty said. "Let's hear one. Just for old time's sake."

"Shouldn't we be getting along?" Tom said. He tried not to look at Louis as he spoke, but glancing down at the street was even worse. For just below him was the sewer grate, rusted, ancient . . . Was it possibly the same grate from twenty-five years ago? Sure it was . . . Nothing stayed the same except the sewers in Baltimore.

"What's a matter?" Louis said. "You don't wanna hear my story, Tom? You only listen to stories now if they pay you, is that it?"

"No, that's not it." Tom felt the weight of Louis's reptilian gaze glowering down at him, but in spite of it, he felt angry now. He really wasn't the helpless kid he'd been back then, with a father who didn't speak to him and an insane mother. Hanging out in bars as he had for so many years, he'd had more than his share of fights, physical as well as verbal. Indeed, the only place he felt really helpless was when he was back home . . . Baltimore was like some great behemoth that he could never quite slay.

"What is it then?" Louis said.

Tommy found himself smiling at Louis, and sticking his own face in the big man's chest.

"It's you, Lou. I know what story you want to tell. But I don't want to hear it."

Wetzel laughed and glowered down at him. "Yeah? What story is that?"

"You wanna tell the one about how you stuck me in the sewer when I was eight years old. How you stepped on my fingers when I tried to push the grate up, and how you found a rat and threw him down there on top of me. And then left me down there for four fucking hours."

Louis looked taken aback. He wasn't used to such impudence from his victims.

"Well, the thing is, Tommy," Louis started, suddenly grabbing Tom by the neck and squeezing, "the story ain't done yet. See, in the earlier version you got away, 'cause Herbert Snyder happened to be home on leave from the navy and the shithead let you out. But this time you stay down there for good, you rich little Hollywood cocksucker."

The pain in Tommy's neck was unbearable. He managed a weak swing, clipping Louis on the side of the head, which accomplished nothing but further infuriated the big man.

"Down we go," Louis said.

He pushed Tommy to his knees, and just for a second Tommy had the optimistic thought that Louis would have to pull off the sewer grate to stuff him inside, and during that interval maybe he could—if he could get his breath—run away.

But now he saw what he should have known all along. The grate had been pulled aside already. Jesus, this had been Ty's plan the whole time.

"Down we go, asshole," Louis said. "Just like days of yore."

Tommy couldn't stand it . . . being thrown into the same hole by the same lunatic bully he'd encountered as a child. He gasped, and bright lights glittered in his eyes. There was only one thing he could do, but if it didn't work it might cost him his life. But why not? He'd rather be dead than go through the sewer treatment again.

Tommy shot out his fist and punched Louis Wetzel in the balls. The big man screeched and let go of his death grip on Tommy's neck. His hand came down to his crotch but Tom hit him again, and the tormentor fell to his knees. Tommy had no idea what to do next . . . Panicky, he punched him in the face, and then took several pokes at Louis's eyes.

From behind him he heard a cheer.

"Brilliant," Ty said. "Fucking brilliant."

Tom looked up and saw Ty's happy, demonic smile framed by the moon.

"You really showed me something there," Ty said.

Then he raised his arm and pounded Louis on the head with a crowbar. Tommy heard Wetzel's skull crack, and saw blood drip down his ears.

"And one for good luck," Ty said. He waved the crowbar over his head and brought it down again on Louis's huge head.

The big man made a horrible gasp and fell off the curb, his head and shoulders dangling in the sewer.

Ty laughed and kicked him the rest of the way in. "Here we go, Tom," he said, in a jovial way. "Give me a little hand with the grate, hey, pal?"

Tommy stood up, rubbing his neck, which was raw and throbbing with pain. "You're out of your mind."

"Well, duh," Ty said.

"Is he . . . dead?" Tom asked.

"Oh, I imagine so. You can't really live all that long without a brain, and I expect what's left of Lou's is a pile of jelly by now."

They put the grate in place, then sat on the edge of the sewer, Tommy gasping for breath and both of them looking down every so often to see if Louis was going to make some kind of horror movie comeback.

"Why . . . why'd you do this?" Tom said.

Ty lit a Camel and smoked in a satisfied way.

"You're gonna get a kick out of this," he said, offering a cigarette to Tom, who took him up on it.

"I am?"

"Yeah, you are. See this whole thing started with your mother."

"Bullshit," Tom said, accepting a light from Ty.

"I swear," Ty said. "See, these days I'm a physical therapist. I work over at Pinecrest, and about a week ago I get a call to go up to apartment 354, and who's there? None other than your lovely mom, Go-Go Flo, as we call her, 'cause she's always up to something. Hugely popular in the dining hall. Anyway, we get to talking about you and she told me you're a big shot now and hardly ever talk to her, and after I'm working on her back awhile, she says to me, 'We oughta take Tommy downa peg.' So we cooked up this little trick to, you know, scare you a little. Just a gag. Believe me, I never expected Louis to go that far. I think when you told him you didn't want to hear his story . . . well, that sent him around the old twist."

"Jesus, Ty," Tom said. "You and my mom cooked this whole sick thing up?"

"Sure did. I followed you to the theater. If you hadn't come out soon, I was going to go in and get you, but your mother was right. She said you always go to the bathroom at least once in every movie. Sometimes two times."

Tom felt himself blush. The enormity of it was too much for him. "The old witch," he said. "And the Ruth Anne thing . . ."

"That was her idea, too. She said she knew you were in love with her when you were a kid, but she never thought the girl was good enough for you, so she told Ruth Anne to buzz off and keep away from you."

"What?" Tom said. "She did *what*?"

"Yeah, Ruth Anne always liked you but your mother pushed her away. Anyway, she knew you'd come with me if I said Ruth Anne was having a party. Your mother is wild. She's so imaginative. Man, she'd make a great con artist."

"Yeah." Tom suddenly felt like he was going to puke. But he had to fight it back. It just wouldn't do to puke on a dead man's body stuck beneath him in the sewer.

"Well, I guess we ought to be getting back home," Ty said. "That's enough fun for one night, huh?"

"Yeah, sure," Tom said. "But Ty, I mean . . . what's going to happen when the cops find Louis's body?"

"In this neighborhood? Nothing. They find five or six bodies a week around here. Gangs, drugs, home invasions. This is Baltimore, son. And Louis was a scumbag. Hey, we just did Charm City a favor. Don't you worry your Hollywood head about it, pal. They only catch killers in the movies."

"Okay," Tom said. "Listen, Ruth Anne? Do you really know where she is?"

"As a matter of fact I do. She's living downtown. I wrote her name and number on a piece of paper for you. The part I told you about her divorce, coming home? That was the real deal. And she *does* want to see you."

"No shit?" Tom said, as they drove away from the moon-lit sewer.

"No shit," Ty echoed, turning down the Alameda and stepping hard on the gas. "But if I were you, Tom, this time I wouldn't say a word about it to your mom. She'll try to sabotage it again. She's the kind of old lady that wants you all to herself, you know?"

"Yeah," Tommy said, suddenly flooded with a terrifying euphoria. "You got a point there, Ty. In fact, I don't think I'm going to be seeing my mother anymore. Ever."

"Now wait. You can't turn your back on your moms. You know that."

"Why, because she's my mother?" Tom said. "Big fucking deal."

"No, not because she's your mother," Ty answered, laughing. "Because she's such a unique kinda monster. I mean, nobody could resist a monster like that."

Tom found himself laughing along in spite of himself. "Well, I'm going to try. I really am."

"Fat fucking chance," Ty said. "Fat fucking chance."

They drove on through the night. Tom looked up at the sky, hoping for some kind of cosmic release. But the stars looked like a patch of teenage acne and the moon was large and bloated, just like Flo's demented face.

PIGTOWN WILL SHINE TONIGHT

BY JACK BLUDIS

Pigtown

Everything had gone up in price since World War II ended the year before. Coddies were a nickel, so were the big, sour pickled onions. Cigarettes cost two for a nickel, but only in the little store across the street from the Carroll Park playground could you buy them by the stick.

I gnawed the first layer of the pickled onion and made a sour face.

"You been here long enough," Mr. Butler said.

"Yes, sir," I said.

I didn't want to leave the store because Knucks was still on the corner smoking one of the cigarettes he had just pinched.

I was what the neighbors called "a good kid." For a few pennies or a nickel I would go to the store for them. From old people I wouldn't even take that. It was the way my mother taught me before she died.

Birute Ludka, the D.P. girl, was coming around the corner from Herkermer Street, watching her feet go one in front of the other and holding her arms under her breasts so they wouldn't bounce. I watched, but I tried not to think about her breasts because I didn't want to tell it in confession. The "e" end of Birute's name had a tough "eh" sound. Most people couldn't pronounce it, so they called her Ludka.

"Hello," she said to me.

I said, "Hi," and stepped out of the way so she could go into the store. She wore her skirt shorter than the other girls. She was growing so fast that her clothes didn't fit her. She went to one of the Catholic schools, Fourteen Holy Martyrs, on the other side of the B&O tracks. She didn't go to St. Alphonsus, the Lithuanian school where I went, even though she had come over from Lithuania.

"What are you, some kind of Romeo?" Knucks said.

"What do you mean?"

"'Hello?' 'Hi?'" He mocked both of us with his exaggerated tones. "I'd sure like to get into that," he added.

He was a big guy who was always beating up other kids. His real name was Billy Hagen, and he lived just on the other side of the B&O bridge. They called it Pigtown up there too.

"How about you?" Knucks said.

"How about me, what?"

"Would you like to screw her?"

"Yeah," I said in self-defense, though I was embarrassed to say it.

"What's *D.P.* mean anyways?" Knucks asked.

"Displaced Person. It means her family got away from the Nazis and came to America."

"How old is she?"

"Thirteen or fourteen." I was guessing that she was my age. She was tall. She might have been older than that, but I didn't think so because she was still in grammar school.

"Old enough to bleed," Knucks said, then grinned.

The last part of it was usually "old enough to butcher." I was not sure what that meant, but some of the older guys always said it about younger girls.

"When she comes out, you grab her and I'll feel her up."

"You're crazy," I said.

"Chicken."

"Yeah, I'm chicken," I said, and I left the corner. It was getting dark and my grandmother wanted me home.

"*Buack, buack, buack,*" he called after me, making the chicken sound from some gang movie. He called out the same sound, only louder, as I approached Cooper the Cop, who was standing on the corner of Bayard and Herkermer, swinging his club. His regular beat was on the other side of the tracks where Knucks lived and Birute went to school, but he spent a lot of time down on Bayard Street with us.

"What's that noise all about?" Cooper asked.

"Nothing," I said.

I looked back and saw Birute coming down the steps from Butler's with an ice-cream cone. Knucks was saying something to her and she smiled. Then he started to follow her.

I turned the corner toward my grandmother's house, which was across from the coal yard.

I thought about what Knucks said about getting into Ludka. I knew the dirtier words for that. I even knew the word *intercourse*. I thought about it a lot but I figured I was too young for that. So was Birute. You were supposed to be married before you did that.

I stood on my grandmother's scrubbed marble steps waiting for Ludka to turn the corner and come down so I could say hello again and see her smile. It was out of the way to her house, but it was the way she always came.

She didn't come that time, and not ever again.

I had trouble sleeping that night because I was thinking about Birute and about what Knucks had said about her. She was pretty, beautiful maybe, but not like a movie star because she didn't wear makeup. I wouldn't mind having a girlfriend like her, but after *"Buack, buack, buack,"* what chance did I have? Maybe she didn't come down Herkermer Street because she was embarrassed to know me.

In the middle of the night, I heard a police siren and the dogs in the backyards started to bark. They did that two or three times a week, usually when somebody walked down the alley.

I had a dream about Birute Ludka and me doing what Knucks said. When I awoke, I changed my jockey shorts and hoped my grandmother would wash them without seeing the stains.

On the way to school, a couple of girls on the trackless trolley were talking about a D.P. girl who was killed in the Carroll Park playground.

"What D.P. girl?" I asked.

"The tall one that lives on Carey Street," one of them said. They were both wearing the white Seton High uniforms that made them look like nurses or waitresses.

"Birute?"

"No. Ludka something."

My face went hot. She couldn't be dead. But I thought about the police car in the middle of the night and the dogs barking.

"You know her?" one of the Seton girls asked.

"No," I said. I had said hello to her, but I didn't really know her.

I guess because she was Lithuanian, there was some talk in school about the murder. I didn't join in, but I paid attention. One of the nuns asked me if I knew her since she lived in my neighborhood. I said that I didn't. I was scared because of my dream, but also because of what Knucks had said: "Old enough to bleed." I didn't think that "old enough to butcher" meant murder though.

When I got off the No. 27 coming home, I walked up Carey Street and saw Knucks was sitting on a set of steps. As I approached, he got up. Then he walked along with me.

"You didn't see me talking to her," he said.

"No," I said. I did see him, though, and I saw him start to follow her.

"Keep it that way."

"Sure," I said. I turned at the corner and he walked up Carey Street toward the bridge.

I wondered what that was all about. It didn't make sense until the police came to my grandmother's door and asked to talk to me.

One was a police detective named Kastel. When my grandmother came downstairs, he talked to her in Lithuanian much better than I could. I had never seen him before, but the uniformed policeman with him was Girardi, who walked the neighborhood beat.

"Did you know Birute Ludka?" Kastel asked. He pronounced *Birute* better than anybody I had ever heard except my grandmother.

"Not very well," I said.

My grandmother was wringing her hands in her handkerchief while Detective Kastel asked me questions. From time to time, he would explain something to her in Lithuanian. She understood some English but she could not speak it.

"But you knew her?"

"I always said hello."

"Did you talk to her yesterday?"

"Just to say hello." I was nervous as I answered his questions about where and when. I was particularly nervous when he asked if my name was Walter.

"Who was with you when you saw her?"

"Nobody," I said. "I was just coming out of the store and she was going in."

I didn't want to talk about Knucks, but Cooper the Cop knew about it. I wanted to correct myself, but I didn't. I could be in trouble for that, but if I told, I could be in bigger trouble with Knucks. Cooper would probably tell them anyway.

"You didn't see her after that?"

"No, sir," I said.

"And nobody was with you?"

"No," I said. *Old enough to bleed.*

"I thought I saw you talking to some other boys on the corner," Girardi said.

"No, sir," I said. I knew he was fishing because I had only talked to Knucks. I would stick to my story unless Cooper, who was on the other corner, confronted me later.

"You hear anything about her?" Detective Kastel asked.

"On the No. 27 this morning. Some girls were saying she was murdered."

"And raped," Officer Girardi almost yelled at me.

"I didn't hear about that," I said. I wasn't even sure what *rape* meant. I would look it up in the dictionary later.

"Did you see her last night?" Kastel said.

"No, sir."

"Mister Butler says you left just before she came into his store."

"I did," I said. "It's when I said hello."

"Then what did you do?" Kastel asked.

"I went home."

"You weren't planning anything?" Girardi said.

"Nothing," I said. *Old enough to butcher.*

Detective Kastel talked about me to my grandmother in Lithuanian and my grandmother started to cry. I didn't understand much of what they said because they were talking too fast. I did hear my grandmother say *"Vladas"* several times, which was Lithuanian for Walter.

After Kastel left, my grandmother talked to me in Lithuanian. I spoke back to her in English. We spoke slowly and we understood a lot of what we said, but neither of us could speak the other's language very well.

I just kept saying no when she asked if I knew anything about Birute. From time to time she would say, *"Dieva mano, Dieva mano,"* spread her hands, and look up. It meant, "My God, my God." I never could figure out if it was an actual prayer or just some kind of cursing.

My grandfather came home later and she started the *Dieva mano's* all over again. He didn't understand English, so we didn't talk much, but she explained to him about Birute Ludka.

I did all of my homework and looked up the word *rape* in the dictionary. I was afraid to go out. I just stayed home and listened to the radio, but I did not pay much attention to it. I was thinking about Birute in my dream. It had nothing to do with murder but it was kind of like rape, because she never said anything. She just said, "Hello," like yesterday, and we did that thing, and she looked up at me with no expression on her face.

It felt good, but I felt rotten too, because she didn't smile.

We did not get the newspaper at my house so I read the *Evening Sun* at a friend's house to learn more about what happened.

"You didn't have anything to do with it, did you?" my friend's father asked.

"Me?"

"You seem to be reading about it a lot."

"It happened in our playground," I said. I decided I would not read his paper anymore.

I wanted to go to the funeral home to see her laid out, but I thought about murderers returning to the scene of the crime and I did not want anyone to think that I might be a killer.

The next day, I bought the *Baltimore News-Post* from the American Store on Washington Boulevard, where the trackless trolley stopped on my way home from school. The paper said that the police found her buried in the sandbox in the playground at about the same time her mother reported her missing. Whoever did it had covered her up in a hurry, the paper said.

Officer Girardi spotted me coming home with the newspaper.

"Hey, you," he said.

"Yes, sir."

"Why you getting the paper? Your grandmother don't know English."

"Movies," I said, thinking fast. "It tells what's playing at the movies. I always go on Saturdays. That's tomorrow."

"Where's your mother and father?" he asked. My grandmother had explained that to Detective Kastel, but maybe Kastel didn't tell Girardi.

"My mother's dead. My father's working out of town."

"Where's out of town?"

"Out west someplace," I said, but the truth was that I didn't know where my father was. My mother died while he was overseas and I only saw him for a couple of months after the war. He didn't want to hang around. He always said I reminded him too much of my mother.

"Did he know the Ludka girl?"

"My father?"

"Who're we talking about?"

"He left us before she moved into the neighborhood."

I don't know why I said *left us* instead of *went out west to work*.

I found out later that day that Kastel and another policeman had interrogated my other grandmother about my father until she cried. I spent time with my father's side of the family only on holidays like Christmas and Easter and sometimes Thanksgiving.

"You saw the girl just before she was murdered," Mr. Butler said when I went to the store. I had been there maybe a dozen times since the murder, but he had never talked about it. Now, it was like he was accusing me of something.

"You saw her last," I said.

"You were on the sidewalk. I saw you."

"I was gone before she came out," I said.

"That guy called Knucks was with you, wasn't he? The one who steals cigarettes."

"I went home," I said.

"They asked a lot of questions about you."

He was getting tough with me, and I decided to get tough back. "They asked me a lot of questions about you too," I said, though I was lying.

"Me?"

"Yeah. You."

"Why were they asking about me?"

I lied and now he had me cornered. "How should I know? Why would they ask about me?"

"Because she said she liked you."

"She *said* that?"

"She said you were a nice boy—not like the others."

That made me feel good, but it also made me want to cry. I gritted my teeth. "Give me a pickled onion?"

"Sour?"

"You know the kind I like."

There were only three in the big jar and he had to poke around with the tongs before he got the smallest one.

"Were you with the guys that raped her?" he asked.

"What guys?"

"You know."

He was referring to Knucks but I didn't know who else, and I didn't say anything.

"Nah, a pussy like you wouldn't hang with them."

When I left the store, I started toward Herkermer Street. Knucks came across from the playground where Ludka was murdered and walked along with me.

"They talk to you yet? Did you give 'em my name?"

"For what?"

"What did they ask you about?"

"They asked if I knew her and I said I didn't."

"Did you tell 'em we were talking about her?"

"I told you I wouldn't."

"So you lied to 'em. Keep it up," he said.

He ran across the street to the lot that ran alongside the coal yard and up toward the railroad tracks. It was the short way to his house from here. I was always afraid of him, but I wasn't the only one.

I was on my way to my grandmother's house when Officer Girardi called after me.

"Yes, sir," I said, and stopped.

"What did he want?" He must have seen us talking.

"Wanted to borrow a nickel. I didn't have one."

"Not even for him?"

"No, sir."

"Mr. Butler says he saw you two talking to her the day they got her."

"We didn't talk. I just said hello. I was on my way home."

"But Knucks was outside with you?"

I didn't know what to say, so I said, "No, sir."

"Knucks says you were talking about banging her."

"Me?"

"That's what he says."

I figured he might be trying to trick me, so I said, "I didn't even talk to him."

It seemed like everybody was ganging up on me: Knucks, Mr. Butler, the police. Even my grandmother was starting to ask a lot of questions.

"She was a good looking girl, huh?"

"Yes, sir."

"Beat your meat over her?"

I felt my cheeks go hot again. I knew what that meant, but I never did it because every time I tried, it hurt.

"No, sir."

"Come on, tell me about Knucks."

"I don't know anything about him."

Girardi had his back to the coal yard. I saw Knucks standing on the railroad tracks where the cars dumped the coal, and I figured I was in trouble no matter what I said.

"Did he tell you he was gonna do it?" Girardi asked.

"He didn't tell me nothin'," I said. I turned away from him and started to walk toward my house. He came after me, grabbed my arm, and turned me around.

"If we don't get him, we're gonna get you," he said.

"For what?"

"For raping and killing the Ludka girl."

"I didn't have anything to do with it."

"You ever hear about being an accessory?"

"What's that mean?"

"Means you're lying to protect a pal."

"He's no pal of mine."

"I guess not. Because he's trying to pin it all on you."

Knucks was still up on the railroad tracks watching us, and I couldn't keep from glancing at him. Girardi turned to see where I was looking, but Knucks had disappeared.

"What were you looking at?"

"Nothin'."

"You see him up there? He trying to intimidate you?"

"I gotta go home."

"Think about what I said and tell the truth next time."

I kept walking and he didn't come after me.

A few nights later, I was in my room trying to do my homework. Some guys were singing and it was echoing down the alley:

Pigtown will shine tonight,
Pigtown will shine.
Pigtown will shine tonight,
All down the line.

I never quite understood why Pigtown would shine, but I didn't understand a lot of things. It distracted me so I didn't have to think of Birute, but I was having trouble doing my homework. Then somebody banged hard on my front door.

"I'll get it," I told my grandmother and grandfather, who

were already in bed. My grandfather worked two jobs and I hardly ever saw him.

"What did you tell him?" Knucks said.

"Nothing, but he was asking about you."

"What about me?"

I told him that Girardi wanted me to say that me and him talked about Birute. "But he almost saw you watching from the coal yard."

"Only almost?"

"He turned around and you were gone," I said.

"They took me in and talked to me all night. I didn't tell them a thing about you, except that you walked past me outside the store. So don't you tell them anything else."

Knucks jumped off the steps and ran up the street.

My grandmother called down the stairs in Lithuanian and asked who was at the door.

"A friend of mine," I said in English. "I told him I couldn't come out."

By the time I was back upstairs, the boys down the alley had stopped singing. I didn't even want to go back to my homework. The last part of it was to look up words in the dictionary. While I was at it, I looked up *rape* again. I did not do that to Birute, even in my dream.

I had trouble sleeping because I was thinking about my mother, who was dead, and about my father, who was gone. I thought about my grandmother and grandfather. Mixed in with all of it was what Knucks had said about Birute Ludka being old enough to bleed and what had happened to her later that night.

When I finally managed to sleep, I had nightmares about Birute. She was coming up from out of the sandbox and she was pointing at me, accusing. Her face was smashed, her hair was crusted with wet sand, and her clothes were torn, especially her skirt. Everything was in black-and-white except that she was bleeding bright red blood from everyplace.

"I didn't do anything," I told her.

"You dreamed about me," she said.

Even in this ugly dream, I remembered how real the first dream had been. I hadn't forced myself on her because she didn't try to stop me from doing it. It was not in a sandbox, it was on a bed.

"But I didn't fuck you, Knucks did." I never said that word when I was awake—I never even thought it. I said it in a dream, but even in the dream it seemed wrong.

"You too," she said.

"Only in the dream."

"It's just as bad," she said.

I woke up sweating and scared. I didn't rape her and I didn't kill her. I only said hello to her that day. I had lied to the police by not telling them about Knucks. I wondered if the lie was a mortal or venial sin.

I hadn't been to confession since before the murder.

"They got your pal," Mr. Butler said a couple of days later. He wore a kind of delirious smile.

"What do you mean?"

"That Knucks kid. They got him sticking up a grocery store out Wilkins Avenue. He tried to shoot it out with a cop and that was it."

He showed me the headline in the *News-Post*: "*Sandbox Killer in Deathbed Confession*." A caption below it read, "*Accomplice Sought*."

"You're next," he said.

What if Knucks said that I was with him? I had seen things like that happen in the movies and heard about them on my radio stories. The cops told lies about what people said so they could get other people to confess.

"Not me," I said.

"Paper says he had somebody with him. My guess is it was you."

"Not me," I said, but I bought the paper.

Apparently, Knucks was trying to rob a grocery store and an Officer C. J. Braddock caught him in the act. When he tried to run, the officer shot him and took a deathbed confession. William R. Hagen, also known as Knucks, died before he reached the hospital.

I decided not to tell my grandmother and grandfather about Knucks. I was afraid I would confuse them with the details and they would think I was in on it.

That night I dreamed I was with Birute again, and Cooper the Cop caught us in the sandbox. I was saying, "No, no, no, I didn't do it," and my grandmother woke me up. I sat straight up in my bed. I was sweating even though it was a cool night.

I thought about the dream all day, and I was still thinking about it when I came home from school. I started to think about other things that happened and I was scared.

The next day was another Saturday, but I knew that cops worked swing shift. They worked every day of the week but at different times. I thought it was dangerous to go up to the Southwest police station on Calhoun Street, because it was on the other side of the B&O tracks. We did not have a telephone in our house, so I used a pay phone and asked to speak to Detective Kastel.

"He works out of Homicide. Who is this?" When I recognized the voice, I got scared and hung up.

I asked my grandmother if she had the number Detective
Kastel gave her, and she went wide-eyed.

"I need it for something," I said.

"No," she replied in English.

"I think I know something," I said.

She told me in Lithuanian that Knucks was dead. She
didn't use his name, though, and I figured she must have been
talking to one of her Lithuanian friends about the murder—
maybe Birute's mother.

"Please, can I have the number?"

The way she tried to hide it from me made me think that
she suspected I was going to confess.

"I need it," I said, but she would not give it to me. She
kept saying no in English and telling me that I didn't have
anything to do with it, but that part was in Lithuanian.

"I didn't have anything to do with it," I said, but she still
would not give me the number.

Finally, I took the trolley downtown. Instead of transfer-
ring, I walked along Fayette Street all the way to the Central
Police Station. When I found the right door to go in, Cooper
the Cop was standing there in uniform.

"Where you going?" he asked.

I did not want to tell him, but I was stuck—I mean, really
stuck.

I had been putting things together. Cooper going toward
the store when Birute came out. Cooper was always friendly
with everybody and always pumping about crimes, but he disappeared from the neighborhood after the murder and didn't
pump anybody about anything.

Apparently, he never said a thing about me and the

"*Buack, buack, buack*" business or about me and Knucks on the corner. We never knew his full name. We just called him Cooper or Cooper the Cop. The officer who killed Knucks was C.J. Braddock. I did not know for sure what the C stood for, but I was betting it was "Cooper."

"Come with me," Cooper said, and he took my arm.

"No." I resisted because he was trying to take me away from the station.

"You're coming with me," he said. Two other officers were approaching the door.

"No!"

"*Now,*" Cooper said.

"This man is trying to kill me!" I called out, and my eyes were filling with tears.

"Gotta take him to Southwestern," Cooper said.

"He killed that girl in Pigtown!" I said, but the other door had already swung shut and nobody else heard.

Cooper was a lot bigger than I was and he was holding my arm tight as he tried to pull me away from the door. I was attempting to stand my ground, but he was dragging me.

"No!" I screamed. "Help! Murder!"

He slapped me across the face, but I did not stop shouting. Finally, he pulled the gun from his holster and pushed me against a wall. There was nobody around. I was sure he was going to kill me.

"I'll be quiet," I said.

"And act calm too," he said through his teeth. I thought he was going to lead me to where the radio cars were parked, but instead he took me in the opposite direction.

"You both did it, didn't you?"

"Shut up," he said, and he continued to push me along.

He was going to kill me and I had made it easier for him,

I thought. I started to resist and he reached for his gun again.

"Hold it there," someone said. It was Detective Kastel from the window of an old Plymouth coupe.

"Gotta take this kid to Southwestern," Cooper said, and he slipped his revolver back into his holster.

"I'll give you a lift," Kastel offered.

"He's trying to kill me," I said.

"Sure he is," Kastel replied and chuckled.

"He's the accomplice in the Ludka case," Cooper said.

"Sure he is," Kastel said, with the same sarcasm. He was out of his car and he had his own revolver drawn. "Let the kid go."

"Hagen told me this kid was with him," Cooper said.

"I didn't do it," I said.

"Let him go," Kastel said.

"These kids are full of lies."

"I know."

"Put that gun away," Cooper said, but he had nothing to bargain with now that his own pistol was in the holster.

"It's homicide, let's go back into the station," Kastel said. He was talking about the Central Station, now half a block away. I guess he was going to leave his car at the curb.

"He killed both of them," I said, and Kastel started to chuckle.

"How about putting the gun away," Cooper said again.

"Kid's dangerous. You go on ahead with him."

Cooper still had me by the arm and he was marching me back to the entrance at Central.

"You don't need the gun with two of us watching him," Cooper said.

"I know," Kastel said, but he didn't put his gun away.

In rapid succession, Cooper swung me around and

pushed me into Kastel. He drew his own pistol and pulled me back. I was in worse shape now, because Cooper had his pistol and he was now using me as a shield.

"You back away, detective," Cooper said.

Something about the way he said it made me think he was going to kill me and Kastel too. Kastel must have thought that as well, because he aimed his gun at Cooper's head. Cooper could no longer afford to hold his own gun on me and he raised it—but he didn't fire.

The flash of Kastel's gun stung my face and blinded me for a moment. I heard the crack, but I heard no sound from Cooper or his gun. He squeezed my arm hard. I looked over my shoulder to see a bloody hole where his left eye had been. He was just standing there, holding his gun with one hand and my arm with the other.

I had no idea whether Cooper held me a few seconds or a couple of minutes, but it seemed like forever before he finally released me and slumped sideways onto the sidewalk. His gun fell into the street.

I did not feel safe until Kastel checked his pulse and told me he was dead.

Apparently, my grandmother had finally figured out that I was looking for Kastel not to confess but to tell him who I thought had killed Birute. A friend who spoke English had found him at home. He was on his way to the Central Police Station when he saw Cooper Joseph Braddock, C.J. Braddock, Cooper the Cop, pulling me along the sidewalk.

He asked how I knew it was Cooper and I told him that Cooper always came down and asked questions but never came down after Birute Ludka's murder. I explained that I didn't go to Central first because I didn't know homicide detectives worked out of there. It was why I called Southwestern in the first place, and accidentally got Cooper on the telephone.

"You could have gotten yourself killed," Detective Kastel said.

"No shit," I answered, and my cheeks went straight to hot. Kastel chuckled.

"You'd better take me home. My grandmother is probably worried about me."

"I'll tell her that you're a hero."

"Yeah," I said.

I would be a bigger hero if I told the truth in the first place—but I might be dead.

OVER MY DEAD BODY

BY ROB HIAASEN

Fell's Point

I n the John Wilkes Booth at Casey's in Fell's Point, I'm drinking Bass Ale on Palm Sunday afternoon. Above the booth, the April 15, 1865 front page of the *New York Herald* is preserved in a dime-store frame: a skinny black number separating at its corners. On the newspaper page, six leggy columns bring us the official dispatches on the *"Death of the President."* Lincoln died at 7:22 a.m., which I did not know. *"There is intense excitement here,"* the paper reported. No intense excitement here today, but I have hope. Fell's Point, once the major shipbuilding spoke of Baltimore, once a nest of sailors, once a place where Labradors could slurp a National Bohemian at the Full Moon Saloon, is now a gentrified waterfront community. At least the neighborhood has preserved, bless my home, its running battle with a roving apostrophe: Fells Point. Fell's Point. I prefer an apostrophe since I'm the possessive type.

Bars along Thames and Fleet and Aliceanna Streets are selling for $1.5 million and $2.1 million, and even Alicia over at Birds of a Feather might sell her license to offer ninety brands of scotch; the knitting club obviously won't be able to meet there anymore. The Whistling Oyster is still open, but I hear they were asking $800,000 for the property. The Dead End Saloon? $2.1 million. Even that hokey schooner, Nighthawk, skipped town—not that I ever wanted to sail on one of its "Mystery!" cruises. See, the urbanites have arrived, the new immigrants. They leave flyers at The Daily Grind coffeehouse that read, *Dramatic Loft Space Available. 20 X 80. Many Goodies for the Self-Indulgent Urbanite.* Soon enough, they'll be calling Fell's Point "Inner Harbor East." Even the panhandlers in Fell's Point are upscale: they don't directly ask for money; they remind you to use the central parking meters and please display the receipt on your dashboard.

Christina still waits in her window, though. Christina, a psychic advisor, must be sixty-eight now, but still waits to sell you a piece of your future. Bertha's bar and her world-famous bumper stickers are still here, and the immortalized The Horse You Came in On, and my favorite watering hole. Casey's is two blocks down from the Recreation Pier, where they filmed the TV drama, *Homicide*. Baltimore's amphibious Duck Tour grinds by, as tourists with duckbill-yellow quackers hope to witness a shooting or maybe just a chalk outline for old time's sake. But all that's left is a plaque: *"In This Building from 1992–1999 a Group of Talented People Created a Television Legend—Homicide: Life on the Street."* The city wants to turn the pier into something called a boutique hotel, according to the community newsletter and my employer, the *Fell's Pointer*.

My name is Michael Flanagan: I'm twenty-three, collect snow globes, eat entire rolls of Butter Rum Lifesavers after lunch, had a girlfriend once who convinced me to paint my toenails cobalt; have promised myself to one day see Aruba; Sundays wreck me (I should be thinking hopefully of the week ahead, but my mood reverses itself: the dull bulk of the past pins me), and I think Herbie Hancock's "Cantaloupe Island" might be better than Paul Desmond's "Take Five."

Since last year, I have been a staff writer for the *Fell's Pointer*, which firmly believes in an apostrophe. I write about bicycle master plans, the harbor's garbage skimmers, and once I wrote a feature about Twiggy, a water-skiing squirrel that is pulled by a remote-controlled boat. My stories have also warned readers about leaving bricks on their property because they tend to be used as weapons during robbery attempts.

My newsletter salary is $950 a month, so I also offer my services at The Love Joint, an adult movie emporium on Broadway, walking distance to Casey's. My employer, Mr. Harland Grimes, and I continue to differ on the artistic direction of the store; I believe Grace Kelly was the finest vision on film, but he stubbornly stocks the store with Paris Hilton home videos. Mr. Grimes often sports avocado-sized bruises on his upper arms. His forehead is large enough to accommodate a second face. Snap beans for legs, icebox chest. And he never wears socks, just old-lady-blue tennis shoes, just the three eyelets on each side.

I work weeknights, stacking Paris videos into attractive pyramids by the front door. My days are spent reporting newsletter stories, investigating the tattoo magazines in The Sound Garden record shop, and having the mussel chowder at Bertha's. By 5 p.m. I'm in Casey's, which is across from a toy store that once featured a bubble machine on the second floor. Bubbles would parachute and pop onto cobblestoned Thames Street—and the "th" is pronounced. I wrote the story when they shut down the bubble machine—an exclusive, you could say.

I accomplish three things in bars: consume quality adult beverages, bribe the jukebox, and form crushes. This Palm Sunday, I had planned to start my novel, but I got hung up again on the title—either *Flight Risk*, *Clumsy Heart*, or *Save the Bows*. Unable to commit, I channeled my creative thinking into imagining a dancer coming in from Larry Flynt's Baltimore strip club. She would make herself at home in the John Wilkes Booth. She would tell me her name is Amber or Savannah or Misty and she has a boyfriend named Ronnie, and Ronnie initially was very cool about this stripping business because the money is extraordinary and she never kisses her customers or tells them her real name. She just takes the money over and over again. But then Ronnie, with his dumb-fuck mind, switches his thinking and thinks she owes him more. He just doesn't know how to confess his loneliness, his jealousy. I could save her! You see why the novel writing is not going well. The jukebox carries Wilson Pickett, so I play "Mustang Sally" and "Funky Broadway" and order another Bass. But this is no novel; this is the truth. A woman does come in.

"I'm Mel."

"I'm Michael."

"Hi, Mikey."

"No, it's Michael."

So, she's no Amber or Misty. I'm way off with the names. (Mel later tells me her boyfriend's name is Steve. Go figure.) Mel says she quit her job today. She was working as a topless cleaning lady for a new company called Dirty Minds Not Houses! She had responded to an ad in the alternative weekly, *City Paper*, and was surprised to learn she could start that day. During a cursory employee orientation conducted via e-mail, she was told cleaning supplies would not be necessary but she would have to provide her own transportation. Her first job was out in the suburbs, one of the new Irish-themed developments along Padonia Road. Mel showed up at the Tullamore Townhouses with a half-dozen rags (her niece's hand-me-down diapers), Pledge (with natural orange oil), and Windex. She'd be damned if she wouldn't get some cleaning done, at least the windows. Maybe if he's got a vacuum . . .

No one was home. Or, no one answered the door, Mel says. Just a note was left: *"Come back tonight after 11,"* with one of those sideways smiley faces people use in e-mails.

"I know, I know. It was stupid to even go. But I thought, hell, why not show some tit and make $75?" Mel says. "Yes, I know! Stupid."

Plus, you can't do business in this world with people who make those smiley faces, we both agree.

Melanie Rogers is twenty-two. Her hair is the color of a metallic brown Hot Wheels car I once owned—either my Camaro or Chaparral. She's wearing brown corduroys with a wide black belt, but she's missed a loop off the right hip. Mel has a man's Timex watch, and some girls look good in men's watches, they just do. She's drinking Miller Light and starts a story somewhere in the middle.

"I put one of them in a Victoria's Secret box. Their boxes are so pretty."

Wilson Pickett is through. I need to hear the Stones, and fortunately the bubble-tube Wurlitzer jukebox maintains a disproportionate ratio of Stones-to-shit music. A dollar will buy me two plays, and I choose "Happy" and "Stop Breaking Down," both off *Exile on Main St.*

"Tino died the next morning. So I put her and the Victoria's Secret box in the freezer."

"Who?"

"My stray cat. She had eight kittens in my basement. All white. I gave them all away except for Tino. The one in the freezer."

Behind the bar, I look at the skyline of Yukon Jack, Southern Comfort, Jack Daniel's, Montezuma Triple Sec. Signs and bumper stickers garland the cash register: "*Street Girls Bringing in Sailors Must Pay for Room in Advance,*" and "*Save the Ales,*" and "*If It Has Tires or Testicles, It's Going to Give You Trouble.*" Lori Montgomery owns the bar and has been kissing off six-figure offers from the suits over at Harbor View Realty, which believes every old bar should be a new bar. Lori doesn't want to go upscale. If she's got to peel away like the Old Point Hotel and Lounge, then to hell, she says. She *likes* her French Tickler condom machine. She doesn't want "No Limit Texas Holdem" tournaments; she wants her John Wilkes Booth. She stole the booth idea from Vesuvio's, a beatnik bar in San Francisco's North Beach neighborhood. Booth, after all, is a native son.

Lori got married at Fort McHenry with a reception at the Clarence "Du" Burns Soccer Arena (it was one of my newsletter items), but I don't know her status now. She's Alison Krauss pretty. But Lori is old enough to be too old for me. I don't want her to sell the bar. If I want upscale, I'll drink in Annapolis.

Tonight's live band at Casey's is Tongue Oil, a dog-eared local group known for its curious and ultimately unsatisfying version of "Stairway to Heaven." I'd rather hear Mary Prankster—why can't *she* drop by Casey's?—when she headlines at Fletcher's, and there's Gina DeLuca Fridays at Leadbetter's and Paul Wingo's trio at Bertha's. What I'm really thinking about is Mel's frozen kitty. I tell Mel I want to see it. She smiles, takes her index finger, wets it with her studded, manta ray tongue, and mats down a twig in my eyebrow. Must have slept on it wrong. This is as close to foreplay as I've experienced in four months (no, six). Her face is nearby.

Mel has an asterisk blood vessel under the iris of her left eye. I imagine someone hit her. "Are you all right?" I ask. The wrong answer is yes. I want her to be lonely and in danger. Lori slides over a bowl of oyster crackers. I question her timing sometimes.

"Why do you want to see my kitty?" Mel doesn't say it dirty.

"I don't know." Liar boy.

I squint to see what must be Steve, Mel's boyfriend, hauling into the bar. I can tell a 33" waist a mile away. He's got these meaty carpenter hands, too. A handsome fuck. Steve can't bring himself to order a beer *in this place,* so he just hands Lori a business card. She doesn't field it. Mel is still fiddling with my eyebrow, which hovers like some randy katydid.

"Are we dating now?" I say.

They say I woke up three minutes later, according to Mel's Timex. I'm on a saggy sofa that has that sofa armpit smell. I was moved to Lori's office, where a white kitten named Marble is playing footsies on my stomach. Christ, does everyone own a cat? I try to sit up but Ravens kicker Matt Stover apparently teed up my brain for a twenty-five-yard chip shot. Lori applies a heated washcloth on my forehead— I take back what I said about her being old. I called the cops on him, she says, the guy that's with the realty company that wants me to sell. "Carpenter hands?" I say, somehow finding the strength to rename the prick. Mel closes in.

"Carpenter hands," she whispers, "prefers we not date."

Casey's packs its urinals in ice. Lori says it's been a tradition ever since her ex-husband's grandfather opened the bar in 1927. The old man's initialed whiskey flask still sits atop the cash register. His beat-up flute is still here, too. I'm here three weeks after boyfriend Steve thumped my head and after a particularly tense argument with Mr. Grimes over the appearance of twenty-five copies of *Rear Window* in the emporium. I had taken the initiative and ordered the shipment because the movie stars Grace Kelly. Mr. Grimes reacted—overreacted, I think—by charging me with a dull oyster knife. My life has become stressful. I don't want any more intense excitement.

"You're too old for your age," Lori says.

"Meaning?"

"Meaning you like Grace Kelly and that Paul Desmond guy, whoever he is. You got old people tastes."

"Your bar is not exactly a youth magnet."

"You're here," she says. She is not being mean.

I go to take a leak in the industrial-strength urinals, where a lumpy tourist in an oversized *Black Dog* sweatshirt says out of the corner of his mouth: "I don't know why they put ice in the urinals, but it's fun to make it melt." One day there won't be a place in Fell's Point where you can melt ice—the bubble machine is gone, after all—and I appreciate these facts, but I need to think about changing jobs, think about, I don't know, doing *something*. My fellow pisser introduces himself as Albert. I have never met an Albert, but he makes a perfect Albert and he seems perfectly happy melting ice. He's back from the Duck Tour and visibly disappointed his group didn't see a homicide.

"Don't feel bad. It's just not a good time of year," I say to Albert. "When the weather gets warmer you might get lucky. And if you can be exceptionally patient, you might see one of the city's garbage skimmers scoop up a body with the rest of the floating trash."

Albert stops melting ice.

"You mean those funny-looking boats with the conveyor

belt and wings? They drag up bodies? What's a good time to see *that?*"

"Low tide is good, trash heads in at low tide."

Albert's spirits improve, and I can't help hoping that one day the Duck Tour won't let him down. Listen, the man passionately wants a *CSI: Baltimore;* he believes that much in Charm City.

Albert leaves Casey's. I don't.

"So, Lori, you going to sell?"

"Over my dead body," she says, planting a Bass Ale for me on a *New Yorker* cartoon coaster. She bought a dozen, mostly dog cartoons. She just has the one coaster out, reserved for me.

"Pretty upscale, ma'am."

"Don't tell anyone," she says. "So, what are you going to do, Michael?"

"Do?"

"Yeah, what are you going to about your porno job? What are you going to do about Mel? Or that boyfriend? He knocked you on your ass, and he wants Casey's, he wants my bar. What are you going to do? What are *we* going to do? . . . Speak up, Michael."

I have to work Independence Day, but it will be my last day at The Love Joint. "Mr. Grimes, I resign my position effective immediately," I announce, as he tapes a sign to the side of the cash register: *"We cannot sell waterpipes anymore. You must ask for tobacco pipes."* Quitting is my strongest career decision yet; two years—where does the time go?—is long enough in the adult store business. A pristine shipment of new Pamela videos has put Grimes in a docile, nostalgic mood. He's even adopted four white kittens from somewhere. He's wearing his blue tennis shoes.

"You talking to yourself again, son?" Grimes says.

"I said I resign immediately."

"Then we should discuss your severance."

One of the white kittens tumbles into the Pamela Anderson video box display, detonating the man's pyramid. It's a staggering architectural loss, but Grimes just smiles, quite the foreign expression on him. The front door opens and it's no customer. I don't understand the presence of Carpenter Hands nor do I appreciate this unsettling interruption. Hadn't I just officially resigned?

"Hey, Mikey."

"It's *Michael.*"

"I'm sure it is," Carpenter Hands says, moving behind the counter. "Mikey, you need to talk to your friend at Casey's. You need, as an objective newsletter reporter, to explain to Ms. Montgomery the practical benefits of selling her bar. I've tried but, frankly, she does not trust me."

"Fuck yourself."

"Well-spoken, and it's not an entirely unattractive suggestion," he says. "But, as you well know, I'm fucking Mel."

Grimes burps a laugh (coughing *something* up), then starts to rebuild the Pamela pyramid to far greater heights. He says something about wanting to expand the operation, make a move to Thames Street.

"You're not going to interfere, are you, son?" Grimes asks.

I scoop up ten copies of *Rear Window* as severance before leaving my job at the emporium.

"She'll sell," Carpenter Hands says.

"Over my dead body."

I walk out, past the Broadway Market and Crabby Dick's and toward my favorite Fell's Point bar. I've always wanted to say "over my dead body," but I now feel under some sort of obligation. I stand at the railing by the water taxi landing and stare at the brown harbor water. It's high tide, the trash is out. The Moran tugboats, with their Goodyear tire whiskers, are all tucked in for the night alongside the Recreation Pier. The briny wind, the drinking people, the subterranean sin— Fell's Point is feeling and looking one quarter French Quarter. Inside Casey's, I hear Tongue Oil close its first set with Zeppelin's "The Immigrant Song." Lori's six, seven customers are speechless, immobilized. One might be weeping.

"Ah, the unbridled power of rock *and* roll," I tell Lori.

"Why no, that's just my shitty house band."

"I quit my job at the emporium."

"I like that decision," Lori says. "Work here. Help me find good music. Please, help me find good music. You heard what they did to 'The Immigrant Song.' Michael, musicians will listen to you—you're old."

When Lori gives you a Bass Ale on a *New Yorker* coaster, when Lori uses your full first name, when Lori offers you a job working with Lori, you don't need a day to think about it. She tells me to start immediately by advising the management (i.e., drummer) of Tongue Oil that a second set and any future first sets will no longer be necessary. During the transitional period, I insert a pressed dollar into the jukebox to hear Springsteen's "Thunder Road" and "She's the One." Lori reimburses me for the money, a gesture far more intimate and sweeter than having your eyebrow groped. I know she's scared to sell, scared not to sell, scared of him. And who knows what happened to Carpenter Hands's girlfriend? Maybe Mel has given topless cleaning another chance; she just needed the right boss.

"Lori?"

"Yes."

"How old are you?"

"Thirty-one. Now help me close up."

The *Fell's Pointer* office is on the second floor of a Fell Street rowhouse. Barry Levinson filmed a scene from *Diner* here, but there's no plaque commemorating the moment. It's the second Friday in August. I'm using one of the office's three Dell PCs to do my listings: The Fell's Point Antique Dealers' Association, the Fell's Point Citizens on Patrol, and the Fell's Point Homeowners' Association all have meetings coming up. I also need to remind readers again to have their recyclables out by 7 a.m. on collection days.

But I don't feel like reporting. I'm exhausted from a late night. I met someone and we ended up drinking, then arguing. He drank way too much, and I don't know if he ever got home. His girlfriend showed up and that was stressful. I left them at the Rec Pier, him still talking his shit. He was one of these cocky dudes—you know, the kind who thinks he owns the place, the kind who would never buy a beer at Casey's. Anyway, the night ended poorly.

We have the windows open in the office because it's so damn steamy. We first heard the sirens at 8 a.m. and now the Baltimore City Police, three patrol cars, are at the Rec Pier. EMT people are here, too. Traffic is stopped, even the Duck Tour had to somehow brake.

"Go see what that's about," my editor says. Paulette means well, but she knows how I feel about covering news. News is stressful. It lacks jazz. "Go," Paulette says. It's a short walk along Thames. It's ninety minutes past low tide but the harbor water is still receded and it's shallow enough to see dismembered crabs swaying in the flotsam. At the water taxi landing, a city garbage skimmer has anchored—its chopsticked wings have locked and apparently stalled on a particularly bulky piece of trash. I'm supposed to be asking questions and taking notes, but I just watch. Albert, my old friend from Casey's urinal, finds me in the crowd. He's back in town and back on the Duck Tour. We both watch as police in gloves peel seaweed, tree branches, Doritos bags, *City Papers*, and four dead gulls off what now appears to be a collected body. The garbage skimmer's conveyor belt holds up the water-logged mass like some Middle River kid showing off a record rockfish.

"Low tide! You were right!" Albert says, zooming his digital camera. "You think the Duck boat can get in the water so I can have a better look?" It's a fair question.

"I'd ask."

At the office, I tell Paulette it was nothing, just another body, maybe a suicide or an accident—some drunk guy from last night toppling into the harbor, getting hooked under a bulkhead. "A mystery," I say. She says to get a name, which I do three hours later from the PIO at the police department. My reporting day is through. I walk to my other job at Casey's. Lori says she has a present for me: Us3's rap version of "Cantaloupe Island." Their 1994 version, "Cantaloop (Flip Fantasia)," is better than the original, she says. Maybe. Either way, I want her.

"I have something for you."

"Oh yeah?"

"You know that body the skimmer choked on today? It was a Steven J. Marsh, thirty-four, of Canton, a commercial real estate agent with Harbor View Realty. Our close friend."

"Carpenter Hands," Lori says.

"You don't have to sell."

"Michael, I was thinking. I mean, $800,000. We could go

somewhere. Aruba. Someplace?" Lori lifts my sleeve over my Timex, a gift from a new friend. She suggests we close early to discuss current events. I tell her I have nothing further to report. I feel I have done enough for us both, and I feel about as happy as a man melting ice. Lori puts Dusty Springfield's "Son of a Preacher Man" on the jukebox, then Marvin Gaye's "Ain't That Peculiar." I'm thinking we might not need a house band.

She brings out two *New Yorker* coasters.

We're so upscale.

THE INVISIBLE MAN
BY RAFAEL ALVAREZ
Highlandtown

C rime in Baltimore was brutal but old-fashioned in those days, before the riots and all the goddamn dope. I blame those longhaired fairies from England. All of 'em.

I had that detail too, standing guard outside Suite 1013 of the Holiday Inn on Lombard Street after they played the Civic Center; all them young girls running in and out, doing Christ knows what when they should have been home in bed with their parents

Brass said: Long as nobody gets killed, let it go. So I let it go.

That Holiday Inn was the first hotel built here after the war. Got a whole lot of attention 'cause the restaurant on the roof spun around while you ate, the full 360. By the time you were done with the crab cakes and started in on your ice cream, you'd get the whole panorama, from Beth Steel to Memorial Stadium.

Hotel's still there, but the restaurant don't revolve no ' more. Or serve crab imperial. Civic Center's named for some bank and we *average* right near three hundred murders a year. Even one of them Beatles caught a bullet. For nothing. Every now and then I hear one of their songs in the supermarket or in the car and it don't sound half bad.

A radio still seems like more of a miracle to me than television, especially when Krupa is coming out of it. I keep it on the AM when I'm down here in the den with the knotty-pine and my citations on the wall, and when the end of the year rolls around, I pull a file or two that walked out of headquarters with me and chew on the ones I can't forget.

Like this one.

She said that she and her "friend" were sitting on a bench at the corner of Light and Redwood Streets late in the afternoon on New Year's Eve, "just passing time," when the call came into the Central District.

Answered all my questions and some I didn't ask; told it better than I'm telling you, so I let her talk.

"We'd just found a bench to sit on when the sun went down," she said in the kitchen of her row-house apartment up near City Hospital; two black eyes, a broken nose, and a lump on her head the size of a quail egg. A bench somewhere once or twice a week, she said, "to watch the day die."

Gray sky bruising to violet, factory lights sparkling in harbor oil, as they nibbled some bread and cheese; the city waiting on the last party of the year.

Pitiful? What are *you* doing on New Year's Eve?

The guy's name was Orlo, a junk collector from the Clinton Street wharves. What he was to her is hard to say, although I could guess. His story checked out. Lucky man, as far as that goes.

"He was peeling an orange," she said, "and the spray chafed his hands."

Chafed . . . who talks like that anymore?

I guess it was a little picnic on the bench. They weren't waiting for a bus, just sitting down. Gave her age as fifty-four—you could have fooled me, even with the beating she took—and said the junk man was "going on sixty-six . . ."

"Orlo Pound?"

"Is he in trouble?"

"Why would he be?"

"Am I?"

"Not that I can see. Except, you know, the reason I'm here."

"It was cold," she said, "so I'd eat a little cheese and put my hands back in my coat."

"Anyone speak to you?"

"Nobody pays attention. People got their own problems."

Headed to their own midnight truths.

They sat and watched people come and go from the Southern Hotel across the street. It had been important once, back in the railroad days, but not anymore. The only thing that revolved was the front door.

Something about the hotel bothered her.

"They were bringing cakes into the hotel and each cake had a big number on it—one followed by nine followed by six followed by four," she said. "Do you remember back in Prohibition when the Southern had orchestras playing jazz on the roof?"

"Before my time, ma'am."

"I begged him to take me dancing there."

"Mr. Papageorgious?"

"Orlo."

"Yesterday you wanted to dance?"

"No," she said, an edge to it. "Back when they had orchestras on the roof."

"Did he take you?"

"*One day I will,* he said. *One of these days.* Then the Depression hit and nobody was going anywhere."

"When was the last time you saw your husband?"

"Yesterday morning. He was going down to the hall to wait on a ship."

"On New Year's Eve?"

"On the way out, he stuck his nose in the pot," and she pointed to a dented stew pot on the drain board next to the sink.

"And?"

"And he didn't like what he saw."

What George Papageorgious saw was awful.

It seems that our Mystery Woman had been up cooking before dawn, and when her old man rolled out of the house, he stepped into a kitchen steamed up with garlic and salt and . . .

"Clove," she said, "I had it on the back burner. Out of the way."

The poor son of a bitch lifts the lid and puts his face to the bubbling water. It don't smell half-bad to him, I guess, so he gets a little closer, shooing away the steam with his hand.

When it clears . . .

"Christ, that's all he was yapping about," said the bartender at the Lorraine Tavern, not five blocks from the bus stop where his wife was having her little picnic. "'Crock of shit—milk blue.' A broken record: 'Crock of shit—milk blue . . .'"

"What?"

"The eyes. The boiled-up eyes of the pig staring at him from the pot."

The Lorraine was on the first floor of the Seafarers Union hall over on Gay Street; between the Great White Way bowling alley and "Your Old Friend Simon Harris" Sporting Goods. All three businesses catered to seamen.

Witnesses said that George had been drinking at the bar since it opened at 6 a.m. and let more than one ship go without throwing in for a job.

"Guess his old lady was making up a batch of head cheese," said the barkeep. "Man, the way he run it down, we could've fixed up a shitload of it ourselves. Didn't have the heart to tell him you're supposed to throw the eyes away."

They said the Greek put away eight or nine shots of vodka and got uglier with each one; shouting questions that didn't make any sense.

"How long?" he bellowed. "How long that goddamn pig in my face?"

Scalded pink snout; pale, sunken eyes; a gun on the bar.

"Everyone's edging out the side door and I told him to put it away. 'Look pal,' I says, 'a sugar ship's gonna tie up over Locust Point in a couple hours. Ain't nobody gonna put in for it on New Year's Eve. Why don't you run upstairs and grab it?'"

"Why don't you mind your own business?" said George, bringing the barrel to his eye.

And I got a cuckold face-down in the sawdust of the Lorraine Tavern with a hole in the back of his head the size of a Kennedy half-dollar.

"When the bread and cheese was gone, we sipped hot tea from a thermos and Orlo asked if I knew how his father died."

"Did you?"

The lovers had shared a long string of delicacies and deceit from the moment the frustrated teenager carried a bowl of steaming pig feet to the King of the Junkmen in her family's diner nearly forty years ago. All that time together— a day here, half a day there—and still their tongues searched out every pebble of cartilage of their mythology.

Leini did not know how Orlo's father had died.

"They had him up on the third floor, eaten up with cancer and crying for his mother," he told her. "I was hiding in the hallway and saw him point to the window and say his dead brother was perched on the sill outside. They told me to go outside and play."

When Eleini Leftafkis was a child of nine on the island of Samos, her parents shipped her to a couple with a prosperous diner at the end of Clinton Street, crying farewell with every intention of following just as soon as they could.

"Before you know it," said her *mintera*.

"Lickety-split," said her *pateras*, practicing his English.

"We love you," sobbed her *ya-ya*.

And they meant it.

Today, all she knows about the deaths of her grandmother and her parents arrived in envelopes bordered in black, first one and then another. She has never seen their graves.

"A bus stopped in front of us but no one got on and no one got off," said Leini, complaining about the fumes, saying how she missed the streetcars. "The driver couldn't get the doors closed, like something was forcing them open. He'd yank the lever and they'd bounce back. He tried to force them but they just hung open."

Staring into the space between, Leini saw herself on the altar of the Orthodox church, barely eighteen years old, saying yes to the man who'd been selected for her and "I'll see you soon" to the man she loved.

I'll do this, she'd told herself, the heart of her absent mother beating in her ears, I'll do what they want and God will give me a life I can bear.

"Orlo wanted me to ride the bus home but the driver

kept banging the doors, and before I could get on, a hinge snapped. The sound it made. Awful. It gave me a chill. It was twenty-nine degrees outside. So I started walking. The cold had worked its way inside the sleeves of my coat, right up to my collarbone. I just wanted to get away."

She asked if she were guilty of anything and I told her the question was irrelevant.

"Well I am," she said.

Orlo watched Leini hurry away but did not chase after her.

You cannot play the games this woman has played all her life—from the time she was traded to a barren couple in America for a couple dozen sewing machines—and be skittish.

Prim, perhaps; the world loves a mask.

But not skittish.

The bus and its broken doors had spooked her more than anything she could remember; more afraid, she said, than the heaving voyage that brought her over as a kid.

I took her story down like a court reporter, page after stenographic page of minutia that had nothing to do with the case.

"I walked fast," she said. "When I hit Pratt Street I stopped to catch my breath, sorry I didn't hop that bus. My knees were aching. Not a cab in sight."

She stopped to watch a couple of tugboats nudge a Norwegian ship up against Pier 5 and moved on, pushing east against a cutting wind, head down, making time.

"I was hoping to catch George before he shipped out and tell him I was sorry."

"For what?"

"For everything."

Between the Inner Harbor and Little Italy, where organ

grinders once kept their hairy beggars in an alley of sheds called Monkey Row, Leini turned toward a rough warren of warehouses and machine shops where heavy springs are forged and hawser line is coiled to the rafters.

A saloon on every corner; pig feet on every bar; a story in every jar.

Leini had not known guilt—pure, inexplicable guilt— since the son she'd conceived with George the week of their marriage was gunned down in the surf of Omaha Beach with the Maryland 29th. The city sparkles cold on a clear night and she remembers how she once navigated its odd turns with ease when summoned by Orlo to assignation.

Walk to the end of Aliceanna Street till you see the side entrance to Maryland Chief . . . Yeah, the packing house . . . They'll be tomato trucks crowding both sides of the street, you'll hear crickets. It's Bawlmer City but them 'mater trucks is loaded up with crickets. Wink at the watchman and he'll point you toward Kai Hansen's Wildflower docked out back . . .

She passed an arching sally port—one of those narrow brick tunnels that separate the older rowhouses—and remembered, as she peeped into one on an especially derelict block, the room of velvet that Orlo had built for them over the summer of '29, a room of skylights where they'd consummated an affair begun before her marriage.

"Looking down that airy way, I started counting up all the lies I'd told and they rattled in my head like nickels in a bucket."

When I told her I wasn't a priest she just kept on talking, a truck whose breaks had given out.

"Then I was in Zeppie's."

"Zeppie's?"

"Thames and Ann."

Zeppie's was a neighborhood tavern where stevedores and deckhands started the day with boiled eggs, raw eggs, egg sandwiches, a shot, and a beer; a Polack gin mill that made a mint on work gloves and sold soup and sandwiches to laborers who settled their tabs with stolen hams and transistor radios.

"George went there sometimes," she said. "I wanted to have a drink with him. That's something I'd never done."

"But he was already . . ."

"Every now and then you could talk to George."

Zeppie's was stag, the only broads you'd find there were Sissy Z. behind the bar, wives looking for their husband's pay, and the busted onions upon whom that hard-earned cash was spilled.

"I found a table in a corner where I didn't think anyone would pay much attention."

Someone did. A tugboat captain who'd just tied up over at the Recreation Pier looked through the crowd and saw Leini and nothing else. He was clean shaven—he'd just washed up on the boat and changed out of his work clothes—handsome and more than a couple years younger than her.

"He asked if he could sit down and then he was sitting down," she said. "When I told him I was leaving, he turned to get me a beer and I was gone."

Out the door and pushing home again, remembering not that she had betrayed George a million times but Orlo only once. It was getting late. There was a pig's head on the stove to deal with.

"I still had the willies, only worse," she said.

Some kind of stick in her back.

Denied passage with the clouds on its way out of this world, the condemned soul of George A. Papageorgious coursed along the crumbling curbs of Baltimore.

From the Lorraine Tavern, where Orlo saw a morgue wagon as he worried his own way home, the ghost hugged the mossy seawall of the harbor, knocked a beer into the lap of a dapper tugboat captain who thought he'd gotten lucky, and bent the tines of his daughter's tongue as she put the family's business in the street.

"It was the eyes that got me," said Little Leini, sneaking out to a New Year's party with a girl she thinks is her friend. "Like a couple of loogies hocked on the sidewalk."

"You eat that stuff?"

"Hell no," said Little Leini. "I don't know who they think they're fooling, but they ain't fooling me."

Not at all.

What remains of George tries to visit the graves of those he'd loved as best he could—a stone honoring the valor of the 29th Division, the tombs of a half-dozen others—and is turned back.

Yet it easily reaches the growling appetites of a couple whose fidelity to one another, something he knew but could never prove, had vexed him for decades.

Sliding up the side of the Salvage House and into the third-floor room where Orlo's father had died, the vapor threw a tiny monkey wrench into every timepiece on the wall, guaranteeing that, for one night at least, the junkman and his slut will not be in sync.

Creeping away, it hovers above a patch of burnt dirt

where Leini's guardians once ran a moneymaker known as Ralph's Lunch.

"It will be yours, George," they'd told him, laying out the deal less than twenty-four hours after catching their young charge parading through the streets in a junk wagon.

The ghost snakes through the exhaust pipes of buses parked near the house where George was absent more than he was home, crosses the street, and hovers before the window of a kitchen where a low blue flame kept a pot of water bubbling around the scalded head of a pig.

Leini's window looks down on row after row of pale green transit buses that have ferried her to many a meal across the arc of her heroic adultery.

The No. 23 to Irvington, where the junkman had open-minded friends among the Xaverian missionaries who ran the orphanage at Transfiguration High; the No. 4 down to the scrap yards of Turner's Station, which might as well have been Mississippi, entire fields of junk where Orlo commanded the respect of men who'd been born to it; and the No. 14 south to the strawberry patches of Anne Arundel County.

All behind Leini as she climbs the stairs and turns the key.

"The house was cold and empty," she said. "I turned the heat up, checked the pot, and put water on for tea."

"What about George . . . wanting to apologize?"

"It passed," she said, the electric Magic Chef clock on the face of the stove humming close to the hour. "I kept my coat on and tried to read."

"What?" I asked, making up questions now just to spend more time with her.

"Se-fah-rye-des," she said, handing me a small green

book with his name on it. "He just won the Nobel."

"For?"

"Poetry," she said. "Seferiades believes it begins in our breath."

Old friend, what are you looking for? It is time to say our few words for tomorrow the soul sets sail . . .

The kettle whistled and she set the book aside, something rare and delicious about to take shape beneath her hands.

"I use every part of the pig but the squeal," she said. "The recipe even sounds like a song."

"How so?"

"When you skim away the fat from the broth, you're not supposed to get rid of all of it. It says to leave 'a little of the nicest.'"

"A little?"

"Of the nicest."

Leini didn't expect to get it all done right away. It was a recipe that required patience, and in the morning she'd listen to the bells of St. Nicholas and take her time picking through the bones, chopping the ears as fine as rice. Using some of the greasy broth to help bind the dish, she'd mix in black vinegar and broken peppercorns, pack the devil into a mold shaped like the head of a tusked boar, dust it with paprika, and slide the treat behind George's beer at the back of the fridge to gel.

"We take turns trying to surprise each other with something special," she said, imagining the pink treat sliced thin across hunks of black rye, moist enough to spare the condiment. She tries to picture the afternoon it might have garnished; which bus would have taken her there.

Near the stove, she reached through the thick mist of

clove and onion and sea salt for a mug above the sink; pours the water, dunks the bag. Standing at the darkened window with tea between her hands, she lets the heat seep into her palms and considers her aging face reflected in the glass.

Neither poet nor teacher nor librarian, as she'd once hoped. Not so much a storyteller as one about whom stories are told.

Or much of anything—though it is said she is pretty good with a sewing machine—but a stubborn gourmand with a sandwich to spare and secrets leeching into the cobblestones of a city desperate to keep pace with progress.

"I never tried, really tried . . . to reverse the hesitation of my misery," she whispered to the glass. "I always took the other way around."

And with that thought, the window shattered and she was thrown across the room, hard against the wall.

"Can you describe who did it?"

"Something yanked me out of my coat like a shot from a sling," she said, nodding to the wall behind me. "You can see the tea stained the wallpaper . . . It was midnight, they started shooting guns on the street."

"Something?"

"I don't know," she said, wincing as she tried to itch her swollen nose, moving a tissue toward the cuts and bruises on her face and then pulling it away. "When I looked up, the pig head was dancing around the room like it was on stilts. It leered at me. I thought . . ."

"Oh brother," I mumbled, and she was quiet.

"I thought it was going to rape me."

Struggling to her swollen knees, spine throbbing, Leini crawled toward the stove, raised herself up on it, and grabbed a wooden spoon for protection.

She did not hear the New Year arrive, the clang of the pie plates and bark of the air horns down on the avenue; did not see the pot that flew across the room to crack her brow.

Blinded by the flow of blood, she falls backward, landing in a hot puddle of souse juice on the linoleum, flecks of flesh and boogers of fat soaking through her dress, sticking to her legs.

Did someone fire a gun through the window?

Some drunk on the street hurl a cast-iron pot at her?

The junkman gone beserk?

"Tell me," I said. "I'll find who did this to you."

Bleeding, confused, and afraid, she was somehow calm enough to think that George would understand this. He saw things sometimes. Swore that he did. But she didn't call out for George.

"I'm frightened," she cried. "*Ya-ya*, I'm frightened."

All of the heat in the house rushed out through the broken window and Leini is cold again, freezing; the skull of the pig resting against the soaked hem of her black dress, a hole the size of a half-dollar behind a wilted ear.

She kicks it away and is alone again; the phantom swirling down the drain in the sink to the bowels of the city; making its way down the storm drains with lost balls and bags of shit before falling into the harbor from the Fallsway; settling into the sleek bed of chrome and magnesium on the bottom of the Patapsco to be held there forever.

"You didn't call the police?"

"No."

"An ambulance?"

"No."

"You . . ."

"Got to my feet and started cleaning myself up."

I closed my notebook and told her she could come down to the morgue to see the body if she wanted, but only if she wanted.

We had plenty of other ways to deal with it if she didn't.

PART II

The Way Things Are

STAINLESS STEEL

BY DAVID SIMON

Sandtown-Winchester

He fought the dragging wheel all the way across Saratoga, then down through the park on St. Paul and over to the viaduct. Rush-hour traffic played around him, the people in the cars seeing him but pretending not.

The boy trailed a few steps behind, lost in a daydream, tossing off some freestyle, trying for some flow. Boy thought he had something with his rhymes, but Tate, being so much older, couldn't really say one way or the other.

"Ain't no one 'bout a song no mo'?" he asked.

The boy smiled. It was a thing between them.

"Singin' an' shit, you know. Key of whatevah."

"Nigga, please." The boy shook his head, as if Tate were beyond hope. "'Cause you old school, I gotta be?"

Tate leaned into the cart, fighting the wheel. The boy followed, still in his flow until Tate made a point of throwing out a loud line or two of back-in-the-day sanctified music.

"Oh happy day . . ."

"Country-ass songs," the boy said. "Please."

Halfway across the viaduct, the bad wheel flopped left, pulling the cart off the sidewalk, hanging it on the edge, spilling some of the aluminum strips onto the asphalt. A parcel delivery truck in the close lane had to slow and wait for them to set things right. The deliveryman stayed off his horn, patient enough, but from the cars behind came all kinda noise.

"Lean down on that side," Tate told the boy.

"Huh?"

"Naw, put weight on it an' I'll lift."

The boy stared at him as more car horns sounded.

"Stand on the motherfuckin' shoppin' cart. Lean on that bitch."

Daymo got it, finally, putting his weight on the front corner of the cart. He was sixteen and maybe 5'9", but built solid, a boy who would tend toward weight if he didn't start adding some inches. He also began wheezing from the asthma. But with the boy standing on the cart, leaning toward center, there was enough counterweight to right themselves on the sidewalk.

Traffic moved again as Tate grabbed the fallen strips of aluminum, tossing them back in the cart. He wiped his forehead with his sleeve, then stole a look at the boy, who turned away, wounded.

Tate had raised his voice. Cursed, too.

"Didn't mean to yell. I was feelin' pressed, you know, with cars an' such."

The boy nodded, wheezing.

"We cool?"

"It's all good."

They rolled down Orleans in silence, crossing near the hospital and then down Monument to the metal yard. Tate tried to get Daymo to throw out more rhymes, but the boy kept inside himself.

"At least forty here, maybe fifty if that door be stainless steel, which I believe it is."

The boy said nothing and ten more minutes passed. By

the time they reached the scales, Tate felt his heart would break from the silence.

The aluminum window strips brought twenty-six dollars, steel belts from a couple radials another six, but the man at the scales said the broken half a door from a warehouse locker was lead, not steel. Bulk metal, meaning only four for all that weight.

"Naw," Tate told him, "that's stainless right there."

"Shit no. Do it look stainless?"

"Yeah, it do. Dirty from the pile where I found it is all."

"Bulk weight," the man said wearily, and Tate snatched the last singles, feeling punked, especially in front of the boy. He walked away calling the metal man everything but a child of God.

"Thirty-six. Ain't bad for the first run of the day."

The sound of the boy's voice took the anger from Tate. He stopped and pulled the cash from his pocket, counting out eighteen and handing it to Daymo, who looked at the bills, then back at Tate.

"You need twenty to get out of the gate, right?" the boy said.

Tate said nothing and grabbed the empty cart, rattling away from the scales with the boy trailing.

"Ain't you need one-and-one to start?"

Tate shook his head. Dope alone would get him right; he could wait on the coke until the next run. "Fair is fair," he told the boy.

"You can have the twenty, man. I make due with the rest."

Tate looked at Daymo, suddenly proud of the moment.

"We partners, ain't we?"

The boy nodded, still wheezing, coming abreast on the

other side of the cart. The sun was high now and they rattled down Monument Street feeling the summer day.

"Even split. Always."

Corelli had no patience for this anymore. He had to admit that much. When he was younger, he could wait the wait, sitting in whatever shithole where he was needed, staying awake with black coffee and AM radio. Once, when he worked narcotics, he stayed put in the Amtrak garage for thirty hours, watching a rental car until a mule returned from a New York run.

He fucking *made* that case. Yes he did. Hickham had come out on midnight shift to relieve him, but Corelli was young then and wanted to show the senior guys in the squad a little something extra.

"I'm spelling you," Hickham had said. "You can still catch last call."

"Fuck it. I'm good."

Corelli tossed the line away like it was nothing to sit in a fucking car for a day and a night and more. He could still see the look on Hickham's face, that fat fuck.

"You wanna sit some more?"

"I said I'm good."

Corelli thought he'd made a point until he got back to the squad office the following afternoon to learn Hickham had pronounced him an idiot. The fuck kind of braindead goof won't take relief after twenty hours in a parking garage?

"Proud to know you, kid," Hickham had said, the sarcasm thick. And the rest of those guys just laughed. Never mind that it was him who eyeballed the mule. Never mind that the case went forward because of it. The joke was on him.

His radio crackled and he recognized the voice.

"Seventy-four ten to KGA. Lateral with seventy-four twenty-one."

"Seventy-four twenty-one?" the dispatcher repeated.

Corelli reached for the radio, keyed the mike, and answered: "Seventy-four twenty-one. I'm on."

"Seventy-four twenty-one, go to three for a lateral."

He flipped channels to hear his sergeant asking what the hell he was doing all afternoon. He answered dryly that he was busy with police work, that he was out in the streets of Baltimore defending persons and property from all threats foreign and domestic. His sergeant, equally dry, remarked on the weakness of the lie.

"Couldn't you just tell me you're drinking at some bar?" Cabazes mused, indifferent to whoever was listening on channel three. "Then I'd know you respect me enough to lie properly and respectfully."

"I'm at Kavanagh's on my sixth Jameson. Feel better?"

"No, actually. Now, because of that admission, I have to believe you are standing in your soiled underwear in a North Philadelphia cathouse."

Corelli laughed, as much at the word *cathouse* as at his sergeant's wit. Cabazes was good with fucking words and Corelli so amused, he nearly missed the white guy in the seersucker coming down the apartment steps. He keyed the radio mike again, even as he watched the son-of-a-fucking-bitch cross the parking lot, headed toward the Beemer, sure enough. He knew it would be the Beemer.

Lawyer, maybe. Or something like a lawyer.

"What do you need, Ray?" he asked his sergeant, releasing the mike.

As he wrote the Beemer's tag, he listened to Cabazes tell him that Lehmann's squad was short a man for the midnight shift, that he could work a double and clock overtime if he wanted.

"I'm good with it. No problem."

The Beemer rolled past him on the way out of the lot. Glimpsed through a windshield, Lawyer Boy looked younger than he expected. Baby-faced even.

"Seriously, Tony, what're you doing out there all the damn day?"

"Police work."

In the pause that followed, he could hear wheels turning in his sergeant's head. "All right," Cabazes said finally, "I'll see you when I see you."

Tate stayed off Division Street, even though the crew on the Gold Street corners was said to have the best coke. He copped instead at Baker and Stricker from some young boys selling black-top vials.

There was no sense going on the other side of the avenue. Or so he told himself until he was halfway down the gulley on Riggs, moving fast, hungry to get the shit home and fire up.

"Where you been at, nigger?"

Tate startled at the voice. Not here on Riggs. Not again.

"I said, where the fuck you been at?"

Tate tried to cross and join the street parade around Riggs and Calhoun, where the Black Diamond crew was working double-seal bags. But Lorenzo followed him, cutting the angle, grabbing him by the throat and forcing him into the wall of the cut-rate. A tout, watching from the other corner, laughed.

"I'm up on Division Street waitin', and where the fuck is you?" Lorenzo was in his pockets now, rooting around, finding nothing. "The fuck's it at? Huh? Where the fuck it be?"

Lorenzo pulled out Tate's shirt, grabbed his dip, then reached down for his socks. Tate tried to run, but Lorenzo snatched him by the hair and threw a hard right, bouncing Tate off the wall. The blood felt warm and metallic in his mouth, and when he finally found some balance, Tate realized that Lorenzo had the dope and coke both: two small zip bags of Mass Destruction and a red-top of good coke; all of it had been curled in the top of Tate's left sock.

"This some low shit," he managed.

But Lorenzo was already walking away, laughing. The whole corner—touts, runners, fiends—was tripping on the spectacle. At Mount Street, Lorenzo turned back before crossing and shouted, "Catch ya later."

Tate gathered himself, wiping blood on his sleeve. Four times in two weeks, and there was no sign Lorenzo was getting tired of the game. Four times he had his shit taken. On Monday alone, it was eight black-tops—a bulk-buy to celebrate the money from the copper rainspouts from that warehouse roof.

"Why you his bitch like that?"

It was the tout, all of fifteen years old, signifying, trying to have more fun with it. Tate turned, started back across the street, and then saw the boy at the mouth of the alley, staring. Tate looked away, then started down Riggs. The boy followed, catching him at Fulton.

"'Sup."

"Ain't much," said Tate. Maybe he didn't see. Maybe he got there after.

"Yeah?"

"Banged up my face a bit."

"I seen."

Walking away, Tate felt shame washing over him. But the boy followed silently for several blocks, until they were passing the corner at Edmondson and Brice.

"Lorenzo jus' an asshole," Daymo finally offered.

Tate gave nothing back, pointing instead to the Edmondson crew. "How 'bout you let me hold ten till tomorrow? First run of the day, I get even with you."

The boy shrugged. "Ain't got ten."

"You ain't got ten dollars? How the fuck not? I gave you thirty-five at them scales not two hours past."

The boy shrugged again. Tate looked at him for a moment.

"What was you doing on Riggs?"

"Huh?"

"What was you doing on Riggs, comin' out the alley?"

"Wadn't doin' shit."

Tate grabbed Daymo's wrist and spun him, pulling the boy's arm behind his back and feeling the pockets of his denims. Right as rain.

"Get off. Get the fuck off me."

But Tate had them out already, three gel-caps of Black Diamond. The boy looked away, hurt and angry both.

"The fuck is this here? You ain't shootin' this shit, I know."

"Jus' a snort now an' then."

Tate looked at the boy and waited. Nothing else was offered, and so, pocketing the caps, he filled the silence with his own words, the softest he could find.

"This shit ain't for you, Daymo. It ain't. You think about what it is you really want an' where you want to be at, an' then you take a look at my sorry ass."

The boy did.

"It ain't for you."

Tate turned and crossed Edmondson. The boy didn't follow.

"So he go an' steal from you," Daymo shouted, "an' you steal from me!"

Tate stopped and wheeled. "I'm holdin' thirty of yours. You gonna see that money first run tomorrow. My word."

He turned and walked down Monroe without looking back, knowing in his heart that Daymo understood, that he had heard his words as truth. And later that night, when the boy came up the stairs of the vacant building where they were laying up, he said nothing further, just nodded quickly to Tate, then undressed and crawled onto his bedroll. The boy knew Tate would have his thirty after the first run. And he knew Tate was real about him not getting high, about the right and wrong of it all.

At the end of summer, Tate told himself, he would find a way to get Daymo back in school somehow, maybe even walk him up to Harlem Park and talk to the people there. Get him some school clothes and a book bag, even.

He had run through his own family years ago, burning them out one after the next, using them all to keep chasing. Shit, he had done a lot to be ashamed about. But he had never lied to Daymo, never cheated him. Not ever. And the boy knew how he felt, though nothing was ever said in all the time they had run together, the boy looking for meal money and finding Tate at the scales one winter afternoon.

"I can work for it if you need help."

"Where you live at?" Tate had asked.

The boy shrugged.

"You ain't got peoples?"

"Had me in a group home."

Tate waited.

"I ain't going back there ever."

Tate nodded at that, asking no more questions, and it was the boy himself who pressed it: "Copper worth more than the rest, ain't it? I know where we can snatch some copper pipe for real."

And each day since, with the boy and Tate sharing everything.

Long after midnight, Tate fired the last speedball after the boy's wheeze got regular and turned to a light snore. Child can't shake that asthma at night, he thought sadly, telling himself that after a couple runs tomorrow, if Daymo was still struggling, they would run down to the university clinic, get some free medicines.

But right now, with good dope and coke running wild in his head, Tate had other work at hand. Yes he did. Reaching into his jacket pocket, he found the rat bait and, from the wax-covered end table, a folded strip of cardboard. He found the first of the empty Black Diamond caps on the floor beside the table and opened it, staring at the space where heroin no longer was.

He would see Lorenzo tomorrow. Most definitely.

Corelli was on the B-of-I computer when he sensed Cabazes behind him.

"For a big man, you're pretty quiet."

"Graceful, like a cat."

"I was thinking more like a ballet dancer or an interior decorator or some shit like that. Someone willing to embrace alternative lifestyles."

Cabazes nodded at the screen and its display of a light

sheet: White, male. Timonium address. A few misdemeanors and no open warrants.

"The fuck are you looking at?"

"Him. That's the cocksucker fucking my wife."

Cabazes frowned. "Lemme guess. You spent the whole day yesterday camped at Trina's apartment so you could mark the new boyfriend."

"Not the whole day, no."

"Fuck, Tony. Grow the fuck up."

"You see this guy? Look at this here. Driving under the influence, D-and-D, failure to obey. Guy's an asshole. Look at this one from '96 . . . solicitation for prostitution, sodomy . . ."

Corelli looked up at his sergeant, mock deadpan. "Guy's a sodomite."

"Who the fuck isn't? By Maryland code, a blowjob is sodomy."

"Seriously, you think I want a guy like this around my kids? You think Trina will want a guy like this around her kids once she knows?"

"Once she knows what? That her new honey once got DUIed? That once in 1996 he took a blowjob from some pro?"

"Right. I'm sure it was just the once."

Corelli hit a button, sending the sheet to the printer on the other side of the admin office. Amid the staccato clatter, his sergeant looked at him for a long moment, then pulled up a chair and sat, leaning close.

"What concerns me here, Tony, is a certain lack of perspective on your part."

"Lack of perspective?"

"How long since you and Trina split?"

"Twenty months."

"Divorce is final, right?"

"Two years, she says."

"Two years."

"Yup."

"Who you fucking now?"

"Me?"

"Yeah, who you fucking?"

"Arlene. The nurse from Sinai." He paused, and when Cabazes waited him out, added: "Among a couple others."

"A couple others. Tony, you been a whore as long as I've known you. You were a whore before you married Trina, you were a whore when you were with her, and with the possible exception of a week or so after she finally walked out, you've stayed a perfect whore. You'd fuck a rathole if it had carpeting around it."

"So?"

"So you're parked outside of Trina's apartment waiting to see who comes out so you can play detective and decide why she isn't right to sleep with whoever the fuck she wants. This is what you do."

"This guy's gonna be around my fucking kids."

"You're around your fucking kids, Tony. And I've known you to drive shitfaced. You're around your kids and I've fuckin' *seen* you take a pro's blowjob once or twice."

"When?"

"Boardman's bachelor party. Remember?"

"Bachelor parties don't count."

Corelli got up, walked to the printer and pulled the sheet free.

"Leave it be, Tony. The problem isn't this guy, and it sure as shit ain't Trina."

Corelli said nothing, folding the printout, tucking it inside his jacket.

"Anyway, I need a witness for a statement. Room two."

"Yeah, what'd we catch?"

"Something a little lumpy. Thought it was a straight overdose, but now I got this little fuck in there putting himself in, calling it a hot shot."

"Huh. No shit."

Corelli followed his sergeant to the interrogation room.

"Rat bait, huh?"

The man nodded, then scratched himself.

"You loaded an empty with the rat bait and then he stole it from you and fired."

The man began to cry. Corelli shot Cabazes a look.

"You're saying you loaded the hot shot on purpose, and that when we tell the M.E. to test for strychnine, it's gonna come back positive for that and negative for opiates."

The man nodded again, then vomited. Corelli shot back in his chair, then followed Cabazes out of the The Box. They walked down the hallway for paper towels.

"The fuck kinda goof puts himself in for a hot shot?" Corelli said. "You keep your mouth shut, it's the perfect murder. Nobody gives a fuck and no jury's ever gonna believe it's anything other than a fiend firing bad shit."

"He says he can't live with it," Cabazes offered.

"Why the fuck not? Why's he gotta bust our balls?"

They found towels in the men's room, but no mop or pail in the utility closet. They went down to the fifth floor, then the fourth, before finding a janitor. Ten minutes later they were back upstairs, Cabazes heading for the interrogation room and Corelli short-stopping at the soda machine.

"Be there in a sec."

He fed a dollar and banged for a diet drink before shouts

from Cabazes brought him running around the corner. The Box door was open and his sergeant was wrapped around the little fuck's waist, holding him. Corelli looked up to see the man's leather belt tied around the ceiling brace, the other end around his neck.

"Get him offa there," Cabazes grunted.

Standing on the table, Corelli fumbled for a few moments before finding and unfastening the buckle. The body flopped against Cabazes, then onto the table. Corelli jumped down and they loosened the other end of the belt. The dead man rewarded them with a cough, then a breath, then another cough. Twenty minutes later, he was sitting in the same chair where they had left him, sipping water from a Styrofoam cup, one arm extended for a paramedic checking his blood pressure.

Cabazes was in the squad room calling the duty officer.

"I don't get it," Corelli said. "You hot shot a guy who stole from you and then you come in to confess. The fuck is up with that? You did what you had to."

The man said nothing at first, then shook his head softly.

"He ain't stole from me. Daymo wouldn't steal."

Corelli waited.

"The hot shot was for this motherfucker Lorenzo. He the one been taking my shit all the time, bangin' me 'round for it. I loaded the shot for him. The boy . . ."

His voice trailed away. The paramedic finished, nodded to Corelli, and left.

"The boy was an accident," Corelli said, finishing the thought.

The man was crying again. "He was living with me, you know? Ain't had no place else to go, an' I was lookin' out for him. I was lookin' out for him more than myself, you know? He ain't got no mother or father to speak of, but I was kinda like a father with him. An' he was starting to use a bit, you know? I seen it. I pulled him up when I seen it. An' I wasn't havin' none of it, so we had gone back and forth on that."

"So he snuck the hot shot from you without you knowing."

The man nodded, tears streaming. He was angry now, his voice louder.

"I was actin' all parental an' shit, like I was responsible for that boy. Like I wasn't who the fuck I been for twenty fuckin' years, you know? Pretending to be something past a low-bottom dope fiend, but you know what? I *am* a low-bottom dope fiend and I kilt that child. I did. So just lock my ass up an' be done with this shit. Jus' lock me the fuck up 'cause I am done pretending. I wadn't no good for that child. I ain't good for no one. So jus' lock me up 'cause I'm responsible for this here."

Corelli backed away, leaving the door open. The smell of vomit followed him into the hall, where he found Cabazes.

"Duty officer is on the way downtown. He wants a twenty-four on it."

Corelli nodded toward The Box.

"Paramedic says he's good to go."

Cabazes nodded.

"So let him."

"What?"

"After the duty officer gets his twenty-four, we let him go."

"He's giving himself up, we can make it a murder."

"You let him go, it can stay an overdose and not even be a stat."

"We could use the clearance."

"Fuck the clearance. In this poor fuck's head, he's been tried, convicted and sentenced. The hot shot was for another asshole. The kid was an accident. This sadass motherfucker's gonna live with more weight than we could ever give him."

Cabazes stared at him for a moment, nodded, then headed down the hall.

Corelli walked into the coffee room, poured sludge from the bottom of a dying pot, then slumped at the corner desk. He stared out the window, watching people and cars negotiate the rush hour below. It was Friday and he thought about calling Trina, asking if she wanted to do something together with the kids this weekend. The zoo, maybe. But he thought on it a moment longer and couldn't see it happening.

Reaching into his pocket, Corelli pulled out the printout and tossed it into the can with the Styrofoam and stirrers and coffee grounds.

"Fuck it," he said to no one in particular.

HOME MOVIES

BY MARCIA TALLEY

Little Italy

P*arents: Please do not allow your children to sit, stand, or lean on the railing surrounding the seal pool.* Angie wasn't counting, but she must have heard the announcement fifty times since she arrived more than two hours ago. The recording was grating on her nerves.

The sun had clocked around to the west, too, so her bench no longer sat in the shade of the National Aquarium, its hulk—all glass and Mondrian-style triangles—looming like the Matterhorn behind her. Sweat beaded uncomfortably along her hairline; it ran in rivulets between her breasts, soaking through the fabric of her Victoria's Secret T-shirt bra.

Damn! Baltimore was hot in July.

Squinting through her Ray-Bans, Angie scanned the bustling Inner Harbor, searching for the sailboat, a Sabre 402 named *Windwalker*. To her right rose the honey-beige tower of Baltimore's World Trade Center, and if she turned her head to the left—past the raked-back masts of the *USS Constellation*, past the red brick walls of the Maryland Science Center—the crimson neon of the Domino Sugars sign, five stories high, glowed like a beacon. Blue-canopied water taxis ferried visitors from the two pavilions that housed the shops and restaurants of Harborplace across the water to dine at the Rusty Scupper, or to points beyond, like the tourist-magnet neighborhoods of Little Italy and Fell's Point.

But there was no sign of Jack or his boat.

Angie had visited the Sabre website, so she knew that a 402 cost almost a half a million dollars. Even a used model could set you back two hundred thou. But it wasn't the price that impressed her; it was the fact that the boat had two separate cabins with doors. That locked. With any luck, though, she wouldn't have to use them.

Angie yanked her cell phone out of its holster and checked to make sure she had her brother Johnny on quick dial, in case things turned sour. Then she punched in the number Jack had given her, but voicemail kicked in right away. Damn! Maybe he was out of signal range, or talking to someone else. She scowled at the phone.

Jack. Jack freaking Daniels!

Angie imagined her mother's disapproving voice. "With a name like that, Ange," she would have warned, shaking a finger, "he's gotta be an axe murderer."

Angie'd argue she found it hard to believe that anybody'd make up a name like Jack Daniels.

"You don't know anything about the man!" her mother would say. "Safer to stay home."

Once, Angie had hitchhiked from Baltimore to San Francisco and back, and lived to tell the tale. "Pure dumb luck," her mother had scoffed, with emphasis on the dumb.

Angie's mother had never approved of blind dates, either, so the idea that her only daughter planned to sail off with a guy after meeting him for the first time on the Internet would have sent her into cardiac arrest.

So Angie hadn't told her.

"I'm taking a vacation, Mama," she'd said. "Got a great rate out of Providence to BWI. I'll visit Johnny in Baltimore, see how he's doing at Harkins, then who knows? Florida, maybe."

The Florida part was practically true. After Baltimore, Jack said he was planning to sail down the Intercoastal Waterway to Fort Lauderdale, then across the Gulf Stream to the Bahamas.

On the bench next to her, Angie had a canvas tote with *Cruising World* stenciled on the side in blue letters. She rummaged inside and pulled out the ad that had been clipped and sent to her post office box in Providence, Rhode Island.

Energetic, forty-eight-year-old Italian American engineer with a comfortable, well-equipped two-cabin, two-head 40' sloop needs an adventurous, athletic female partner to island hop in the Bahamas, year round if possible. Safe sailor, good navigator, I dive, fish, cook, and clean. Healthy, intelligent, 5'11", 185, lots of salt and pepper hair. Previous female mate references available.

Angie had responded that she was an adventurous, free-spirited young lady who wanted to sail where the weather is warm, the wind is steady, and the islands are beautiful. After a flurry of e-mails, they'd agreed to meet.

She hadn't called his references.

Angie lived life on the edge.

Parents: Please do not allow your chil—

Someone pulled the plug on the recording, thank God. Angie joined the crowd around the outdoor pool as aquarium staff prepared to feed Ike and Lady, the gray seals who lived there. She rested her forearms against the railing and watched Ike flounder onto a rock, snap up the fish tossed his way, and honk appreciatively for the crowd.

When feeding time was over, Angie strolled along the seawall, past the grinning black hulk of the USS *Torsk* permanently tied up there, wondering where the hell Jack Daniels had gotten to. He was coming from Annapolis, he said, so she'd timed their meeting carefully, taking the crowds into consideration. Maybe Jack was already on island time.

So she wouldn't mess up her cutoffs, Angie selected a relatively clean spot and sat down on the granite wall, her legs dangling over the water. Her feet ended in Docksiders. No one could say she didn't dress like a sailor.

The water taxi came and went, its canopy flapping as it chugged through the still, humid air. Motorboats flitted about the harbor, weaving around the fleet of paddleboats that puttered around like ducklings. Sailboats bobbed quietly at anchor, suddenly swinging wide, facing into a puff of wind that rippled a path along the water.

"Stevie! Stay away from the water!" A woman's voice, screeching. When Angie turned her head to check out the kid, she saw it: a Sabre motoring in under bare poles, its blue hull bright against the greenish-brown mound of Federal Hill. It would be ten, twenty minutes maybe, before the captain found a spot to anchor amid the sea of tethered vessels.

Angie extracted a digital camcorder, smaller than a paperback, from a plastic bag in her tote. She flipped it open and centered the sailboat in the viewfinder. She zoomed in, waited for the cam to focus. No mistake. *Windwalker* was stenciled in gold letters on its hull; an inflatable dinghy bounced along in its wake.

She panned aft to where the captain, his features indistinct in the shadow of a baseball cap, manned the helm, then forward along the life lines. *Well, that's a surprise.* Jack Daniels had crew. A young man in chinos and a blue polo shirt stood on the bow, his foot resting lightly on the anchor chain as it screamed over the windlass and snaked into the water, pulled along by the weight of the anchor as it sank into the muck at the bottom of the Patapsco.

When the anchor was secure, the two men piled into the dinghy, cranked the outboard to life, and motored to the dock where they jostled for a spot, bouncing off the other inflatables like oversized inner tubes.

Through the viewfinder Angie watched the men disembark, watched the young guy shake Jack's hand, watched as he seemed to be saying goodbye. Good, she thought. One less Y chromosome to worry about.

From behind the camera, Angie stared, comparing the man coming toward her to the photo from the e-mail attachment. The man in the photo had darker hair, a wider nose, a less prominent chin. Angie sat on the seawall, puzzled, her knees pulled up, hugging them, studying the man with the salt-and-pepper hair who *had* to be Jack from under the brim of her hat. Son of a bitch knew he was late, too, hustling along the pier, glancing at every female face, probably wondering if she'd given up on him. Let him sweat. Angie had the advantage, after all. She hadn't sent Jack a picture—only a description. One couldn't be too careful.

Jack reached the end of the pier and stopped to gaze out over the water, big hands hanging at his sides. She stuffed the videocam into her tote bag, stood, and followed.

"Jack?" she called, settling the strap of the tote comfortably against her shoulder.

He turned. His sunfrosted eyebrows lifted. "Mandy?"

"That's me." She smiled ruefully. The name sounded strange pinned on her, rather than on the drugged-out cousin to whom it actually belonged. Angie extended her hand, and he took two steps forward to take it.

"Shall we go somewhere to talk?" she asked, eager to get

on with it.

Walking side-by-side, chatting casually, they crossed the brick-paved causeway to Barnes and Noble, the ho-hum of its chaindom somewhat mitigated by being sandwiched between its trendier cousins, the ESPN Zone and Hard Rock Cafe. Once inside, they wound through smokestacks tattooed with rivets, rode up the industrial-style escalators to Starbucks.

"My treat," Jack said, and bought them each a mocha frappuccino.

"Do you want to see the boat now, before you make up your mind?" he asked, sitting down at the table opposite her.

"How about the other guy?" She jammed a straw into her drink.

"What other guy?"

"The guy I saw riding in on the dinghy."

Jack actually blushed. "You must mean Tim. He works for the yacht broker."

"Tim, then."

"He installed a self-steerer in the Sabre. Wanted to make sure it worked."

"Self-steering will come in handy on the ocean," Angie commented, taking a sip from her mocha frappe. "So, tell me about the trip."

While Jack extracted a map from his fanny pack and smoothed it out on the table, Angie studied his face. The eyes were right, and so were the ears, but the nose and chin bothered her. Plastic surgery? If so, the scars were hidden in the tiny creases of his well-tanned skin.

Jack anchored a corner of the map with his drink. His finger traced a line from the Abacos to Eleuthera, down the long Exumas chain to Great Exuma. Angie smiled and nodded and asked all the right questions—about sending and receiving mail, about satellite phones and how they'd divide up the duties and the costs—but knew it was time to move on.

She leaned over the map. "I'd like to see the boat now, Jack."

His eyes, dark as cinnamon, locked on hers, and something went *ka-plump* in her chest. Goddamn. She hoped that wouldn't be a problem.

Minutes later, opposite the aquarium, Angie held back. "Wait a minute!" she said, grabbing Jack by the arm and dragging him along. "You have to see the seals!" She led him to the seal pool, where they stood side-by-side, leaning against the railing, the crowds pressing in around them.

Ike and Lady eeled soundlessly through the water in their idyllic, 70,000-gallon world. Mounted on the railing was a sign—*Caution: Throwing coins or objects in the pool can kill the seals.* Well, not so idyllic, maybe.

They watched in companionable silence for a while, then Jack turned to face her.

"Mandy," he said. His eyes seemed to drink her down. "This'll probably not sit too well, but you could be the figurehead on my ship of life."

"That's bullshit," she said, smiling.

"No," he said. "Gilbert and Sullivan."

"About the figurehead. I don't think so . . . *Bill.*" Her voice dropped an octave on his name, like a late night DJ. Her smile evaporated and she waited, giving him time to let the significance of her words sink in.

"Shitfuckdamn." He blinked slowly. "How the hell did you find me?"

"We're betrayed by our buying habits, Jack. Take me, for example." She plucked at the collar of her gauzy shirt. "If I wanted to disappear, I'd have to stop shopping at Chicos."

Jack relaxed against the railing. Perhaps he was relieved. "So what gave *me* away?"

"The West Marine catalog."

"No way." He actually grinned.

She slipped a hand into her tote, easing it down deep along the side. "I called their 800-number to complain that we hadn't received our catalog since we moved, and were they still sending it to the Providence address." She shrugged. "'Oh, no,' the woman told me, 'it's going to your new address in North Carolina.'" Angie smiled. "Of course she confirmed that for me."

Jack laid a hand on her shoulder, and again she felt it, like a jolt of electricity straight to her heart. "But why you?" he asked.

"Not me," she said, leaning closer, so close that her nose was filled with the Tide-washed freshness of his shirt. "It's Michael Cirelli who's looking for you. He wasn't amused when you ratted. When your testimony sent his son to jail." She paused. "It irks him that Danny's cooling his heels at Lewisburg while you are . . ." Angie waved a hand in the direction of *Windwalker*, bobbing quietly at anchor in the harbor behind them. "Sailing off into the proverbial sunset."

"I'd like to be sailing off with you," Jack whispered.

She stood on tiptoe, her lips warm against his cheek. "I'm really sorry, Jack."

The knife cool in her hand. Its blade, long and thin, penetrated his shirt and the skin of his chest, slipping cleanly between his ribs, piercing the left ventricle of his heart. Still leaning against the railing, Jack only looked surprised as she withdrew the knife and dropped it back into her tote. Jack slumped against her—another amorous couple enjoying the summer evening. Her lips brushed his ear as she whispered,

"But if I'd sailed off with anybody, it would have been with you."

With a fluid, practiced move, she lifted and pushed, gently tumbling him over the railing, onto the concrete skirt that surrounded the seal pool, where he lay still, one hand trailing in the water, his eyes wide, locked on hers. It would take several minutes for his heart to bleed out, flooding his chest cavity. Plenty of time for Jack to call out—*Help! Murder!* or even her name. But he lay quietly along the skirting, defeated, dying.

Lady surfaced, the water sleeking off her mottled fur. She snorted, her whiskers twitching curiously next to Jack's hand. Bobbing, she studied the dying man with dark, sorrowful eyes.

"Sorry, Lady," Angie whispered, thinking about the warning sign. Then, "Call 911!" she screamed. "He's having a heart attack!"

In the subsequent confusion, she slipped away, weaving quietly through the crowd, moving confidently against the grain.

Near the causeway between the power plant and Baltimore's Public Works Museum, the wig came off with the hat, in one quick swoop. By the time she crossed President Street, Angie had fluffed up her flyaway copper curls, and the disguise was tucked safely into the plastic bag that had once held her videocam.

She strolled down Fawn Street, almost to Gough, before finding a dumpster where she ditched the bag. She doubled back to Exeter. Angie wasn't worried. Two thousand people were crowded in Little Italy tonight, out to enjoy the film festival. *Cinema al fresco* would generate tons of garbage. Nobody was going to be pawing through the dumpsters in the morning.

On Stiles, at the far end of the bocce court tucked between High and Exeter, she found her brother and his team, all duded up and slicked back, their asses being whipped by *paisanos* on Social Security, wearing team shirts, Bermudas, and tube socks. She perched on a park bench painted red, white, and green to watch the massacre, wondering, not for the first time, how Johnny could bet serious money on a game that was a cross between lawn bowling and horseshoes. After a while, she wandered off and bought herself a meatball sub and ate it at the corner of High and Stiles, where Johnny found her later, just as it was growing dark. He carried a couple of lawn chairs.

"Sorry I'm late, sis."

She presented her cheek for a kiss.

He unfolded a chair, placed it on the sidewalk, and held it steady while she sat down. "Glad you stopped by."

"I'm starving," she said. "What's in the box?"

"Dessert," he said.

"From Vaccaro's, I trust," she said, holding out her hand for the box.

"How's Mom?"

"Just fine," Angie replied, liberating a chocolate-dipped cannoli from a square of wax paper. "She thinks I should get a life."

"And Providence?"

"Not so good as when Buddy Cianci was mayor, but thriving." She took a bite of the cannoli, savoring the sweetness of it on her tongue, feeling giddy. "You should visit sometime, Johnny."

"Maybe I will," he said, "if I'm not on call over Thanksgiving."

From the third floor bedroom of John Pente's apartment directly over their heads, a blue stream of light projected the opening scenes of *Moonstruck* onto a blank white billboard across a parking lot crammed with people: a street festival meets the drive-in, but without all the cars.

"They always start with *Moonstruck*," her brother explained, "and end with *Cinema Paradiso*."

"All Italian?"

He nodded, chewing, his mouth full of amaretto tiramisu. "Mostly." He fished in his pocket and pulled out a printed schedule.

"So if it's mostly Italian, how come they're showing *A Fish Called Wanda* next Friday and not *The Godfather*?" Angie asked after reading it over.

Johnny licked whipped cream off his fingers. "The neighborhood would never go for *The Godfather*," he said.

"Why not? It's classic."

"You know." He tucked his hands in his armpits and tipped his chair back to rest against the formstone.

"What?" Angie said, comprehension dawning. "Too much like home movies?"

Johnny snorted. "Yeah. Everybody thinks we hang out on street corners with stupid meatheads named Vito saying 'fahgedaboutit' all day."

Angie laughed out loud. "Does any rational person *seriously* believe that every Italian-American family has a mobster or a hit man somewhere on their family tree?"

"Stereotypes," said her brother.

"Cultural bias," said his sister, settling back to enjoy the movie. "Fahgedaboutit."

Author's note: When the seal pool at the National Aquarium in Baltimore closed for renovation in early 2002, Ike and Lady were sent to live at the Albuquerque Biological Park. Ike died several years ago, at the ripe old age of thirty-two, but Lady, now thirty, thrives in New Mexico.

LIMINAL

BY JOSEPH WALLACE

Security Boulevard-Woodlawn

As always, the rabbi had spoken in calm, measured tones. "If we could learn to see them, we'd recognize that our existence is full of liminal moments," he'd said, "times when we've already left our previous life behind, but have yet to take the step into a new one. A liminal moment represents the space between an ending and beginning—a critically important gap, and of course potentially a very dangerous one."

That had been three days ago. Now Tania Blumen's head banged against the motel's bathroom wall, unloosing a blue-green flash deep within her skull. Pain followed after a respectful pause, radiating along her jawline and cheekbones like thunder pursuing a lightning bolt.

"God, I'm sorry, sweetie," the man said to her, his voice wet, his hands grasping the waistband of her panties and tugging. Something stung her on the hip: his fingernail tearing her skin. "I didn't mean to do that, I'll never do it again, I promise," he said. "If you'd just listened to me, trusted me . . . Didn't you know this was going to happen? You must have known. I'm asking so little, and you're making it so hard—"

Liminal moments.

Tania guessed this qualified as one.

"Room 213," the teenage clerk at the Round Tripper Inn

said. "Out that door into the courtyard, up the stairs on your right." His eyes were on her face. "You need help, come back and ask."

"The room," Tania replied, "it says the number on the door?"

The clerk blinked. "Sure."

"Then I'll find it," she told him.

"Oh, wait," he called as she hoisted her bag over her shoulder and turned away. "I forgot to tell you."

She looked back.

"Mr. Sims isn't here yet. He called to say he'd be a little late."

Tania stood still, thinking. Thinking: Still time to turn around. Still time to get on the bus and head back home.

And face Yoshi. And tell him she'd lost her nerve.

She went out into the courtyard.

Two bus rides, that's all it took to get from Falstaff Road to Security Boulevard. Yet it was a different world.

Tania stood blinking in the milky spring sunshine, the pounding in her head competing with the ceaseless roar, like a river in flood, of the boulevard a block away. No one she knew would ever find her here. The people from her neighborhood didn't work at the Social Security offices, those giant buildings that towered over the neighborhood like active volcanos. They didn't shop at the Old Navy, rent movies at the Blockbuster, buy sandwiches at the Subway and cars at the Chevrolet dealership over there, with its giant plaster fox.

And they didn't stay at the Round Tripper Inn.

But that was the point, wasn't it?

The room was suffused with brownish light filtering through

closed curtains decorated with crudely stitched crossed baseball bats. The queen-sized bedspread displayed a repeating
pattern of gloves, and the lampshades were designed to look
like baseballs. Two garish paintings of a tubby Babe Ruth
hung on the wall, a mirror with an inexplicable seashell frame
between them.

Tania felt shaky. She hadn't been able to eat breakfast
this morning, or even dinner last night. Tzom, Yoshi had
named it. The ritual fast. Purification, it was said, was an
essential part of the journey. But looking at her face in the
mirror, at its pallor in the room's earthy light, Tania didn't feel
pure.

"In the midst of a liminal moment, you are out of the
world," the rabbi had said. "For that time, it is as if you no
longer exist."

A keycard hissed as it slid into the slot outside the door
of Room 213.

Almost at once, Tania knew.

"You're so beautiful!" Gary Sims spoke in tones of awe.
"Even more beautiful than the photographs your uncle—"

"Yoshi."

"Your Uncle Yoshi sent me. Beautiful!"

"Thank you," Tania said.

Her face was hot. It did not feel like her face at all.

"Don't thank me," Gary said, placing a heavy shoulder
bag and a smaller, flatter case on the bed, then turning back
toward her and clasping his hands in front of his chest. "I
should thank you, Tania. For giving me this chance."

Gary smiled, nodded his head, made a little bow toward
her. He was maybe thirty-five, but looked younger, with a
round face, a wispy beard and mustache surrounding red lips

that stood out against his pinkish skin. Just an inch or two taller than Tania's 5'8" and always in motion, hands knotting and releasing, foot tapping, head tilted to one side, then the other, as he looked at her and away.

Making Tania feel like something heavy and ponderous, a cow, an elephant, in comparison.

But Gary seeming to think otherwise. "I couldn't tell from the photos, but your nose is perfect," he said. "Those little buttons—they just don't show up well. And those girls who get their noses broken and reset—" His hand went up and pushed at the tip of his nose. "They look like pigs, don't you think?" Another quick glance. "With you, though, I was worried about a bump. You know, a lot of girls like you have that bump right here—" Touching the bridge of his nose now. "But not you."

A lot of girls like me.

"I'm so glad to be here," he said. "It was worth the drive." Looking suddenly shy, he reached into his pocket. "I brought this for you."

A long silver necklace, interlocking links, a chain. Hanging from it was a Jewish star.

He placed it around her neck, arranged it so the star rested in the little indentation between her breasts. It shone against the navy-blue of her Goucher sweatshirt.

Tania knew then.

She understood exactly how this worked.

And why it worked.

"Your uncle told me you don't have a computer at home."

She shrugged.

A sympathetic grimace. "Why not?"

"My parents won't let me."

"Yes, that's right." He laced his fingers, pulled them

apart. "And I'll bet that's not all they're unfair about. You probably even have a strict curfew, right?"

She shrugged again.

"I guess I shouldn't be surprised." He looked thoughtful. "How old are you, Tania?"

"Seventeen," she said. "Like my uncle told you."

He shifted his weight from foot to foot. "So beautiful, so bright, but so . . . stifled. Held back. Distrusted," he said, shaking his head. "Believe me, I've heard it before, more times than you could believe." His gaze touched gently on hers. "Seventeen is old enough to start making your own decisions, don't you think?"

"Yes," she said. Then: "That's why I'm here."

"I know." His eyes were full of sympathy and understanding. "I'll help you, Tania," he said. "I swear it."

He sat down on the edge of the bed, unzipped the smaller of the two bags he'd brought, and pulled out a laptop computer. He unfolded it, rested it on his knees, and pushed a button. The computer hummed, and a moment later the screen turned from black to gray to blue.

"Let me show you what we'll be doing together." He gave her a slantwise look, then patted the bedspread beside him. "You won't be able to see from way up there," he said. "Sit."

When she hesitated, his face turned solemn, as if he was on the verge of taking offense. "Sweetie, I feel like we already know each other so well," he said. "I understand you. I know what you're trying to escape from. But you have to trust me. So keep me company. Sit."

She sat.

It was called TeenHeaven. The letters were spelled out in a flowing script with a pink heart where the "a" should have been. "The Place Where All Your Non-Nude Dreams Come True," a second line read.

"Whose dreams?" she asked.

He turned his head to look at her. She could feel the heat of his leg just a few inches from hers, and all at once she was aware of her body. Her heart pounding beneath her breasts, the band of her panties digging into her hip, a tickle of sweat snaking down the back of her neck.

"Yours," he said softly. "Your dreams, Tania."

"And theirs too." She glanced at him. "The members."

"Yes," he said. "And why not? Why shouldn't we please them? They're men and women who appreciate the energy and spirit and beauty of youth, and are willing to open their wallets to prove it."

His smile was warm on her face.

"But deep down they're nothing to me—just ghosts, phantoms out there in cyberspace. Numbers on a credit-card slip. You . . ." he sighed. "You're real. You're sitting right here with me. And your dreams are the only ones that matter."

A row of portraits, eight in all, each contained within an oval of a different pastel color. Cameos, they looked like, or popsicles, or candy eggs with girls trapped inside.

Pretty girls, fifteen years old, sixteen, seventeen. A name below each portrait, with the i's dotted with smiley faces: Jessica and Kristi and Nata, Suz and Miki and Beatriz. Smiling at the camera or giving it a pouty look.

"This is where I'll be?" Tania asked. "Here?"

"At first," Gary said. "Just at first."

He reached up and brushed the side of her face with his fingers, the lightest of touches. "I'm amazed by you," he said. "You must be the most beautiful girl in Baltimore. I know that the camera will love you as much as I do."

She blushed.

He turned back to the computer. His fingers moved across the touchpad, the moisture from her cheek leaving momentary trails on the gray surface.

"Here's how it'll go," Gary said. "We'll do the first few shoots today, here. I'll introduce you on TeenHeaven as my newest discovery—" She heard him take a breath. "Boy, will the members be happy to meet you. And then, in a couple of weeks, we'll get together again and do a full-scale session, maybe ten, twelve different outfits. Get a thousand great shots, easy, and use the best of them for the grand opening of your own site."

He paused, thinking, then smiled at her. "What say we call it 'Blooming Tania'?"

Glorious Gloria was tall and slender, with dark, wiry hair and olive skin. She often wore short-shorts, halter tops that were a size or two too small for her, long dangly earrings, brightly colored headbands. She always looked only half-awake, smiling sleepily over her bony shoulder at the camera or lying on a tan sofa in a living room with splintery floors and peeling wallpaper, her toes pointed to accentuate the length of her legs.

Starlight Stacy lived on a farm someplace warm. Even in winter she was always outdoors, feeding the chickens in her shorty pajamas, posing in muddy boots and a bathing suit amid rows of vegetables, scraping the flesh of an orange off the peel with her even white teeth, swinging on a tire in a miniskirt.

Dream Jeannie had freckles everywhere: her face, her arms, between her breasts. All her photographs were taken indoors. She almost always wore bathing suits, and had moved from tankinis in her earlier galleries to thongs in her most recent, suits so insubstantial as to leave her practically naked.

Tania felt her face grow hot again.

"I know," Gary said. "Not until you're ready. But you'll be amazed at how fast you become comfortable with the . . . more revealing outfits. Everyone does."

Joyful Jane, though, didn't look comfortable. In fact, her modeling name seemed like a joke, or an indictment. She never smiled, never once, as she posed. Her large, dark eyes and prominent cheekbones gave her a vulnerable look.

"My shy one," murmured Gary. "Popular because she's shy."

"She looks like me," Tania said.

Gary glanced up from the screen at her face. "Not a surprise, really."

Tania looked at him.

"Sweetie, you come from the same tribe."

"Everywhere," he told her. "They're from everywhere. Gloria is from Sandy, Utah. Melanie—I didn't show you her—lives in Froid, Montana. Stacy hails from Balm, Florida—"

"Are those real places?"

Gary laughed. "Yes, and there's a million more just like them. All filled with girls desperate to get out."

Tania thought about that. "So all your other models are from small towns?"

"Uh-huh. Big-city girls cause too many problems." Then he shook his head. "Well, Jane lives in Milwaukee, but she's the exception to the rule." He smiled. "Just like you are. The same exact kind of exception."

He gave a fond laugh at the confusion on her face. "Where did your family come from, Tania? Russia?"

"The Ukraine."

"Same thing." His hand touched her knee for emphasis, withdrew. "Look, sweetie, I know about Jews. Immigrant Jews. They don't move here looking for big-city lights. Wherever they settle, even if it's New York or L.A., they build their own small town."

Again that quick touch. "Take you. Your address says you live in Baltimore, but I know that you're really from the village of Park Heights. It might as well be a thousand miles from anywhere. You shop at your own stores, eat in your own restaurants, keep with your own kind. It's true, isn't it?"

She nodded.

"Especially for the girls," he said. "I mean, you don't even get to have a computer. Too busy learning to cook while the men read the Bible, right? You wouldn't even know about me if your uncle hadn't broken away from the tribe and told you."

He smiled at her silence. "Let me ask you something," he said. "Those jeans, that sweatshirt—is that how you get to dress at home?"

"No," she said.

"Of course not. You have to, like, cover up everything, right?" He frowned, on her side. "And do they ever tell you you're beautiful?"

She shook her head.

Radiating warmth, he leaned toward her, reached out and rubbed the back of her neck. "Well, you are," he said. "I love Blooming Tania, my girl from the Baltimore shtetl."

He pronounced it "shteedle."

There would be enough money for everyone to be happy, he said.

"You'll earn fifty dollars an hour for the shoots, which will usually take two or three hours." He looked up from the camera he held on his lap. "Imagine—a hundred dollars, two hundred, for just an afternoon's work! Have you ever had that much of your own?"

She said no.

"But that's just the beginning. Just the beginning, Tania! Once I set you up in your own site, you'll get ten percent of each membership fee. Right now, memberships go for twenty-five dollars a month, but it's heading up up up." His face lit up. "Think of it! Starlight Stacy has almost twelve hundred members—I write her a check for almost three thousand dollars every month from memberships alone. And, Tania, I think—I *know*—you'll do even better."

He put the camera down on the bed, stood, came over, and clasped her hands in his. "And even that's just the start. Then there's CD collections, DVDs, webcams—so many opportunities," he said. "You'll have more money than you ever dreamed of, enough to go out to restaurants, to buy the clothes you want—and wear them without anyone telling you otherwise." His grin was full of eager complicity. "I'll even buy you your very own computer."

He released her. "Now, sweetie, let's get to work."

So here it was at last.

"When you take my pictures," she asked, "will anyone else ever be . . . there? In the room?"

He shook his head. "No. Never. I promise. Just you and me—" He bent over and unzipped the larger of the two bags and pulled out a camera. "And our little witness." He pushed a button and the camera made a whining, dissatisfied sound.

A glance at her body. "I hope your uncle gave me your

measurements right." A smile. "Of course, we won't mind if the outfits I brought are a little tight, will we?"

"Can I . . ." She hesitated. "Can we start with what I'm wearing?"

Eyes narrowed, tapping his chin with a forefinger, he studied her, then aimed the finger at her sweatshirt. "Take that off," he said.

She removed her new necklace, wrapped it around her right hand, and took off the sweatshirt, static electricity snapping around her ears. Handed the sweatshirt to Gary and put the necklace back on over her gray turtleneck.

Scanning her body, Gary pushed his tongue into the side of his mouth, making a little mound in his left cheek. "Hmmm," he said.

He stepped close to her. "This will do," he decided, "with an adjustment or two."

Reaching out, he pulled the turtleneck tighter, tucking the extra fabric into the waistband of her jeans. She felt the pressure of the material through her bra against her breasts. "Better," he said.

Head tilted to one side, he walked around behind her. She felt his hand on her hip, on her waist, on her bottom. She stepped away from him, saying, "Stop that."

He seemed not to have heard her. "Next time, wear jeans a size smaller, 'kay?" he said. The camera whined again. "I think we'll start next to that chair over there."

On your tiptoes. Now lean forward a little. Good. Smile. No, try again, you look like you're eating soap. That's better. Jane has crooked teeth—that's why she keeps her mouth closed. Yes, she's planning to get them fixed. But your smile is perfect, we don't have to hide it. There! Excellent!

Now, come here. Yes, on the bed. Lie back—good! This leg up. No, like this. Your left foot here. Hmmm. Let's try it with your shoes off. Who wears shoes to bed, silly? Don't worry, only the shoes. Well, the socks too. Most people don't find socks to be a turn-on, even cute little white ones like yours. See, I'll put your shoes and socks right here near the door, where you can find them when we're done.

Oh, Tania, you have the most gorgeous feet! Our members will just love you. Some of them get very excited by feet, you know. Well, yes, I agree, it's weird. I mean—feet? But that's people, you know. You can't ever tell what will raise their temperatures. Though I have to say, when I look at you, your feet aren't the first things my eyes gravitate toward. Tania, you're blushing! Great . . . a bit of shyness, embarrassment, are perfect for your first shoot. Your cheeks are like little apples!

Okay, now, sit up. What? Don't worry, I'm not taking it off, just rolling it up a little. Just to here, so they can see your bellybutton and the bottom of your rib cage. Just a smidge higher. Now let's loosen the belt, just a couple of notches, and open this. I promise, not too much, just enough for a glimpse. I always think the glimpse is sexier than the full view, don't you?

I remember watching a comedy show on TV years ago, and there was this scene set in a nudist colony. Everyone was naked, of course—though they made sure we didn't see anything—but no one was aroused because there was, like, too much skin everywhere, you know? All the men were really bored until this dressed woman came to visit, and then, boy did they go wild, trying to figure out what she looked like under her clothes! Too funny.

You see, that's why my sites make so much money, even

though they're non-nude. It's all the power of imagination, seeing how far we'll go, always expecting, hoping, dreaming they'll catch a glimpse of something we didn't mean to show. That's why they'll love you, Tania, with your shyness and reserve and hints of something more. Oh, great. Perfect.

Now lean back. Wait, let me adjust the pillow. Good. Now arch your back. More. Excellent! You're so toned . . . do they have a gym for young Jewesses down Park Heights way? Okay, roll this way a little and look over your shoulder at us. Play with your necklace. Great. Lips apart, teeth just barely showing. Eyes open wider—we want that half-innocent, half-whore look. What, they didn't teach you that at the yeshiva? Doesn't matter, it comes natural to you. Good. Good. Good!

As Tania got off the bed, Gary stepped close and kissed her on the mouth. A quick kiss, done almost before she could react, leaving behind the impression of his soft lips and the smell of his sweat and the salamander sensation of his tongue.

"Don't do that!" she said, but he had already turned away and was back at work. Rummaging through the larger of his bags, he pulled out something white and lacy.

He came back toward her. "This next," he said, holding out the nightgown. "Give everyone a look at those lovely long legs of yours."

"I don't know," she said. Her voice was hoarse.

Something set in his face, a tightening of skin around his eyes. But when he spoke he sounded just the same. "Oh, sweetie," he said, "don't start getting all Red State on me now. It's just a nightgown. I'm not making you wear a thong or a see-through or anything like that, yet. I know you're new, which is why I didn't bring anything too . . . too *much*. But you have to work with me, Tania, you have to meet me part-way. You can't expect to show nothing, you know?"

His words washing over her.

"The opportunity provided by liminal moments is that they give you the chance to shed the skin of your past life, and be reborn," the rabbi had said. "The danger is that you may leave your old existence behind, but be unable to find your way into a new one. Then you can be lost forever."

Gary dropped the nightgown on the bed, reached down, and yanked her turtleneck out of the waistband of her pants. She felt the goosebumps rise on her newly exposed skin.

"No!" she said. Then, more quietly, "I'll change in the bathroom."

"Okay." He smiled, rubbed the back of his hand against her belly. "Take your bra off, but leave your panties on," he instructed her. "We'll give them something to dream about!"

Her face looked simultaneously chilled and feverish in the blue fluorescent light of the bathroom, her hair tangled under the headband, a vein pulsing in her forehead. Did the members find such discomfort sexy? She thought they did. That's why they liked Jane, the girl who never smiled, who looked like she was posing against her will.

Tania's eyes traced the scattering of birthmarks on her chest above her bra, the small scar on her belly, the extra flesh above her hips. Already her body didn't seem to belong to her. Already she was studying it as if she were one of *them*.

She hung the lacy white nightgown on a hook and took a closer look at it. At most, it would come down only to mid-thigh. Gary was no doubt planning future ones to be shorter still, to reveal even more.

Turning away from the mirror's accusing gaze, she

reached back, unhooked her bra, and put it down on the counter beside the turtleneck. Unzipped her jeans, pulled them down and off, folded them, and placed them on the counter as well. Took the nightgown off the hook.

She was dropping it over her head when the door swung open and Gary came in. The whites of his eyes had a yellowish sheen and his lips were very red. As she stood there, frozen, he closed the door, raised the camera, and started shooting, the repeated clicking of the shutter like a bird pecking at her skull.

"Get out!" Her voice emerged as little more than a whisper. She struggled to slide the nightgown on, but the hem got twisted around her neck. "Turn off the camera!"

He focused below her waist, the camera clicking. "You have too much hair," he said. "Our members don't like so much hair. You'll have to shave."

Suddenly the camera was on the counter and he was close to her, so close that she could smell his sweat. One hand rested on her hip while the other moved, searched, probed, further down. "Let me shave you," he said into her ear. "I love to photograph my girls as I shave them. It's the most intimate thing—"

"No!" She twisted away from him, stumbled toward the door. But before she could get it open, he grabbed her shoulder, spun her around, and hit her.

Not in the face, not where it might leave a mark during the next shoot. In the stomach. She fell back, her head slamming against the wall. And then he was up against her, his fingernail scratching her flesh as he yanked at her panties, his wet, confident voice apologizing, begging, muttering incantations that she no longer wished to make sense of.

She'd waited long enough. It was time to reenter her life.

She brought her right knee up, felt it slam into something hard and something soft. The breath whistled out of Gary like he'd sprung a leak, and then he was rolling on the floor, grasping himself, moaning and cursing, his red face suddenly white with shock and pain.

Tania stood over him. Men are amazing, she thought, rubbing the back of her head. All you have to do is keep your mouth shut, nod at everything they say, blush a little, and they assume you're whatever they want you to be. A runaway, a slut, a victim, a whore.

The one thing they never seem to expect is for you to fight back.

She untangled the nightgown and pulled it down, the soft cotton brushing against her skin. Then she stepped over the writhing, gasping Gary and walked out of the bathroom. Found her bag. Reached inside and pulled out the pistol, the .22 she'd had for three years and knew how to use.

She returned to the bathroom, stood near the door, waited for Gary to notice her. When his eyes finally stopped watering and he saw the gun, he grew very quiet and still, even as his hands continued to clutch his groin.

"Didn't anyone ever teach you," she said to him, "that when a girl says stop, she means stop?"

He stared up at her, startled by the sound of her true voice. Then he took a deep breath, another, made a nodding motion with his head. "You're right," he said, filled with contrition. "I'm sorry, Tania. I lost control. It won't happen again. I don't know what came over me. I thought you wouldn't mind. I thought you understood. My mistake. My terrible mistake. It's just that you're so beautiful, so gorgeous . . . I mean, look at yourself! Just look. Any man would have—but I know I shouldn't. I know, I know, I'm so sorry, it was like . . ."

She glanced at the mirror, saw no great beauty, just a tall girl with strong arms and long legs and lots of hair down below. Then she squatted beside Gary and put the gun to his head.

"If you apologize one more time—" she said. "In fact, if you say one more word before I tell you to, I will shoot you."

He opened his mouth, closed it again, kept quiet. At last he was learning to listen.

In the sudden silence she heard a thud, a knocking sound, a muffled curse, another thud.

Finally.

"Don't move," she said to Gary. "Don't speak." She stood, looked at the gun, back at him. "You don't know me well enough to know whether I'll use this or not."

She walked across the room to the front door, swung it open just as the man on the other side was hurling himself against it again. He came in fast, catlike, somehow keeping his balance in his heavy leather boots, his wiry hair a mess, his eyes wild beneath his tangled eyebrows. Staring at her, then scanning the room, his gaze resting briefly on Gary lying on the bathroom floor before coming back to her. His sharp-featured face turning murderous as he saw the streaks of blood on the nightgown.

Tania put a hand on his arm. "I'm okay, Yoshi," she said. "It's nothing, a scratch. I'm fine."

"It was the traffic," he said with furious frustration. "I was stuck on the Beltway, and then this boulevard—I didn't know what to do. I finally left the car at a hydrant and ran the last eight blocks, and then the guy at the desk wouldn't give me a key." His eyes were still frantic. "I was going to call you, call the police, but—"

"It would have ruined everything," she said. "You did right."

She went up on her toes and kissed him on the cheek, which at last seemed to calm him a little. "Check the bags," she said. "I'll see what he has to say."

Yoshi took a deep breath, another, and nodded.

She went back into the bathroom, where Gary had propped himself against a wall. His face was flushed a deep red, but his eyes were like blue glass beads.

"You set me up," he said. "Both of you."

Tania made a scornful gesture with her hand. "It was easy."

"You're robbing me," he said.

"Among other things."

She sat beside him, reached into his pocket, pulled out his wallet. Glanced at the address on his driver's license and sighed.

She could tell that he was looking at her. Tania thought that, despite all his praise for her beauty, he probably hadn't paid much attention to her face till now. It was her body, and how much of it she would expose to the camera, that had mattered.

He said, "How old are you?"

She raised her gaze to his. "Twenty, Gary. I'm twenty. Much, much too old for TeenHeaven."

She heard someone enter the room behind her and got back to her feet. "Gary Sims," she said, "this is my uncle, Joshua Blumen."

"Pleased to meet you," Yoshi said, and planted his boot in Gary's face.

"Shut up," Tania said.

She was wearing her own clothes, the clothes Gary had assumed were a costume or a sign of rebellion. Herself again, though not quite. Each time she emerged she was changed.

Gary lay there at her feet, hands on his face, exploring the jagged edges of his broken teeth with his tongue, blood from his cut lips streaking his fingers. He hadn't said anything.

"I'm sick of hearing your voice," she went on. "I feel like I've spent half my life listening to you babble. It's my turn to talk now. My turn."

The rabbi always said that any class that had Tania in it automatically ran a half hour late. People who wanted to see Jews as stereotypes saw her as one of the pushy, noisy types, only concerned about herself. But they were wrong too.

"First of all," she said, "if you say one more word about Jewish girls—if you ever even use the word 'Jewess' again— Yoshi will find you and kill you."

"Can I?" Yoshi asked. Then he scowled. "*Jewess?*"

He'd gotten most of his good mood back after breaking Gary's teeth. But not all of it. Gary cowered away from his dark gaze.

"You don't know a thing about Jewish girls, if you believe every one of us is hidden away, protected, pure, and innocent—" She brought her face close to his, jabbed him in the chest with a forefinger. "Helpless under your hands." She made a fist, hit him harder. "Some of us know more than you think. Some of us go to temple and wear jeans and read the Bible and have computers too. We live here—" Another blow. "In Park Heights, yes, but also in this city. In the shtetl and in Baltimore at the same time. Understand?"

He moaned.

"And for those who choose a different way, it's *their* choice," she said. "So next time, you keep your fantasies of peeking under the dress of an Orthodox Jewish girl to yourself, okay?"

Gary's head lolled. Yoshi said in a mild voice, "I think you made your point, T. And you want him to stay awake for a while, don't you?"

She sat back, breathing hard. "*God*," she said. "No, I don't."

Then she sighed, reached into the pocket of her jeans, pulled out and unfolded the sheet of paper she'd printed out the night before. Yoshi squatted beside her as she showed it to Gary.

Gary moved his lips. "Jane?" he said.

"Yes, Joyful Jane," Tania replied. "The one who never smiles. Is she still your model?"

Gary nodded.

"You still see her—work with her?"

Another nod.

"You swear?" She poked him. "You can talk now."

"Yes," he said. "She's my model."

Tania felt herself open up. Blooming Tania. "Where does she live?"

He licked the drying blood from his lips. "I told you. Milwaukee."

"Where in Milwaukee?"

"I don't know."

She slapped his face. Fresh blood flew. "Tell us where Jane lives," she said.

"I told you." His voice was thick. "Milwaukee. I've never—never seen where she lives. We meet—in a motel."

Tania raised her arm again. "But you do have her address somewhere, don't you?"

He spat bloody saliva onto the floor beside him, then slumped back against the wall. His eyes were dull. "It hurts," he said.

"Concentrate, Gary," she warned him.

He let out a breath that bubbled at the end. "At home," he said vaguely. "My desk."

"He lives in New York City," Tania told Yoshi. "Queens."

"I know." Yoshi gave a resigned grunt. "Could have been Kansas City, I guess."

Gary lifted his head. His eyes focused a little. "Jane," he said. "Why?"

"She is my cousin," Tania said.

"My niece," added Yoshi. "My brother's youngest daughter. Zhenya."

Gary's gaze went from the picture to Tania's face.

"You saw it too," Tania reminded him. "Remember? Zhenya and I, we come from the same tribe."

She splashed water on his face. Pink rivulets got caught in his patchy beard.

"Now you better talk," she said in a low voice.

They could hear Yoshi on the phone. "Yes, this is Mr. Sims in 213," he was saying. "There's no 'Do Not Disturb' sign here to hang on the doorknob. I want to make sure no one bothers me till I check out tomorrow morning . . . You sure? . . . Great. Thanks."

"He learns what you tried to do to me, I tell him the details, he really will kill you," Tania said.

Gary's tongue ran around the inside of his mouth. "What?"

"Those pictures you took of me—the ones in here." She clasped her hands to keep from hitting him again. "Do you take ones like that of Zhenya?"

He nodded.

"And the other girls?"

"Most."

"Do they ask you to stop?"

He just looked at her, as if the question made no sense.

She touched him with a forefinger. "Do they want you to stop?"

Fresh sweat broke out on his face. "Sometimes," he said. The unspoken words in his mind: *As if that mattered.*

She sighed, weary of his presence. "Just one more question. Those pictures? The ones of—of naked bodies. What do you do with them?"

"I sell them," Gary said. Even now, he couldn't quite keep the pride out of his voice. "Special clients buy them."

Tania had heard enough. "Not anymore they won't," she said.

Panic made him more alert. "You can't leave me here!"

Yoshi grinned, twisting Gary's arms behind him and expertly binding his wrists. "Just for one day," he said. "Just long enough for us to find what we need without you getting in our way. Tomorrow the cleaning lady will come in to make the bed, and she'll find you. You won't die before then."

But Gary was barely listening. "I'll shout—I'll tell the cops."

"Really?" Yoshi leaned in close. "I don't think so. You seem like a smart guy. I think what you'll do is disappear, turn up in another city, find a new line of work." He yanked on the rope and Gary whimpered. "If you tell a soul about us and what happened here today, we'll deliver everything we find in your apartment—and in your cameras—to the police."

That got through.

"And you're never going to post another picture online, ever, right?"

Yoshi picked up the wadded strip of cotton he'd ripped from the nightgown and the duct tape he'd brought with him.

"Wait," Gary said.

Tania, leaning against the wall, was ready to leave. "Make it fast."

He took a deep breath. The words came tumbling out, indistinct but comprehensible. "You—you feel so proud of yourselves, but nothing's going to change."

"Sure, Gary."

"I'm not the only one doing this," he went on. "There's others, taking pictures. Just like me. Looking for an edge. I'm gone, there's a dozen ready to jump in, take my place—and my girls."

"Just like you jumped in," Tania said calmly, "when a couple of other photographers left the business last year."

Gary nodded.

She got down beside him and looked into his eyes. "Like Phil at Young Beauties." She glanced at Yoshi. "And who was that other one?"

"Silverteen Models," he replied. "Guy had a funny name."

"Rogelio." She switched her gaze back to Gary. "Gone for good, both of them, just when they were getting successful."

Gary slowly understood what she was saying. His face went yellow.

"We've been searching for Zhenya for a long time," Tania said. "But she keeps moving on, and until now we were always a step behind."

"But Phil—" The smell of Gary's sweat and drying blood filled the room. "Phil was—"

"In the hospital for weeks," Yoshi said. "He almost died."

Tania shrugged. "Phil didn't cooperate, but, you know, I think you will."

Yoshi looked at her and she nodded. He pushed the cotton past Gary's bruised lips and into the clotted mouth, and began wrapping the contorted face with tape.

When he was done, they picked up the trussed body, Tania grasping the legs, Yoshi the torso. Together, they hauled the trembling form across the room. In a few seconds Yoshi had tied it tightly to the pipes under the sink. Gary wasn't going anywhere until someone found him.

Under the wild gaze of the shot-red eyes, they washed their hands with plenty of soap and left the bathroom for the last time.

"How could she do this?" Yoshi asked. "Zhenya. How could she be with such men?"

They were walking through the early-afternoon sunlight on Security Boulevard, Yoshi carrying Gary's two bags, Tania her own. Unless they hit bad traffic on the turnpike, Yoshi's Miata would get them to Queens by nightfall. They'd find Zhenya's address and see what else Gary's apartment had to offer.

The sun gleamed off the windows of the Social Security mountain up ahead. Horns honked and brakes squealed along the boulevard, the flood of cars carrying people toward snacks at Dunkin' Donuts and antacid at Rite Aid. But the noise and bustle seemed remote, distant to Tania, as if she were just a projection of herself placed here and the real girl was somewhere far away.

"They told her she was beautiful," Tania said. "They offered her money. They swore that her family would renounce her, would never welcome her back, not after what she had done. They put their hands on her until she thought they owned her."

Yoshi gave her a sharp look. "Is that what Gary did to you?"

Tania shrugged. "Close enough."

"I wish I'd killed him!" Yoshi knotted his hands. "You should have pulled the gun out as soon as he walked in the door."

She smiled. "Then we might not have learned anything. And anyway . . . after what happened with Phil, we agreed I'd wait till you got there."

"I know," Yoshi said. "I remember."

Phil's raging response had been . . . unexpected. Even with the pistol, Tania probably couldn't have handled him alone.

"We were lucky Gary turned out so easy," she said.

Yoshi stared at the traffic as if he wanted to challenge each car to a fight. "Security Boulevard," he said with loathing.

"And anyway, it was good." She caught his expression. "No, it was. Now I know what Zhenya heard. And the other girls too. What they heard when they were poor and scared and hungry, when they'd run away and thought everyone back home hated them."

"But we don't—"

"What was it her parents said after she left?" Tania said. "'We have no daughter!'"

Yoshi shook his head. "My brother Avi. That fool."

"And how was she to know they'd changed their minds, Avi and Rachel?" Tania asked. "She was out of reach."

They walked in silence for a while. The wail of distant fire engines wove in and out of the traffic's tidal surge. Then Yoshi spoke: "When we find her, will she come home with us?"

Tania thought about the unsmiling face, the dark,

haunted eyes she'd seen in image after image.

"I think so," she said.

Yoshi nodded. "And then, finally, we'll be done."

But Tania barely heard him. She was listening to another voice, the one that had been with her all day.

"Most of us make the mistake of thinking that such experiences occur only very rarely," the rabbi had said. "But it isn't true. Every wedding, every birth, every death, takes you out of one life and into another. Even the Sabbath lets you escape for twenty-five hours, every week of the year. And each week, the world you join is different from the one you left, just as you, yourself, are different."

He'd smiled then at all of them sitting in the pews. "Despite the risks," he'd said, "some of us find these liminal moments the most fulfilling of our lives. We welcome them, cherish them, even come to crave them. Life would be a cold, barren place if they did not exist."

They reached the Miata. There was a ticket fluttering on its windshield.

"And then we'll be done, right?" Yoshi said.

Tania felt the memory of Gary's hands on her skin. She thought of all the other girls he'd touched, and all the girls these new photographers—the eager replacements he'd brandished at them in his last gesture of defiance—would touch as well. Girls who would listen to the serpent words, and through fear or desperation or self-hatred would believe what they heard, just as Zhenya had. Girls who might want to put up a fight, but who weren't lucky enough to have an Uncle Yoshi or a .22.

She looked up, watched his eyes widen at the expression he saw in hers. "Uh-oh," he said. "We're not done, are we?"

Tania smiled at him. They came from the same tribe.

"Not quite yet," she said.

ALMOST MISSED IT BY A HAIR

BY LISA RESPERS FRANCE

Howard Park

Had it not been his body in the huge box of fake hair, I like to think that Miles Henry would have been amused.

At least, the man I once knew would have seen the humor in it: a male stylist who made his fame as one of the top hair weavers in Baltimore discovered in a burial mound of fake hair at the Hair Dynasty, the East Coast's biggest hair-styling convention of the year. It had all the elements that guaranteed a front-page story in the *Sunpapers,* maybe even a blurb in the "Truly Odd News" sections of the nationals. Television reporters swarmed the scene, desperate for a sound bite from anyone even remotely connected to Miles. Yes, it all would have been sweet nirvana to Miles, publicity hound that he was. If only he had lived to see it.

I knew him pretty well. In fact, I knew him when he was Henry Miles, the only half-black, half-Asian guy in Howard Park, our West Baltimore neighborhood. His exotic looks ensured that he never wanted for female attention, although they also made him a target for the wannabe thugs who didn't much cotton to a biracial pretty boy spouting hip-hop lyrics. He was a few years older than I was, so our paths crossed only rarely. Besides, he was the neighborhood hottie and I was a shy chubby teenager with acne. The difference in our social statures, as well as the difference in our ages, limited us to the socially acceptable dance of unequals. Meaning, I stared at him and he didn't know I was alive. It was only when we were grown and found ourselves cosmetology competitors that we began to talk to one another.

Not that my little shop, Hair Apparent, could ever be considered a true threat to Miles's chain of mega-salons, His and Hairs. There were four His and Hairs in the Baltimore metropolitan area, combination hair-and-nail emporia where Baltimore's celebrities went to get their 'dos done. In our city, celebrity is defined as female television anchors, the wives of the pastors at the mega-churches, and strippers, although not necessarily in that order. Miles had started doing hair in college as a way of meeting women and discovered he was actually good at it, especially when it came to taking a woman who was close to bald-headed and transforming her into Rapunzel. He was the king of the weave.

He shared his empire with his older sister Janice who had renamed herself Kylani and taken to playing the role of Dragon Lady, complete with super-long talon nails and makeup that emphasized her Asian features. I had never much liked her and I wasn't alone. She was condescending to everyone and she made a big show of how much money she and her brother were raking in. Miles oversaw the beauty shops, she managed the nail business, and they both joked that their success was based on combining all the salon stereotypes—African-American stylists on one side, Asian nail technicians on the other, gossip everywhere.

Kylani was ambitious, always pushing Miles to expand the business into Washington, D.C. or maybe even New York. Vain as Miles was, he at least recognized that it was better to be a big fish in Baltimore than a small fish anywhere else. He was all about expanding the businesses they already owned and plowing the profits into better equipment, the newest technology, and anything else that made the salon more upscale. Kylani seemed to be all about directing her share toward her wardrobe, trips, and cars. Miles told plenty of people that the nail side of the business would never have been profitable without his constant improvements.

I was privy to such confidences because I was publicity chair for our local branch of Cosmetology Representatives and Appearance Professionals—an organization of hair-dressers, makeup artists, nail technicians, and fashion stylists that is known by the unfortunate acronym CRAAP. Miles was president of CRAAP, so we spent more time together as competitors than we ever had as kids growing up in the same neighborhood.

"Now Jordan, I know this is way more than you're used to handling," he had told me at our last planning session, pick-ing pieces of lint from the oversize sweater he wore. These Bill Cosby throwbacks were Miles's trademark, an odd choice given the fact that his salons were so ultra-chic. The joke around town was that he did it to reinforce the image that he was straight because no gay man would ever allow himself to be seen looking so unstylish. Maybe so, but the things were dust and dirt catchers, picking up more stuff than a Swiffer.

"I'm on top of it," I said. "I've got Cathy Hughes's local radio stations on board and you're going to be on Larry Young's talk show on 1010."

"You're doing fine *locally*." Pick, pick, pick—the sweater and me were both getting raked over. "But we have to pull this thing off with class. So no ghetto fashion shows or tacky discos. Think high-end. See if you can get the D.C. stations and maybe Philly to cover this. You have to reach beyond your usual comfort level."

Just who did he think he was talking to, I seethed. Whose marketing plan had landed us Hair Dynasty? I may have been only twenty-three, but it was my brainstorm to send crab cakes, Utz potato chips, and gallons of "half-and-half" to the organizers. Half-and-half is a local concoction, a mix of iced tea and lemonade, and it is pure ambrosia. I was positive that it had sealed the deal.

Half-and-half is a good analogy for hair shows—you didn't have to grow up in a black neighborhood to get it, but it sure helped. Black hair care is big time, a billion-dollar-a-year business these days. But a hair show is more three-ring circus than sedate gathering of professionals, with every stylist scheming to steal the show. Demure chignons and sleek pageboy cuts were not the norm at Hair Dynasty. You'd be more likely to see a woman with the Statue of Liberty rising from her hairline, woven from suitably patriotic red, white, and blue hairpieces. Or a model strutting the catwalk in an haute couture "hair dress" that started at her temples, criss-crossed around her neck, and extended down her body to form a sweeping floor-length gown. The overall effect made the wearer look like a slightly less hairy version of Cousin Itt.

Wefts of hair were sewn or glued in, blow-dried, sprayed, teased, and pinned. There were perms and curls, braids and weaves, and more dyed-color combinations than they have at Sherwin-Williams. People still talked about the year a Chicago stylist sent out a model with a weave designed to look like a satellite dish and a television. The thing actually worked and got pretty good reception. We never figured out how he pulled it off without showing any wires or electrocuting the girl who had to balance it.

And now the whole circus had come to Baltimore, whose motto could be: *A Small Town With Big Hair.* We take hair very seriously in my hometown. I'd taken the credit for getting the show here and now I had to take responsibility for making it a success. It was all going according to plan—until Miles's body was discovered.

It was late morning on the first day of the convention and I felt I looked like quite the young professional in my cream-colored linen suit. Sure, almost everyone else would be in basic black, the calling card of the beauty business, but I wasn't working any heads that day so I thought I could afford to dress up. Besides, as publicity chair, I needed to be camera-ready. Just because I was barely 5'4" and about twenty pounds overweight didn't mean I couldn't be fly.

I walked the exhibition floor with pride, enjoying the happy buzz of a convention in full swing—flamboyant demonstrations of new styling techniques, salespeople hawking the latest shampoos and conditioners absolutely guaranteed to give the user thick, glossy, long hair in two days. Loud was good, a sign of people enjoying themselves. Unfortunately, the happy din of the convention center wasn't loud enough to drown out the screams of the unfortunate young woman who found Miles.

His impromptu shroud of fake hair was behind some dividers that had been used to create a storage area and her screams bounced off the convention center's concrete walls. The acoustics made it hard to figure out exactly where the ruckus was. By the time I got there, security was cordoning off the area with those elastic stands usually used in banks and airports. The ones where if you lift the top portion, the band snaps right back into the pole like a hyper rubber band. Several people had surrounded the woman and were trying to quiet her hysterics.

It was looking more and more likely that I would be on television, but not in the celebratory manner I had envisioned.

"Let me through," I said, as I attempted to squeeze by what looked like a crowd trying to make it into a hot nightspot. "I'm with the organizing committee and I need to know what's going on."

Luckily, my best friend and business partner Jennifer was close by. She waved me over as she tried to dispense tissues in the general direction of the weeping.

"Listen up," she said loudly, trying to be heard over the now gulping sobs of the crying girl. "This is Jordan Rivers and she is going to escort this poor child to a quiet area where she can relax and prepare herself to speak with the authorities."

The girl was wearing the standard stylist uniform of black T-shirt and black slacks, and she looked up from the center of the group with red-rimmed eyes, which were set off nicely by the black lines of mascara streaking her face. "Authorities," she moaned. "I have to talk to the cops?"

"That's usually what happens when you find a dead body," I told her, trying to reach through the others to grasp hold of her arm. "You have had quite a shock. Let's find you someplace to sit down and relax."

"Suppose she don't want to go with you." A glowering young man whom I hadn't noticed had his arm firmly wrapped around her waist. "Do you have some identification or something?"

"I'm not the police. I'm Jordan Rivers and I'm in charge of publicity here. I'm not going to take your friend far, just to an office on the next floor to get her away from the crowd. Security is having enough trouble keeping people away from the body, and in a minute they are going to figure that getting the details from the person who found the body might be the next best thing. Now, sweetie, what's your name?"

"It's okay, Chris," she hiccupped in the direction of her

protector, before turning to address me. "I'm Diana. I'm a wash girl at Divas Salon and I had just went to get some hair for my boss when—"

"No need to explain it all right now," I said, aware of how gossip would sweep through this crowd. "Let's go find you a chair and get you a glass of water or maybe some tea."

Like a child trying not to lose a parent in a crowd, she reached out and grabbed hold of the back of my suit jacket. I guess I was about to find out how "wrinkle-free" my linen suit actually was. I guided her through the maze of people to the elevator and up to the third-floor meeting room used as our nerve center for the event. Along the way, I stopped to ask a security guard to send the police up as soon as they arrived. Several of my colleagues tried to catch my eye and some even called out my name but I kept moving, concentrating on trying to radiate serenity to Diana who had the back of my jacket balled up in a death grip. I shooed a few people from the room and grabbed a bottle of water for Diana out of the mini fridge in the corner as she dropped limply onto the beige couch that dominated one wall. I pulled a rolling chair from the conference table in the center of the room and turned it so I sat facing her.

"Are you okay?" I asked. "Is there anyone I should call for you?"

"I should call my mom and tell her what happened," she said. "Shoot! I left my purse downstairs, and my cell phone and everything is in it."

"Don't worry about it. Your friends will watch out for your stuff, I am sure. And in a minute this place will be crawling with Baltimore's finest and I doubt that thieves will be making off with much today. So why don't you tell me what happened."

"I was washing hair for Cindy. I'm in cosmetology school and I work for her at Divas. A lot of us like to work the hair shows because you can make extra money and pick up some tips. I want to have my own salon someday. Anyway, Cindy had run out of hair and asked me to go get some more. I couldn't find the color she needed in the top of the box and so I kept digging, and that's when I felt something hard. I pulled my hand out and it was sticky. I realized that it was blood and I started pulling hair out of the box, and that's when I saw him. I just started screaming and I couldn't even talk. It was awful."

"How was he laying?"

"He was on his stomach," she said, before covering her hands with her face as if trying to blot out the memory. "He had a pair of scissors sticking out of his back." She wrapped her arms around herself as if to warm her body. I sympathized with her, having found my beloved Aunt Tilly's body. And while her death hadn't been a violent one, I knew the shock which accompanied seeing the shell of a person after the spirit had fled. It was a sight that could chill you.

Before I could ask anything more, a pair of police detectives walked in and I suppressed a groan. Did I mention that Baltimore was small?

"Jordan," my sister said with that girl-don't-give-me-no-mess tone I knew all too well. "Can you excuse us please?"

I know, I know—what are the odds of my sister catching the body at my convention? Actually, in Baltimore, about one-in-five. Census says 600,000-plus in the city proper, over a million in the metro area, but I swear there are only sixty, seventy-five people tops, and I know them all. So, anyway, my good luck, right? Wrong.

You would think my sister Euphrates and I would be closer despite the fifteen-year age difference. She knew the agony of being saddled with a name that elicited guffaws and corny jokes, even though she had used her middle name, Patricia, ever since she was a teenager. But we couldn't be more different. At 5'9" she was way taller than me, and where I could pinch way more than an inch, she was thin and muscular. I was a glam girl who loved the latest hairstyles and fashions and she looked like she had been wearing the same outfit since 1991, though the colors rotated among blue, black, and army-green.

But our differences went more than skin deep. She's always been as straitlaced as they come and more of a second mother to me than an older sister. As my mama liked to say, "Euphrates don't stand for no types of nonsense," and that's probably what drew her to the police force straight out of high school. When she made detective, she was the youngest African-American woman in the history of the department.

But the wildest thing she ever did was marry a white Jewish guy and set up house in a semi-Orthodox neighborhood in Pikesville where they were raising my gorgeous niece and nephew. While I considered myself a bit of a free spirit, my sister never met a rule she didn't like. Sometimes it seemed like she would purposely set out to do the exact opposite of what I did. If I went right, she went left. Even though she opted for a career just like I did, she still managed to get her Bachelor's in Criminal Justice by going to school at night, and I knew she was disappointed that I didn't go to college. It was as if she thought everything I did or didn't do was personally directed at her. I felt the same about her too, some days. I was convinced that she kept her hair cut short in a natural as a direct slap at me as a stylist. Like she would much rather go to a barber shop than have her own sister do her hair.

Now her partner, Ahmad Johansen, was another story. I had long ago decided that Ahmad was my soul mate, though he has been a bit slower at coming to that realization. Ahmad means "greatly praised" in Arabic, and Detective Johansen had a lot to be praised for. Six-foot-two, chiseled physique with café au lait skin, gray eyes, and a voice that rivaled Barry White, the man was the epitome of *fine* but carried himself in such a way that you knew he had no idea why women had a tendency to stop and stare at him when he walked by. He was as easygoing as my sister was stiff. They made quite a team.

After a few minutes, the office door opened and my sister and Ahmad came out. "U", as I liked to call her to remind her that someone hadn't forgotten where she came from, motioned to a uniformed officer further up the hallway. He looked all of twenty years old and scrambled to do my sister's bidding.

"We are going to transport the witness to the station to take a formal statement," she told the cadet. "Until then, make sure no one talks to her."

She looked right at me when she said that, then added: "Jordan, where can we chat?"

We walked down the corridor into another meeting space, this one small, and probably more importantly to my sister, unoccupied. U motioned for me to sit in one of the chairs, but I chose to lean against the meeting table instead. No way was she going to make me feel like a suspect by towering over me during questioning.

"So," my sister said, "what do you know?"

"I know that Miles is laying dead in a box full of hair. Other than that, you probably know more than I do."

"I doubt that, Jordan. You looked like you were deep in conversation with the witness when we arrived."

"Said witness has a name," I replied, crossing my arms. "All Diana said was that she was going to get some hair for her boss and that's when she found Miles. If I knew more, I'd tell you more."

"Look, Jordy," my sister said, reverting to my childhood nickname, "we may need your help with this one. You know all the players here and I suspect that this thing with Miles was personal. The uniforms say he still has his wallet on him so we can rule out robbery. And besides, it would be more likely that we would be dealing with a pickpocket with a crowd this size than a robber who would take the chance on knifing someone in a convention center filled with people. Plus, he was stabbed with a pair of scissors that had some type of ivory inlay on the handles. Very high-end. Can you think of anyone who might want to hurt Miles?"

"I hate to speak ill of the dead, but the man could be a jerk," I said. "He was a massive womanizer to start. And seeing as how he had poached clientele from just about every stylist in B-more, anyone here could have had a motive."

"That's why we need you to help us narrow down the field," my sister said. "You are always up in everybody's business so I'm sure you know if he's been having problems with anyone lately."

"First of all, I dislike the implication that I am nosy," I sniffed. "It's not my fault that people confide in me. I just have an air of trustworthiness that I exude."

Ahmad stifled a laugh. I tried to give him my best dirty look, but was distracted by his gorgeousness.

"It might help if I could see the body," I said, tapping my cheek as if I was speculating about something.

"Jordan," my sister practically yelled, "this is not an episode of *Murder, She Wrote*. I am not going to have you traipsing all over a murder scene!"

"Look," I huffed, "do you want my help or not? I promise I won't go running through the blood and mess up your precious forensics. Maybe I'll recognize the murder weapon or see something that might be out of the ordinary. I helped plan this whole event, in case you have forgotten!"

"Jordan might have a point," Ahmad piped in. "She can't do much damage if we are right there with her."

I looked at him with a combination of gratitude for recognizing the value of my insight and irritation for his insinuation that I needed to be baby-sat.

"Let's go," my sister said, turning quickly and practically barreling out of the room.

Downstairs had turned into a bit of a madhouse with police swarming the area and everyone craning to see what was happening. Some young women I recognized as His and Hairs employees were crying and comforting each other near the three booths that had been set up to showcase designs from the salon. My sister flashed her badge to clear a path for us and we stepped gingerly around the dividers that had been shielding Miles's corpse from view.

I'd seen him looking better. His face had already taken on that ashen look of the dearly departed, and a small trickle of blood appeared to be coming out of the corner of his mouth. Or it could have been a strand of hair, as he was laying on a pack of "Ridiculously Red, Number 38." A police photographer was snapping away, periodically pushing the bottom of his Baltimore City Police Department jacket to the side to avoid the zipper as he crawled around and laid flat to get multiple angles. Miles was on his stomach, head turned to the side, his hands on either side of his head, as if he had tripped and was trying to soften his fall.

Most of the plastic packets of hair had been cleared from on top of him and I could make out the black crocheted sweater he was wearing over a T-shirt, and the handle of the scissors was sticking out through one of the holes near his left shoulder blade. Those sweaters had been the bane of the planning committee's existence because Miles insisted that the center be kept well air-conditioned so *he* wouldn't swelter. Not much of a problem, except that it was unseasonably cool outside even for a Baltimore April and many of the models were running around wearing next to nothing other than tons of hair. Maybe, I thought, one of them wigged out and killed him. The old "I-murdered-because-my-brain-froze" defense. Johnnie Cochran, may he rest in peace, could have taken that one on.

"See anything out of the ordinary?" Ahmad asked.

"Well, he's dead all right."

"Other than that, Columbo."

"It's hard to tell," I said. "Maybe if I could get a little closer look." There was something about Miles's sweater that seemed off. Were those holes part of the design, or had they opened up in a struggle?

"Forget about it, Jordan," Ahmad said. "I'm surprised your sister even let you get this close."

That's when I realized that U was no longer with us. I stepped around the divider and caught a glimpse of her through the crowd about ten feet away talking to C.P. Murray, hairdresser and drama king extraordinaire. No one knows what the initials C.P. are short for, but my theory is that it stands for "Chile, please" because that's what I feel like saying every time he opens his mouth. Forty-five if he was a day, but he claimed he hadn't crested thirty yet.

He gave himself away reminiscing about the old-style hairdos he used to craft. He had cornered me more than once during the weeks before the show to chat about his glory days, clutching his little two-ounce Chihuahua, Bouf (short for bouffant). "We really must figure out a way to get national coverage of the absolutely fabulous salons we have here. Baltimore is the place to go for the latest styles and no one seems to know it. Forget New York and L.A., honey. We set the trends when it comes to black hair! Was I not the first to do the asymmetrical cut with the deep finger waves and the glittery bangs? Tell me that wasn't fierce!"

It did no good to explain to him that we were lucky enough to get *any* coverage for Hair Dynasty, and I had only managed to pull that off because I convinced the photographers that they would get colorful shots of creations like the "Domestic Goddess," which entailed a model with a hair-sculptured kitchen sink on her head complete with wet and wavy hair coming out of the "faucet" to simulate running water. And unless Oprah or Halle Berry started jetting to B-more to get their hair done, I doubted that the national media was going to pay much attention to us.

Although, now they would. *Death by scissors, buried in hair.* Miles had a shot at the cover of his beloved *Weekly World News.*

U raised her hand and made a come-here motion, but when I started that way she shook her head vigorously and mouthed "Ahmad." I stepped around the divider again and tapped him on the shoulder. "She who must be obeyed beckons," I said. But I was right behind him. My sister was out of her mind if she thought I wasn't going to listen in on what C.P. had to say. Jennifer had spotted me tailing Ahmad and she caught up with me, linking her arm with mine.

"Yes, we argued, but we always argued," C.P. was whining as Ahmad, Jennifer, and I strode over. "Ask anyone. He was very jealous of my business." He motioned to the large black banner on the booth which contained the name of his salon, Isn't She Lovely, in gold letters. "But I wouldn't have killed the man." He shifted his dog under his arm and held him like a purse while he looked to two of his employees who were doing hair at the booth for confirmation.

"We have information that you threatened Mr. Henry just a few hours ago," U said calmly.

"Me?" C.P. asked incredulously. "Why in the world would I threaten Miles?"

"Remember, you said you would slit his throat if he kept coming over here stealing your hair spray," piped up one of C.P.'s employees, a petite honey-colored woman with chunky fuschia highlights in her hair. C.P. shot her a venomous look over his shoulder.

"Figure of speech, Mona," C.P. said, a little louder than necessary. "I am a nonviolent animal lover." He patted Bouf for emphasis.

"We were also told that you changed clothes, Mr. Murray," U further explained. "Now why would you do that?"

C.P. whipped around to face Mona. "You are deliberately trying to destroy me!" he screeched. "It's because I wouldn't give you last Friday off, isn't it?"

"Calm down, Mr. Murray," Ahmad intoned. "No one is accusing you of anything . . . yet."

"Do you own a pair of ivory inlay scissors?" U asked, studying C.P.'s face closely.

"I do, and I can show them to you," C.P. said quickly, walking over to his work station where he dug through his many supplies. "They were right here this morning. Mona! Did you steal my scissors? I swear, when this is over we are having a very long talk, you and I."

At that moment, a uniformed officer with a name tag that read "A. Jenkins" escorted a visibly distraught Kylani over to where we were. "Detectives, this is the victim's sister and she's demanding to see the persons in charge of the investigation," the officer said.

"Arrest this man!" Kylani screamed. "He killed my brother."

C.P. paled and opened and shut his mouth so hard that I thought his teeth were going to shatter. He sputtered and managed to choke out, "I have no idea what she is talking about."

"They argued this morning," Kylani continued. She was actually wringing her hands, holding one fist tight inside the other. Given the length of her nails, it had to hurt, but she seemed too distraught to notice.

"I was standing right here when it happened. C.P. said Miles had stolen the last client he was ever going to take from him. He promised he would get even. I'll never see my brother again!" she wailed, then collapsed against the police officer.

"Where's the shirt you were wearing earlier, Mr. Murray?" my sister asked.

"I got some dye and perm on it so I asked my assistant to wash it with the last load of towels," C.P. stammered. "She left an hour ago to go to the laundry. I swear to you, I would never hurt Miles. I was one of his mentors."

"I think we should continue this discussion at the station," U stated, all business.

"How could you, C.P.?" Kylani cried, as the officer propped her back up on her feet. "How could you stab my little brother with your special scissors after pretending all this time to be his friend?" She threw her hands up to her face and tilted backwards as if she were about to swoon again.

"U, wait," I said. "Officer Jenkins, did you take Kylani to see her brother's body?"

"No ma'am," Jenkins replied. "The crime scene is still being processed."

"Kylani," I tried to boom in my most authoritative voice. "Give it up. Once the police review the security tapes, they will know that *you* killed Miles."

Her head shot up and the tears magically disappeared. "Are you nuts?"

"The jig is up, girlfriend," I said. "You stole C.P.'s scissors and stabbed your brother. Either you lured him to the storage area or he was already back there, but you shoved him in that box of hair and covered him up, probably because he was too heavy to drag someplace else and you couldn't chance somebody seeing you."

"Why would I do such a thing??" She was good at mock indignation, I'll give her that. But then, the whole performance had been top-notch, undone by only one little detail.

"I have no idea," I said confidently. "But I can assure you that the police will find evidence on his body that connects you to the murder. You messed up and left something behind."

With that, I grabbed her right hand and held it up to her face.

She wrenched away from me and tried to run, but both Ahmad and the uniformed officer grabbed an arm and snatched her back. She rained down curses on me as they cuffed her and led her away. Jennifer gave me a high-five and C.P. reached out and hugged me, squeezing Bouf between us. He promptly yelped and nipped me. Bouf, not C.P.

"Well, little sister," U smiled, "that was quite a bit of investigative work. How did you figure it out?"

"I got suspicious when she mentioned the scissors," I said. "How did she know that? Even if someone had said he had been stabbed, she wouldn't necessarily know that it had happened with a pair of scissors. But the clincher was her nails."

"Her nails?" U questioned.

"Yeah. Two of her tips were broken off. She probably snagged them in Miles's sweater dragging his body into that box of hair. I thought I saw something stuck in the crochet. Her nails were her calling card and there is no way she'd be at a hair show with them looking a hot mess like that."

Jennifer started giggling, C.P. guffawed, and U rolled her eyes. Bouf even gave a high-pitched bark of amusement.

"Well," U said, "good thing you knew about the tape from the security cameras."

"Umm, yeah," I grinned sheepishly. "If that even exists. I was bluffing. It always works on the TV shows."

My sister actually cracked a smile and said, "Okay. But next time, find a show with better dialogue. *The jig is up, girlfriend* was a bit much, even for you."

Before I could respond, I felt a tap on my shoulder. I turned around to find Olive, my vice-chair for publicity, wringing her hands and looking distraught.

"Jordan, you've got to come," she said in a rush. "We have, um, a situation."

"A situation other than a murder?"

"Yeah," she said. "See, I was being proactive and I thought we should do something to take folks' minds off this mess, so I made an executive decision. I mean, I couldn't find you and you are always saying, 'Be empowered,' so I thought, 'WWJD. What would Jordan do?' People are here to have a good time as well as network and show off their skills, and I started thinking, *We need to refocus here . . .*"

"Olive." I used all my will not to scream at her. "Please get to the point."

"Well," she said, "I sent out the specialty hair models."

"So?" I actually thought it was a good idea. The local-themed 'dos included an Oriole and a black-eyed Susan.

"It's the crab," she sighed. "It went haywire."

Someone had come up with the beyond-obvious idea to construct a huge steamed crab, orange-red as if it had just emerged from the pot. The "Crustacean Creation" was to be the *pièce de résistance* of all the hair art. I had vetoed the Old Bay seasoning glitter on the grounds that it would create a mess, but gave in on the rigging that allowed the small, black beady eyes and long claws to move. The stylist, who had majored in mechanical engineering before dropping out of Morgan State University, was to follow at a discreet distance and work the contraption using a wireless remote.

"Define *haywire*," I said, feeling a massive headache starting behind my eyes.

"Just come see," Olive said, as she grabbed my upper arm and led me forward.

Yet another crowd had gathered, this time around local newspaper photographer Sal Dorsey, one of the old-timers. Sal was tilted forward as if he were about to take a header into the floor, and his camera swung like a pendulum from his neck. His bald patch had reddened until it was almost the same color as the hair crab that had him in its grip. Yes, the only thing keeping Sal from sprawling face-forward was a giant claw, which was giving him a crustacean wedgie. Even as the stylist pushed multiple buttons, trying to loosen the hair crab's grip, the model continued to smile robotically at Sal's colleagues, who were busy snapping photos even as they shook with laughter.

What can I say? The only thing more hard-shelled than the local delicacy are the locals themselves. And while I was sorry for Sal, I realized these photos would get far more play than the murder, just another Baltimore domestic, already fading in public memory with Kylani's arrest.

Poor Miles—upstaged by a crab.

ODE TO THE O'S

BY CHARLIE STELLA

Memorial Stadium

A light drizzle had just started to fall when the two men moved their conversation from the waterside tiki bar to an inside corner table still overlooking the Inner Harbor. James "Jilly" Cuomo brushed his thin gray hair back with both hands after sitting with his back to the windows. Tommy "Red" Dalton, a tall man with broad shoulders, positioned his chair so he could see the boats docked on the far side of the marina.

A short waitress with a big chest and a long ponytail had followed them with their drinks. "Anisette?" she asked.

Jilly pointed to a spot on the table directly in front of him. The waitress set a napkin down first, then his drink. She smiled at Tommy before placing his glass of water on a napkin in front of him.

"I guess this is yours," she said.

Tommy winked at her.

"Anything else?" she asked.

"Not right now," Jilly told her.

She was still looking at Tommy.

"No thanks," he said.

Jilly glanced at her ass when she left. "Nice rack, but she could use a little more meat, you ask me," he said. He turned to Tommy and the conversation that had been interrupted by the rain. "He's got you in the car, yeah, and . . . ?"

Tommy said, "I says to him, I says, if you're thinking she's out there, she pro'bly is. There's nothin not gut-check about it, what we're talkin. A guy knows, same as a broad, it comes to that. You just do. Junior says to me, he says, 'I'm pretty sure something is going on.'"

Jilly was mid-yawn. "The moron," he tried to say.

"This is that day couple weeks after I first meet him at the party down here, this place. I figure he figures I'm around his age and all, he can talk to me, it won't go nowheres. This is before I get sent for by the old man, of course, which, I gotta tell you, I first get that call, I'm thinking, uh-oh, the fuck I do to deserve this? Sometimes you get sent for, you get dead."

Jilly nodded. "It's a smart assumption. A guy should be prepared for whatever, especially these days."

Tommy was enthusiastic. "Right, exactly, but at the time I get the call, I'm not thinking straight enough to figure that out. I'm just thinking I fucked up and now I gotta pay for it. Maybe get whacked for whatever the fuck and I got no clue what it is, it might be. Makes it even tougher to think, that happens, you get sent for out the blue like that."

Jilly sipped at his anisette. "Yeah, so . . . back to Junior."

Tommy said, "Right, so, Junior has me there in that old tank he drives, the Lincoln, he turns to me, he says, 'Look at my eyes.' I do and they're all red, bloodshot from crying it looks like, or he didn't sleep the last hundred years, maybe he's a vampire or somethin. Anyway, I see they're red and he says, right out there, just like this, 'I think my wife is fucking around.'"

Jilly frowned.

"Exactly," Tommy said. "I mean, all due respect, it's a tough thing, you find your wife is out there and all, but Jesus Christ, Junior, grow a pair."

"The kid is weak," Jilly said. "He's always been weak."

"Yeah, but what the fuck am I doin there listenin to it? I mean, Jilly, I know the guy less than two, three weeks, he picks my shoulder to cry on?"

"What he say?"

"This and that, her routine the last couple weeks since she got some promotion at work, whatever. Makin excuses, findin reasons, I don't know. He's losin sleep, he don't wanna confront her, he don't know for sure. He's all fucked up in the head, which I know for fact because I'm sitting there listenin to it. It's pathetic is what it is. Not for nothin, he's my kid, I gotta think about takin him out the Gunpowder River there and lose him."

"I'm sure it's crossed the old man's mind more'n a couple times," Jilly said, "except it's his son."

"What I figure, yeah," Tommy said. He stopped to drink most of the water in his glass.

Jilly noticed the waitress watching Tommy from across the room. He motioned toward her with his head. "I think you got a fan."

Tommy glanced her way and smiled. "She isn't half bad," he said, "except it's a headache I don't need right now. The wife says to me the other week, she says, 'Don't forget our anniversary is coming.' That turned out to be a week ago and of course I forgot. Now I'm paying for it in spades. Every night I go out I'm not dragging one of the kids, I gotta hear it full throttle on the way out and all over again when I get back."

Jilly motioned at the glass. "Sure you don't want something stronger?"

Tommy waved it off. "Positive," he said. "I never drink on a job. Never ever."

"You're not working now," Jilly said. "Not yet."

"Irregardless."

Jilly downed his anisette. He spit a coffee bean into his open palm and then slapped the empty shot glass on the table. "Better you'n me," he said. "Not drinkin, I mean."

"Anyway," Tommy continued, "Junior tells me this sob story about his wife and what he thinks is going on and how he feels he can trust me because he asked around and so on. And this is all confidential, what he says to me. He says it's to stay between us, me and him, but that his father is aware of the situation too. Which now I know, or why'm I here tonight with you?"

Jilly yawned again before looking at his watch. "Be grateful there's an end to this nightmare," he said, "this New York prick ever gets here."

Tommy gathered his thoughts. "I says to him, I says, what about her routine? She buy new clothes? She getting her hair done different? She wearing new shoes? You know, obvious shit. 'Yeah,' he says, 'come to think of it.'"

Jilly smirked. "Dumb cocksucker."

"Please, you don't know the half of it," Tommy said. "No wonder, what I'm thinking, his wife is out there. The fuck can blame her, she's dealing with that mess every end of the day."

"So, what, he sent you out looking?"

Tommy nodded. "Which is another thing I didn't appreciate," Tommy said. "Sittin around waitin on a guy, a job, whatever, is one thing. Followin some broad around, see who she's bangin in her spare time, that I can live without. Felt too much like the law, spying like that. It's lowlife work. Bad enough I gotta do it, but then I gotta give him a call, Junior, and meet him at the diner over West Mulberry off Forty, give him a report. Knowin she's out there, just knowin it, wasn't enough. This fuckin loser wants details."

Jilly made a face. "Details?"

Tommy threw up his hands. "I says to him, I says, 'I'm not there in the room with them, Junior. How do I know what they're doin inside?' What most people do, they meet at some motel on the sly, middle of the fuckin afternoon, they're supposed to be at work. Not good enough. The jerkoff wants to know were they holdin hands before they went in. Did they kiss? Were they touchy-feely?"

"Asshole," Jilly said.

"I couldn't make things up, but I didn't watch that close, tell you the truth, what they did before and after they screwed each other's socks off. I said I didn't know, but they seemed chummy."

"He get a rise out of that?"

"If his eyes turn to a pool of water count for anything, yeah, I guess."

Jilly shook his head. "This is too familiar, tell you the truth, although Senior didn't sit around take it up the ass, I'll tell you that much."

Tommy seemed surprised. "The old man, the boss?"

"Was '69, the year New York fucked us from both ends, the Jets over the Colts in the Super Bowl there, and then the Mets over the O's in the series. You pro'ly weren't born yet."

"Don't think I was. I was like, six, that other thing happened, midnight run, the Mayflower vans, whatever."

"Don't get me wrong," Jilly said, "we all earned. Anybody taking action made out that year, but then there's that other thing, the pride issue. Bitter fucking pill to swallow, losing to New York twice the same year. Made Angelo crazy, that's for sure."

"What happened?"

Jilly glanced around the restaurant before he leaned forward to whisper. "Senior gets wind his old lady is out there with some guy with the Erioles," he said. "Had me and Eddie Bats, which was the muscle end of his crew back then, had us thinking it was one of the team we was gonna have to whack. This is the same night the O's take game one down Memorial. Cuellar beat Seaver, goes the distance on a six hitter. Buford nails Seaver first inning, home run. Great fucking game."

Jilly sat back to savor the memory. He saw Tommy was waiting for more, and then leaned forward again. "Anyway," he continued, "Angelo gets wind it's somebody with the Erioles organization with his wife, but there's only two of us he comes to this with. He wants it dealt with quiet, no muss, no fuss, but serious, no bullshit either."

"Was he runnin his own crew back then?"

"Yeah and no," Jilly said. "We were his guys, me and Eddie Bats. Like I said, his muscle, but we weren't a formal crew. Things was different back then. Why the books never reopened here. Baltimore fell outta the loop when it came to families and so on, what they got there in New York."

"I hope it was better'n it is today," Tommy commented.

"Today you got rats riding shotgun," Jilly said. "Makes it hard to get serious about taking a blood oath, the guy giving it is wearing a wire. Another New York phenomenon, the bosses rat now."

"Yeah, well, makes it hard to earn sometimes, what we got down here," Tommy said. "There's strength in numbers."

Jilly said, "Weakness, too, but you're young yet, you'll learn. More guys on a job, more you got to worry about. I did two bids at Maryland Pen before it become a transition center, whatever the fuck that means, because a couple too many guys on a job couldn't hold their water."

Tommy nodded.

"Just sit tight about earning," Jilly said. "You'll get your play soon enough. You're with tight people now."

Tommy said, "So what happened, the old man?"

Jilly leaned forward again. "Angelo was married a few years," he whispered. "Maria was what, I don't know, twenny-five, maybe? Twenny-six? Anyway, Angelo sends me and Eddie to the stadium see what's what after the game. He had some guy from the dock workers' union there feeding him tickets down to the field boxes he hands off to Maria. She was a big fan. Where he met her originally, an Erioles game."

"No shit?"

"I shit you not." Jilly stopped to push his empty shot glass closer to the edge of the table for the waitress. "She takes her eyes off'a you a minute, maybe she sees I'm dry over here."

Tommy turned to the waitress and pointed at Jilly's empty glass. She started over.

"Anyway, winds up Maria likes them young," Jilly continued. "She married Angelo, and he was up there in age compared to her, but the kid she's with out the stadium lot there a couple times a week, one of the kids hawking the beers and soda and whatnot, working the stands there, he's gotta be twenny-one, I guess, he was selling the beer, but that's a lot younger than she is, or Angelo was. Bottom line, it's not Boog Powell, Brooks Robinson, or Jim fucking Palmer she's banging. It's some kid hawking shit in the stands. The time Angelo musta been thirty-five or so. Imagine what he felt like, his wife is out banging some kid sells hot dogs, pro'ly in the backseat of his father's car."

"Jesus Christ, was this, like, common knowledge?" Tommy asked.

Jilly stopped and waited for the waitress to replace his drink with a fresh one. She smiled at Tommy again. He returned the flirting with a wink before she left them alone.

"Yeah and no," said Jilly. "I mean, a few more people than us knew about it, me and Eddie Bats. Some might've seen them at the game there, or afterward, whatever. Somebody brought it to Angelo's attention the first place, where to look for the guy and all. She was hanging around the stadium, getting fucked in the car for Christ sakes. She didn't try hard enough to hide it, you ask me. And it was like twice a fucking week there, whenever they were home, the O's."

Tommy was shaking his head in disbelief.

"I mean, Eddie wound up dead a few years later, so whoever he told must've known after the fact, but don't forget now, this was more'n thirty years ago." He paused to sip at his drink again. "Anyway, long horror story short, the Mets take game two, then three and four, and Angelo, while he's making it hand over fist on the local book, everybody and their mother was all over the O's, huge favorites they were going into the series that year, two twenny-game winners, that lineup and all, like I said, we all killed on that series, anybody taking action."

"What my old man said," Tommy interjected. "Big money year that was, the sports book."

"Right," Jilly said. "But it was Angelo's pride killed a guy. After the Colts lost to the Jets, Angelo hated anything New York. Anything had to do with the place. Even though we made on that game, too, all the local money was laying the eighteen points, some guys were giving nineteen, even with the money we made off the Super Bowl there, it was after the Mets upset the O's he went completely crazy. He tells me and Eddie after the O's drop game four, if they lose game five, which they did, we was going back to the stadium there with the kid his wife was banging and toss him off the roof. 'Let the cocksucker see if he can fly like an Oriole,' he tells us."

Tommy sat up straight. "Holy shit," he said. "That was you?"

Jilly put a finger to his lips. "Easy does it," he said. "No need to announce it here."

"Holy shit," repeated Tommy, a little lower this time. "Holy fuckin shit, Jilly. I remember my old man talkin about that one day. He was explainin to me the worst thing he ever witnessed, the Erioles losing to the Mets like that. He said some guy was so depressed, some kid worked the stadium there, he went up the roof and jumped."

"It's better that's what people think," Jilly said.

Tommy chuckled. "I wished the old man was still alive. I could straighten him out on that, him and his fuckin Erioles."

Jilly took offense. "What, you got something against the O's?"

"I couldn't care less," said Tommy, waving the question off. "Fuckin faggots making telephone-number salaries to play games. Please. I like to shake them down is what I'd like to do. I put it to a guy a couple years ago, about shakin down some of those clowns, see how tough they are with a gun in their mouths, see if they wanna part with some of that cash they make for jerkin off half speed around the bases, but he says it'd bring federal attention unless we went after the home team guys lived in Baltimore, and he wasn't about to shake down a couple of home team guys."

Jilly was expressionless.

Tommy said, "You can relax, Jilly, I didn't do it. I never bothered. Need a crew to get away with somethin like that, at least a partner with big enough balls."

"Yeah, well, just pick another city, you're gonna do something crazy like that. 'Less you wanna make a couple hundred thousand enemies."

"It was an idea. Nothin ever come of it."

Jilly was still staring. Tommy opened his hands and said, "What, I burn a picture of the Pope?"

Jilly rubbed his face.

"What happened afterwards?" Tommy asked. "The kid dove off the cliffs there? Angelo is still married, no?"

"Different broad," Jilly said. "Different Maria, come to think of it. The original was let go shortly thereafter, the difference between the father and son, you ask me. One has balls, speaking of them. The other don't."

Tommy was confused. "Let go how? What, his old lady isn't the same one back then?"

"He gave her walking papers and not a fucking dime to go with them," Jilly said. "I get the call to drop her off the Travel Plaza, give her the scratch for a bus ticket, like the Peter fucking Pan, one fucking way, and that's what I did. She had two bags with her, suitcases, that was it. Her eyes were red like what you says Junior looked like."

Tommy was incredulous. "This was Junior's mother? Are you shittin me?"

"I shit you not one more time," Jilly said. "It was indeed Junior's mother. Didn't make a difference. She made Angelo look bad there, embarrassed him, he took care of things. How this came about tonight, us waiting here. The old man stepping in, or you'd be dealing with Junior the next ten years with this bullshit, like some fucking shrink pro'ly. Why we're here waiting on this New York guy now, the old man."

"So the old man's wife now, she's a Maria too, but not the original, not Junior's mother," Tommy said.

"You're quicker'n you look," Jilly said.

"Okay, I get that, but there's another thing I don't get," Tommy said. "Why we're farmin it out the first place. I mean, what the fuck, we can get a couple guys down the docks put on a couple masks, go to work, shove'm in a container there, send it across the ocean someplace."

"Angelo's got his reasons," Jilly said. "The man knows what he's doing, although I don't like the idea reaching out to New York either, tell you the truth."

Tommy shrugged.

"Who knows, maybe he's thinkin ahead," Jilly said. "Let it go. Angelo's no dope."

"You know the guy, the one from New York?"

"Nope," said Jilly, looking away then. "I don't like he's from there is all. Shit fuckin city it is." He stopped to sip his drink again. He set it down and remembered something. He pointed at Tommy. "We're sure they're down the Tidewater Marina, 'Napolis there, right, the two of them?"

"Where they been the last two nights," Tommy said. "Since Junior is out to Vegas for some convention." He pulled a set of Polaroid pictures from his pants pocket and showed Jilly the top one, the back of a cabin cruiser. The name *Tina Marie* was clear across the rear of the boat.

"Guy's got a pair," Tommy said, "I give him that much. Names the boat after his wife and fucks his girlfriends on it."

"Not after tonight he don't," Jilly said. He took the pictures and flipped through them quickly. He stopped to stare at one of a topless woman being groped on the deck of the *Tina Marie*. He said, "Fucking twat, look at her."

Jilly handed the pictures to Tommy. "Make sure you lose those later."

"Will do," said Tommy, stashing them. He sat back in his chair and stretched through a yawn. "I never much minded it, though, New York," he said after the yawn. "It's got a lot to be said for it, all the things you can do there anytime the night."

"It's a pisshole," Jilly said. "And it's got them fucking teams I hate."

"What, the sports thing? You're not serious."

"As a fucking heart attack. I hate the place. They could flush it down the toilet all I care."

"So, what, like you don't care what happened there, nine-one-one? That didn't bother you?"

Jilly pointed a finger. "That's an entire other matter, what happened there. And it wasn't just them, either. Pennsylvania got it too. And the capital. That was an act of war against the country, something completely different. I'm talking in general here. I hate the fucking place. I hate the city and both baseball teams play there. And don't get me started on the Jets, those cocksuckers."

Tommy shrugged again. "Okay, fair enough. I hear ya."

"Shula starts Unitas, it's a different game altogether," Jilly ranted. "Maybe we don't cover the spread, but there's no way that faggot white-shoed cocksucker and his nylon commercials beats Johnny U. Wearing nylons, for Christ sakes, a football player."

Tommy didn't know what Jilly was referring to. He left it alone while the old man finished his fourth anisette.

"What time this guy supposed to get here?"

"Half an hour ago," said Jilly, suddenly seething. He slapped the shot glass down loud enough for the waitress and several other people across the room to hear. He said, "Back when you were six, whatever, '84 it was, I think, Colts up and left middle of the night? That all started when they lost to the Jets back in '69."

Tommy tried to get him off the subject. "Who's he with in New York, this guy we're waitin on?"

Jilly wiped his mouth with the back of a hand. "Vignieri," he said.

"Aren't they having their own problems?"

"Who isn't? Fucking deals they offer today, the government, guys are lining up like it's the lotto to make a deal."

Tommy noticed the rain coming down harder, but didn't mention it. "Angelo tight with New York?"

"Used to be very tight with them," Jilly said. "I suppose he still has something going there, or why he reached out inna first place?"

"The one coming here a made guy?"

The waitress was back with another anisette. She set it on the table and picked up Tommy's glass to refill.

"Fuck knows," Jilly said when the waitress was gone. "I'll tell you a good one, though, you wanna hear a war story about a made guy come down here from New York to do a thing a few years ago."

Tommy moved his chair in. He set his elbows on the table and smiled.

Jilly smiled too. "Guy comes here to do a job, take somebody out from Philly was hiding the Camden Yard. Was between the bosses, something do with the casinos in Atlantic City, back when they first went up. Anyway, the New York guy comes down, has dinner with a few of us, he don't shut up breaking balls about the Jets, the Mets, and then I think it was the Knicks too, I'm not mistaken. They won it too that year, but not against the Bullets. Bullets were gone early, I think. Anyway, he's going on and on about the greatest city inna world, a couple of us get an idea, we get up to piss and make a call over to Lombard Street, some crazy kids hanging out there. A few of them go back to the hotel this New York hot shot is staying and fuck up his car."

Tommy laughed. "Now I know you're shittin me."

Jilly made the sign of the cross. "I shit you never," he said. "It was kid stuff, don't get me wrong. We'd all rather have put a couple in his big fat mouth, the cocksucker, but it turns out, the kids they sent to the garage there, the hotel garage the guy was staying, they slash the four tires plus the one in the trunk, they rip up the upholstery, all the leather there, and they carve *Erioles* and *Colts* all over the hood, the fenders. Shoved a golf ball or some shit in the gas tank too. The guy was fucking livid when he gets back from whatever he did. It was dumb shit, but we all pissed our pants the next few days after. Angelo heard the story and sent the kids fucked the car up some kegs of beer and a few of the older broads from one of the strip joints."

"Who was the guy? You remember him?"

"Agro something. Somebody Agro, I think. He's a big shot there now, I'm not mistaken. Skipper with the Vignieri crew."

"That's one I gotta remember," Tommy said. "It's a great way to fix a ball-breaker."

Jilly looked up toward the front door and spotted a man wearing sunglasses. "Look at this mamaluke," he whispered. "Middle of the fucking night, he's the nightrider with those shades."

Tommy turned to see who Jilly was talking about.

"He puts on a white baseball hat, he's our guy, which he is, I can tell," Jilly said.

The man in the sunglasses pulled a white baseball cap from his coat pocket. He took his time looking around the restaurant before putting it on.

"Cocksucker," Jilly said.

"What?" Tommy said.

"Fucking Mets hat."

Forty-five minutes and thirty-five miles later, which was all that separated Baltimore from Annapolis, Jilly sat in a stolen Taurus half a block from the Tidewater Marina while he waited for Tommy Red and the guy from New York to return from their visit to the *Tina Marie*. The rain was coming down hard. It had just started to thunder when Jilly spotted the white Mets hat.

He flashed the headlights to get their attention. The two men ran back to the car. Jilly unlocked the doors when they were close. Tommy sat in the back. The guy from New York sat up front.

"How'd it go?" Jilly asked.

"Done and done," Tommy said, "the both of them."

"Which means you have something for me now," the guy from New York said.

Jilly said, "You can take that hat off now, it stopped raining soon's you got in the car."

The New York guy wasn't amused. "Where's my money?"

"Under the seat," Jilly said.

The New York guy reached down under his seat at the same time Jilly pulled the Walther from between his legs. The mousetrap he had set under the car seat snapped shut and the New York guy barely gasped before the first of three bullets entered the left side of his skull.

Tommy froze on the backseat. Jilly had to yell to get his attention.

"Oh! You wanna sit here with him, be my guest, but I suggest you come with me before it stops raining, some fucking plebe on a midnight jog finds you."

Tommy was nodding, but hadn't moved.

"Grab the handle and pull," Jilly told him. "Then the door'll open, you can get the fuck out."

Tommy finally realized what Jilly was saying and got out of the car. He circled the back end slowly until he saw Jilly was wiping down the Walther with a chamois cloth.

"We just leavin him here?" he asked.

"Unless you wanna invite him home," Jilly said. He started across the road toward a minivan parked at the curb. "Come on. That one's ours. You're driving."

Tommy tried the door and found it unlocked. He got in behind the wheel and waited for Jilly to get settled.

"Key's in the ignition," Jilly said. "You gotta turn it to start the thing."

"Right," said Tommy, before he started the engine. He glanced back at the stolen car before he pulled away from the curb. "Where to?"

"Me, home," Jilly said. "But first I gotta get my car. I was you, I go back the Inner Harbor and catch that waitress before she goes home with one'a the kitchen help."

Tommy drove toward Interstate 97. He didn't speak again until they were pulling off the exit where Jilly had parked his car near Route 50.

"What was this tonight?" Tommy asked.

"Something between bosses," Jilly said. "Not that you need to know."

"Right," Tommy said.

Jilly lit a cigarette. "You okay?"

"Yeah, almost."

"You did good."

"I'd've done better, I knew what was comin."

"You thought you were next, after the prick?"

"For a second, yeah. Yeah, I did."

"Angelo likes you," Jilly said. "Or he don't send you."

"Right."

"But this is where it ends, make no mistake. What happened tonight, that's the end of it. Should never come up in conversation, okay?"

"Got it. Course not."

"Your old man wasn't Irish, you might get straightened out, be what used to be a made guy."

Tommy forced himself to shrug. "Ain't what it used to be, like you said."

"We're not flashy down here, but we look after our own," Jilly said. "Remember that."

"Yeah, I will. I appreciate it. I do."

Jilly pointed to the curb near the entrance to a parking lot. Tommy pulled over. "Here good?"

"Yeah, I promised the old lady I get her bagels for the morning," Jilly said. "She likes to toast them, she don't need them fresh."

Tommy put the transmission into park.

"One thing," Jilly continued. "I didn't like that scam shaking down the Erioles. The guy steered you straight, you don't do that to the home team. If nothing else, learn that tonight, huh? You ever get a bug like that again, you wanna go after some baseball players, go pick on the Yankees in that shit city. They're all fucking millionaires anyway, they can afford it."

"Right," Tommy said. "I'll go to New York."

Jilly was about to get out when he stopped. "Leave this thing a block from wherever you parked your car. At least a block. Wipe down whatever you remember you touched and take the keys with you. Grab a ferry ride in the morning and drop 'em in the bay."

"Got it," Tommy said.

Jilly opened the glove compartment. Tommy flinched.

"Easy, kid," Jilly said. He pointed to a thick envelope. "There's eight grand in there. Take it with you, unless you don't need it."

Tommy managed a smile through his nervousness.

"I'll see you around," Jilly said. He closed the door, knocked on the window twice, and was gone.

Tommy swallowed hard a few more times before he removed the envelope from the glove compartment, jammed it between his legs, and drove off. When he looked up at the rearview mirror, he noticed he was still smiling.

"Go O's," he said.

DON'T WALK IN FRONT OF ME

BY SARAH WEINMAN

Pikesville

I wanted honest work and got it at Pern's. A Jewish bookstore is a strange place to work for a guy like me, but I didn't have much choice; a month of job hunting left me frustrated and ready to break things, and the ad stuck on the store's main window was as close to salvation as I could get.

Though Sam—we were on a first-name basis from the beginning—was very particular about which items I could handle and which I couldn't ("Anything with God's name on it, leave it to me"), he left me to my own devices when it came to handling the cash register, stocking the books, and helping out customers. I hadn't known much at all about Judaism, but I sure learned fast.

When I told my mother where I was working, she was understandably confused, but got over it quickly enough. I had a job, and a pretty decent one, and that was what mattered to her most.

"I worried about you, Danny, the whole time you were *incarcerated*." She articulated each syllable, just as she did every time she used the word. Which was a lot, because my mother adored big words. It was her way of showing how much more educated she was than the rest of the mamas in Little Italy.

"Why'd you do that?" I said. "I was going to be okay. And I am, right?"

She touched my face. "Danny, I know that *now*, but not then." The silence afterwards was telling. I hadn't written her much in the six and a half years I was gone. Only when she made the four-hundred-mile trek with my cousin Sal did I learn just how sick she was.

"I don't want to think about then, Ma. It's over, I made my mistakes and I don't want to make them again. You have my word."

Only a slight narrowing of her eyes gave away the hurt she still felt. She'd forgiven me a long time ago for shaming her, but wouldn't forget. I still had to work on forgiving myself before I could truly let go.

The task was made easier with the day-to-day work. Some customers gave me an extra look, scouting my face for some recognition of familiar features, but most people weren't nearly as blatant because they were too preoccupied with making sure they had the right item to buy. I followed Sam's advice and was courteous to each and every person who walked in, from the prominent members of the Jewish community who liked to act the part to the giggly teens who "accidentally" broke things, to frazzled mothers of crying groups of children. It was an education.

A couple of months in, I was working alone on a Thursday morning. Sam couldn't show up till later in the afternoon because his granddaughter was starring in her school play. He was so proud of her that even as he feigned reluctance over giving me full responsibility for the store, I knew he had confidence in me. I knew what I could and couldn't handle or touch, what advice to give, and when to keep my mouth shut.

A wiry, bearded middle-aged man wearing a black hat with an upturned brim strode in with a purposeful gait. The purpose being me.

"You're Danny Colangelo," he stated in a surprisingly deep voice. Surprising because I'd expected a higher-pitched tone to match his skinny frame.

I never heard my name during working hours. Right from the start, Sam insisted I use a different moniker because "it's easier for you, and easier for the customers." I didn't argue, so if anyone needed to know my name, I was David. I flinched at hearing my true name spoken.

It must have shown, because the man added, "Look, Sam Levin said you'd be alone at the store and it'd be the best time to speak to you. So don't worry about it."

Whenever anyone, except my mother, said, "Don't worry about it," my guard went up even more.

"Who are you?"

"My name later, my problem first, if you don't mind."

I folded my arms. "Actually, I do mind. I'd prefer it to be the other way around, uh—"

"Oh, all right then," he said in an exasperated tone. "Chaim Brenner."

I cut him off before he continued introducing himself. "I know who you are."

His eyes widened. "Sam's already told you about me?"

"Sam hasn't told me a damn thing. If he was supposed to, then he's probably acting like the cagey bastard we both know, but I doubt it. Anyway, even a *goy* like me knows you run Ner Israel."

The principal of Baltimore's prestigious school for young rabbis and scholars-in-training laughed. From the sound of it, he didn't do so very often.

"All right, I think that's enough male posturing from the both of us. I'm not really very good at it." He chuckled softly, a more genuine sound. "Probably why I chose my path and you chose yours."

I wondered if he'd ever get to the point. "How can I help you, rabbi?" I emphasised his title.

He apologized, then began his story. "My daughter Beryl is to be married next month. She's the second youngest in the family, and a lovely girl. Beautiful, really. If you saw her you'd understand what I've had to deal with."

"Fighting off the boys with a stick?" I said only half-ironically. Some of the yeshiva boys who showed up in the store talked about the same things any guy would. Namely, women. And not necessarily in the nicest of terms.

"You might say that," said Rabbi Brenner tightly. "I should be happy she'll be settled down soon."

"But you aren't."

"Correct." The door swung open and a young, heavily pregnant mother wheeled in a stroller containing two crying toddlers. The rabbi briefly stepped away from the register to say hello to her. She responded, looking at the rabbi with undisguised awe. Her stay was brief: She wanted candlesticks, I found them for her, and five minutes later, having paid a small fortune, she left.

The rabbi resumed his story. "On paper, my future son-in-law is very desirable. A decent young man, attends a yeshiva in Cleveland, went to Israel last year, and comes from a good family with *yichus* . . ." That word I didn't know. He hesitated briefly before translating it as, "Breeding, good lineage. It's hard to express in English, but this boy, he is perfectly acceptable. On paper. And he's always been a gentleman with Beryl, and extremely respectful of me and my wife."

"So what's the problem?"

"In the last two or three weeks, I've heard . . . rumors.

Usually I wouldn't dare take unsubstantiated gossip, *loshen hara*, into account, but too many stories are repeating themselves from different sources. I've tried to warn Beryl but she won't listen to a word I say. The girl believes that because she's getting married, she won't have to answer to me anymore!"

I can't say I blamed the girl's reasoning, but I said nothing and let the rabbi continue.

"Anyway, this boy, Moshe, everywhere he goes, trouble seems to follow. In Israel, the rabbi at the yeshiva he attended in Be'er Sheva couldn't prove anything wrong, but any time a boy was beat up—and there were four incidents like this—he'd clam up as soon as Moshe reappeared. I called up the principal of the school in Cleveland, and after some serious questioning I received even more stories along the same lines, but even worse." Rabbi Brenner trailed off, his face twisting in sudden pain.

He dropped his voice to a whisper even though no one else was in the store. "One boy had to go to the hospital, the beating was so bad. They hushed it up and made it clear Moshe would not be welcome to return once he'd finished the year. This happened three months before my daughter met him, and now it's too late. She insists on marrying him and refuses to listen because all I have are *bubbe-meises*, 'fairy tales,' as she says.

"There's no other way to put it: Moshe is a blot that must be rid of."

I tried to process what the rabbi was saying, and it didn't make any sense. Or at least, I didn't want it to make sense in the way I thought he meant.

"Look, rabbi, you're going to have to be a whole lot more specific. Because if you're asking me to do what I think you are, then you've asked the wrong person."

"Sam said I could count on you!"

"And I'm very glad my employer trusts me. But killing someone's going way too far."

The whisper was gone now. "That's not what I meant!" Rabbi Brenner blushed. "My God, how could you think that of me? That I'd hire a . . . hit man, or whatever it's called. Never mind that to do so would be illegal and immoral, but it's a sin."

"Not like it hasn't happened before," I pointed out. "Look at the guy in New Jersey."

"He was not a real man or a good Jew. No, this is what I want: Follow Moshe around. Find out what he does. Find out if the rumors are true and do so before he marries my daughter."

What Rabbi Brenner proposed shocked me more than if he'd asked me to kill his future son-in-law. "You want me to play private investigator?"

He smiled. "If that's how you want to think of the task, then yes, I do. You already know how to blend in, else how would you have worked here so long?"

"Good point," I acknowledged. Blending in was a talent I'd developed when I was little. I'd never looked stereotypically Italian, thanks to a smattering of Irish inherited from my maternal grandmother and some stray Scots ancestry on my father's side. Instead, I grew up to look like a taller, stockier absentminded professor. Granted, one who could alter his perceived appearance depending on whether the situation was benign, neutral, or dangerous. I'd harnessed the ability even more when I'd taken up space in certain city corners to deal, and it was even more of an asset in prison.

I was good at fading into a crowd. And this, in a perverse way, sounded like a fun thing to do.

"I'll do it, but are you sure Sam will let me take so much time off the job?"

"I've already procured a substitute: my youngest daughter, Sara."

That was easy. "Fine, but I'll warn you, I might be good at the chameleon business, but I've never followed anyone around before."

"You could always find a mark, correct? Someone to whom you could sell your wares?"

Rabbi Brenner had an interesting way with words, and as soon as those were out of his mouth, he winced. "I'm sorry. I didn't want to remind you of your past."

I shrugged it off. "That's why it's the past. I'm trying to move on, but I guess I'll never leave it behind."

We quickly negotiated payment and a next meeting, scheduled for a week before the wedding. I only foresaw one major problem.

"What if I don't find anything out before the wedding takes place?"

The rabbi fixed me with a look that chilled me. "Then we'll figure out something else."

With Sam's blessing, I spent the next three weeks tailing Moshe Braverman from Rabbi Brenner's home to wherever the boy—because he wasn't more than about twenty-one—went to. When I followed him to a religious neighborhood, I wore clothing similar to my Pern's uniform. If it was an area I knew better, like Baltimore Highlands or the Northwest sections, I ditched the white dress shirt and glasses and opted for all black. And if I happened to be in a nicer part of town, closer to the downtown core, a quick trip to a restaurant bathroom to change into jeans usually did the trick.

Except all that clothes-switching didn't amount to anything at all, because from what I could see, Moshe was clean. When he was with his bride-to-be, he was the epitome of the lovesick suitor, telling Beryl whatever she wanted to hear without ever breaching the social codes of where to touch and how much distance to keep. Because of their engagement, the couple was allowed to go around town unchaperoned. An irony, then: Maybe all Rabbi Brenner wanted was a glorified bodyguard for his daughter, the last vestige of an overprotective parental instinct.

When I asked my mother, whose illness was worsening, she seemed to agree.

"Some parents just don't know how to let their children go, to be adults," she declared between hacking coughs.

"Yeah, that's why I'm still here with you, Ma," I said, mopping her brow. I didn't like that her fever kept spiking, but any time I brought up the idea of admitting her to the hospital, or even a nursing home, she refused.

"Danny, in spite of everything, you're a good son. A good man. Even for this crazy, overbearing rabbi, you'll do the best you can."

"You really think so?"

"Of course I do. You think other people would have been so determined to look for a decent job when they left prison? Would they have spent weeks driving up and down the city looking at want ads, even though not a single person wanted to hire you?"

My mother's words brought back the humiliation of those early weeks. I'd been back maybe a month, living in a basement apartment just outside of Pikesville. A part of town I would never have set foot in when I was younger, but the shabby, poorly lit one-bedroom I now called home belonged to my cousin Sal. Still, it was a step up from an 8' x 8' cell, so I didn't care too much if the kitchen was tiny and there was barely room for a bed and a desk. I didn't cook, and once I got a job I'd hardly be in the apartment at all.

But weeks of frustration took their toll. I didn't want to lie, but telling the truth about my stint in prison made prospective employers antsy, leaving them to reject me outright or not even bothering with a response. After yet another ill-fated interview where my past came up, I wondered whether I was qualified for anything but selling small bags of powder to desperate customers on shitty street corners. All I had to do was call up a couple of old contacts and I'd be back in.

I didn't want to do that. I couldn't face my mother's disappointment when she'd believed in me the entire time I was in prison, and I couldn't quit on myself and take a step back when all I wanted to do was keep barreling forward. Something had to come along.

Thanks to Sam Levin, something had.

I leaned over and kissed my mother on the forehead. "You're the best, Ma. I'll come and see you soon."

She shook her head and smiled ruefully. "Just do the best you can."

Later that afternoon, I met Rabbi Brenner at a kosher Italian place further south along Reisterstown Road. I didn't shy away from the truth: that I'd found absolutely nothing to prove Moshe Braverman was a bad match for Beryl.

Of course the rabbi didn't like what I had to say. "And you checked? And double-checked? Did you interview people?"

"Even though you didn't ask me to, but I figured it couldn't hurt. Your daughter's friends gushed about Moshe, about what a nice boy he is. A couple of them seemed pretty jealous that she landed him and they didn't. Some of the boys at Ner Israel—"

"You were on the premises? I never saw you."

"It wasn't too hard." I let that sink in, because the school was known for its excellent security. "Going there didn't yield me much in the way of information, though. Since he's not a student there, most of the boys I spoke to could only offer impressions formed when he'd been in town. All of which were of the 'decent young man' variety."

I took a spoonful of fettuccini—surprisingly good—and swallowed. "I'm sorry, rabbi, but I think you might have to accept Moshe as your son-in-law."

Rabbi Brenner slumped in his chair, taking the news worse than I'd expected. But his eyes burned. It occurred to me once again that this man wielded considerable power within his community, and was regarded as a scion, a man of absolute respect. I had given him bad news and he didn't like it. I didn't like what this could mean for me.

He sat back up and held my gaze. "If there isn't anything to be found before the wedding, there will be something found *at* the wedding."

"Forgive me," I said, "but is it possible you're taking this just a bit too personally? Let her marry Moshe. He could turn out to be a good guy, after all—"

"That's just not possible, Mr. Colangelo. And to think of him fathering my grandchildren," his face turned sickly white, "is something I cannot even consider. No. You'll go to the wedding and keep an eye on him there."

"What?" It was definitely the strangest invitation I'd ever received.

"Just continue your decoy act, the one you've been doing

all month. But this time you'll have to wear what I'm wearing." He signaled downward toward the fringes, the *tzitzis*.

"Oh," I said, understanding.

"After all, it's not like you'll be the only outsider there. Many times, we need to add men to the group in order to increase the number of dancers, to make it look more festive, more *freilach*. You'll just be another member of this group."

He explained further: There was an agency responsible for finding able-bodied young men to add to the corps. Being Jewish was an option, not a requirement. In order to blend in, yet again, I'd have to register with this agency and use Rabbi Brenner's name.

"They don't ask questions, so it shouldn't be a problem." The rabbi gave me a meaningful look. "Nor should your task."

"I can only try, rabbi."

We finished our meals in silence. He picked up the check and stood first.

"Rabbi, one more thing," I called.

He turned around.

"I hope you're wrong."

"And I hope I'm not," he said, before leaving me to stare at the last strands of fettuccini on my plate.

Many families went for the pomp and circumstance that a hotel could provide, but not Rabbi Brenner. A synagogue was the only place for a wedding, he'd told me during our meeting the week before, and the Beth Jacob Synagogue on Park Heights Avenue was his choice. By the time I arrived, the place was packed. I hadn't wanted to drive in my rented tux so I'd brought it with me, assuming I'd be able to find a bathroom to change in.

I wasn't the only one with the same thought. A couple of other dancers from the agency I'd paid lip service to a few days earlier were also changing in the bathroom. A young boy who couldn't have been more than twelve or thirteen looked completely stunned at what he was seeing.

"Why are you changing into your suits?" he asked.

The other guys exchanged looks so I elected to answer the question. "We're here to dance. You been to a wedding in this synagogue before?"

The boy shook his head. "Not here, usually at a hotel in Pikesville."

"Well, anyway," I continued, "they want people to be really excited for the bride and groom, but sometimes there aren't enough invited guests. That's why we're brought in to help."

"Wow, that's really cool!"

When the boy finally took off, the other two ringers laughed.

"Couldn't have explained it better," said the first, a short, stocky bruiser with blond hair.

"Poor kid," said the other, taller man. "He might be traumatized!"

"I hope not, and hell, someone had to." I didn't want to make small talk: I had work to do.

What work exactly, I still wasn't sure. Moshe would be sequestered in a back room somewhere, being prepared by his family and friends. There was no way I could just walk in and make myself a part of the group. I thought about trying to watch him during the pre-wedding ceremony where he would "uncover" Beryl's veil to show she was his real bride and not an impostor, but couldn't find an opportunity. All I could do was watch, and wait for some signal, whatever it was.

But all that watching allowed me one extra pleasure: checking out the girls. This was a wedding, so they'd be dressed up more elaborately and formally than girls I hung out with. I didn't know what was in the water, but Beryl was far from the only beautiful girl present. There were plenty, most of them obviously preening for the mostly male crowd.

The girls waited by the canopy where the bride and groom would be married. Unlike more ultra-Orthodox places, this synagogue's seating was allowed to be mixed when the wedding, like this one, took place on a weekday, so everyone could mingle freely. As a girl passed a boy, she flashed her brightest smile and hoped it would be reciprocated in turn. I even benefited from a couple of those smiles, so I did the only proper thing: I smiled back.

"What is this, a meat market?" I asked Sam, who was sitting next to me. The rest of his family was on his other side.

"You might say that," he replied, a faint Russian accent inflecting his voice. "But how else are young women supposed to meet men? Weddings are the best times to do so."

I certainly knew that. When my best friend got married right before I was sent up, I'd become instant friends—well, if you call it that, though after several rounds of JD I certainly didn't—with the maid of honor. Never saw her again after the next morning, but I'd always remember her, and her mouth, vividly.

The ceremony began with the cantor's intonation and the room quieted down. I'd never been to a Jewish wedding before, and the rituals fascinated me. The prayers, which I couldn't understand, had an ancient rhythm that appealed to the buried part of me still well-versed in Latin liturgy. Seeing Beryl circle her husband seven times amused me, and I winced when Moshe broke the glass, wondering if he'd hurt his foot.

When the crowd clapped, so did I. Beryl and Moshe made a beautiful couple, and the ceremony was elegant and dignified. The only thing marring the celebrations was Rabbi Brenner's expression of absolute disappointment. He couldn't know where I was sitting but it didn't matter. I felt that expression on me and a responding pang of guilt. I hadn't done my job, even though there was no job to do.

And then chaos broke out.

It lasted maybe a minute, two tops. First there was shouting, then there was screaming, and then there was a shot. When it was all over, a man was tackled to the ground, and another one—Moshe Braverman—lay dead under the *chupa*. Because of security issues, police were already at the synagogue, so an arrest was quickly made, but the story wouldn't fully emerge until a few days later, when Sam and I attended the *shiva*. We'd closed the shop up early in order to get there in mid-afternoon, when hardly anyone else was around. Even though Beryl had barely been a bride (there'd been some question as to whether the ceremony was truly valid, but a signed document was a signed document), she was an active mourner and wept over the loss of her husband.

Rabbi Brenner's emotions were far more controlled. Even though he'd spent much energy, and a fair amount of money, on me to prove him right, he hadn't expected the evidence to occur in such a dramatic fashion.

"I watched it unfold and couldn't do anything," he told us in hushed tones, so his wife and daughter, sitting on the other side of their living room, couldn't hear. "I couldn't stop that boy from confronting his tormentor, the one who'd put him in the hospital and crippled him for life—silencing him with such finality. I'm not sure how I'll live with myself."

It wasn't appropriate, but I put my hand on his shoulder nonetheless. "You didn't bring this upon your family, rabbi. You had no way of knowing."

Rabbi Brenner looked at Sam, who knew the entire story after I'd filled him in the day after Moshe's death, then me. His face was tear-stricken. "The ways of God are far more complex than you, or even I, can possibly understand. Perhaps you are right, Mr. Colangelo, and my actions or thoughts didn't lead to a ruined wedding and a traumatized daughter and community. But I'll never know."

We left soon afterwards, saying a brief but awkward hello to a still-weeping Beryl and her more stoic mother.

"Do you need me around for the rest of the afternoon?" I asked Sam, as I drove him back to Pern's.

"No, go ahead. I'll get one of my older grandchildren to help me out. See you tomorrow, Danny."

I stopped Sam before he left the car.

He turned around. "What is it?"

An old memory had come flooding back. "The way you said it reminded me of the first time you used that expression."

Sam laughed. "The day I hired you, you mean. You were so stunned I knew who you were and took you on anyway."

"No one else would take a chance on me."

Sam said nothing. Another memory came back.

"There was something else you said then, something about not being surprised what develops as a result. I wish Rabbi Brenner could say the same."

When Sam looked at me, I realized just how old he was. His spirit and old-world jokes carried him through during working hours, but without them, he was every inch the man who'd survived pogroms, two World Wars, and losses I had no idea about.

His voice was unnaturally grave. "Me too, Danny."

I put my hand on his forearm. I hoped that by gripping it, I could convey the message I didn't dare speak aloud: that I was proud to work for him and always would be.

After I dropped him off I took the interstate back to Little Italy. My mother was waiting, and she didn't have much time. I wanted to spend as much of what was left of it with her.

I turned the key and walked upstairs to her bedroom. My cousin Sal had spent the morning there and his wife Theresa usually picked up whatever slack we couldn't.

My mother was awake and beamed when she saw me enter the room. I knelt at her side and felt her forehead. Clammy, but not feverish. Not a bad sign.

"How are you doing, Ma?" I said softly.

"Better now that you're here. How are *you?*"

She heard my story with a mixture of shock and reproach, the latter for getting mixed up in such a "crazy situation."

"I've been in them before and I managed to get out of them. And this one didn't even involve me going to prison."

She held my gaze, the light in her eyes blazing. "Just promise me you'll continue to stay out of them."

I held her hand. "That I can promise," I said, the man who always tempered promises with realistic expectations, because it wasn't just what she wanted to hear: it was the truth.

My mother died three days later. It wasn't easy, but I know she passed in peace and suffered a lot less by the end than beforehand. I still work at Pern's, and I work hard and Sam trusts me with more tasks. I'm moving out of my basement apartment soon, and Sal's set me up with a girl he knows, someone "from the neighborhood." I haven't seen Rabbi Brenner and don't expect I will unless he comes into the shop to buy something. Sometimes I wonder how Beryl's doing, but I try to keep from thinking of her.

It's a start. Not much, perhaps, but in this town I'll take whatever I can get.

PART III

THE WAY THINGS NEVER WERE

AS SEEN ON TV

BY DAN FESPERMAN
Fells Point

T he Baltimore of Branko's dreams was a killer's paradise, a bleak landscape of wet streets after dark. To his mind, it was the one city in America where even a restless soldier fresh from the wars might feel at home, patrolling the long, deep trenches of its row-house streets, entire blocks walled off by bricks the color of mud. Someone who was handy with weapons could get mighty comfortable there, and that certain someone, of course, would be Branko. Like most Europeans, he tended to embellish any fantasy involving America with touches of the Wild West. Thus, he saw himself ruling Baltimore in the manner of a desperado, careening over the potholes and sewer grates in an old nag of a Crown Vic, riding the range to the clip-clop of gunshots.

The endings to these flights of fancy never varied. Word of his murderous exploits would filter down through desk sergeants, cop reporters, and neighborhood gossips, and inevitably make its way to a script writer for *Homicide*, the television show that had first brought Baltimore to Branko's attention. The resulting episode would make Branko a legend, because who could possibly resist the exotic lure of his tale: Branko Starevic, the Balkan hit man who traveled 5,000 miles for a single commission.

Imagine the disappointment, then, of Branko's first real view of Baltimore as his plane circled to land at BWI. It was a Friday afternoon in October, and the sunlight on the fall foliage below was almost shocking in its luminescence. Flak bursts of orange and yellow were everywhere, overflowing from parks and hillsides, assaulting streambeds and riverbanks, and spilling from the cracks of neighborhoods. When the big jet looped out across the bay, the glare from the water almost blinded him. He shifted in his seat to see clean white sails in formation. A ribbon of trestled highway passed beneath them. Then the towers of downtown winked smartly, as if to seal the jest, and in quick succession Branko spied a tall-masted ship at harbor, two big stadiums, and more highways, teeming with cars, coursing arteries of a place that looked disturbingly vital.

He fidgeted uncomfortably, the airline lasagna from three hours earlier executing a barrel roll, then he shut the plastic shade in disgust. For ages he had looked forward to this moment, anticipating a gloomy approach through factory smoke and low clouds. He had expected to behold a city rendered in the colors of a bruise—*once upon a daylight dreary, as he pondered weak and weary*—yes, he knew Poe as well, from a translated copy lent by a friend at the beginning of his Baltimore fixation.

The weak and weary part he had cold. Branko had been traveling for twenty hours, a low-budget itinerary from Sarajevo via Zagreb, Frankfurt, and JFK, with lengthy layovers at every stop.

Here is what the passport control officer saw as Branko lumbered forward with his overnight bag and his documents (his boss, Marko Krulic, had fixed the visa with a cooperative consular officer, paying twice the amount Branko would be earning for the commission): He was a tall man, about 6'3", with the rangy build and sharp cheekbones of those Slavic

toughs the NBA favors for their Euro guile and rigid funda-
mentals. Pale skin with the translucence of boiled cabbage.
He wore a black leather jacket, too large and with too many
silver buckles. His black pair of acid-washed jeans sported a
label no American had ever heard of, and his lank black hair
was a longish version of a style from 1957.

But it was Branko's eyes that prompted the passport officer to ask a few extra questions, just before they took his
prints and snapped his photo. It wasn't the bleached-out blue
that demanded your attention; it was their chilly quality, as if
he were staring up at you through an inch of frozen pond.
The war had done that for him, the war and all its enthusi-
asms of killing on the run, house by house.

Krulic, his commander, was now his boss, and in the
manner of most war profiteers he had diversified into the
multiple rackets of peacetime—drugs, stolen cars, bootleg
designer wear, and duty-free vices of every ilk. Branko was a
hired gun, and the target in Baltimore had only recently
come to Krulic's attention. It seemed that war-crimes investi-
gators in The Hague had finally made their way down the
pecking order to Krulic and were struggling to collect evidence. Krulic knew something that they didn't: that the most
incriminating witness now lived in the States, having made his
way to an apartment on the fringes of Fells Point back in '98.

Branko had to have the job the moment he heard about
it. Dubbed episodes of *Homicide* were an obsession, and he
felt he knew the entire cast by name. He spoke just enough
English to believe he would be able to engage them in witty
conversation, should he happen across them in a bar. And,
who knows, now maybe he would.

Krulic was aware of Branko's television addiction, but figured that a killer was a killer. His bigger worry was Branko's

inexperience with handguns. Most local jobs were dispatched with AK-47s or RPGs.

"You won't be able to just blow up his house, you know," Krulic had said. "Well, not unless you can arrange some sort of gas leak. But be tidy, be smart."

To Branko, being smart meant carrying out the deed in such a fashion that, one day, he would settle down on his couch before his Soviet-made television to see his exploits immortalized by the actors he knew and loved. Perhaps the killer—the one modeled after him—would even have a fling with Melissa Leo, or at least a flirtation. He liked it when she talked tough, although he suspected from the clothes she wore that maybe she didn't like boys. But surely, he had thought, as he scanned the credits of an episode only two nights before his departure, some of those writers must be yearning for a breakout idea. Well, he was about to give them one.

These were the contents of Branko's pockets and overnight bag as he exited customs: two changes of clothes, a toothbrush, $50 in cash, a credit card (he was under strict orders to use it only to rent a car), a fake New Jersey driver's license, the address for a homeless shelter where he was supposed to sleep, a telephone number for a contact who would supply his gun, a Fells Point address for a bar called Flip's, and a return ticket to Sarajevo, reserved for Sunday. That gave him only two nights, but he was a fast worker.

The target was Dusko Jevic. Branko knew only that the man worked at Flip's, at 1900 Aliceanna Street, where he supposedly swabbed floors, hauled garbage, killed rats, and did a little bouncing. His name was pronounced "DOOSH-ko" and, barroom clientele being what it was, the regulars called him "Douche Bag" or just "Douche." Not being particularly fluent in English, Dusko didn't seem to mind.

Branko's expectations took another hit at the Hertz counter. Instead of a Crown Vic he got a Ford Focus. An upgrade to make things right would have cost $39.50 a day, and Krulic wouldn't have approved. So he grabbed the keys, bought a map from a newsstand—at $6.95, it was obvious his $50 wasn't going to last long—then plotted a course for Fells Point.

At first, the drive into town only depressed him further. The procession of colorful trees continued, straddling the highway. There was even a welcome sign, painted on the sort of rustic timbers you normally found at alpine retreats.

Then he reached the fringes of Westport, and his spirits began to lift. He got only a glimpse, but it was enough. To his right, battered rowhouses were bunched like the cars of a derailed train. To his left was a small slag heap. Just ahead, a lane was shut for repairs, lined with unsightly orange barrels. The pavement seemed to have suddenly gone to hell, rippled and rutted and scarred. This was more like it. His mood brightened at every alarming jolt of the axle.

The clincher was a huge factory-like building that reared up suddenly on his right, just as the downtown skyline came into view. He slowed for a better look. It was sheathed in brown corrugated metal, at least a dozen stories high, with three chimneys belching steam and a fourth, taller and thicker, pouring white smoke a good half-mile into the blue. But the best part was the sign out front. Someone had actually had the balls to tout this monstrosity as an *"Empowerment Zone."*

Well, Branko certainly felt empowered now, and he drove onward with spirits revived, unflagging even as he skirted the touristy attractions of the harbor—that damned tall-masted ship again and those long pavilions with cheerful green rooftops.

It took only a mile before he was back in his milieu. Crossing Central Avenue, he entered a gloomy block of low-slung homes built of dark brick. Their flat rooftops and barred windows made them look like prisons. Yet children played in the streets, and the homes extended for blocks. Could this, perhaps, be "the projects"? His pulse quickened in excitement. He half expected to come upon a bleeding body at curbside, surrounded by yellow crime-scene tape. Then a cruiser would round the corner, and Bayliss and Pembleton would leap from either door. Okay, okay, he knew they were just actors, so he accommodated reality by also imagining a film crew. *Lights, camera, action.* A cameo of Branko in profile, idling by in the car, a first and ominous sighting of the mysterious man in black from the Balkans.

"Stay in your lane, asshole!"

A honking horn ended his reverie and he swerved to let a Jeep Cherokee roar past, some white guy on a cell phone who flipped him the bird. Branko was out of the projects now, but fortunately the view was no happier. Over the next several blocks, in fact, the nicest house to be seen was a *mural* of a house painted on the side of a vacant one. As if on cue, a police helicopter throbbed past overhead. Perfect.

In his growing enthusiasm, Branko missed the turn for the shelter, so he doubled back after heading north on Broadway, reaching his destination a few blocks later. Krulic had instructed him not to park too near the shelter, lest any-one realize he was an impostor. His contact, a Balkan émigré whose name had not been revealed, arrived within minutes of Branko's call from a pay phone. They met on the shelter's front steps.

"You're good for two nights here," he said. "I told them your name is Bob King, and did the paperwork for you. They think you're out of a job, so act depressed. Here's the gun."

The bag seemed ridiculously small, no heavier than a couple of potatoes. Branko started to peek inside.

"Not here, stupid! They'll kick you out before you even get inside. The doors open at 6, in twenty minutes. Here, put it in your overnight bag. It's already loaded—one clip, don't waste it. Dusko the Douche Bag gets to work at 7. Give me the phone number."

Branko handed it over.

"Don't call me again. You're finished with me, and I'm finished with you."

"But . . ."

The man was already walking away. Branko watched him go half a block before climbing into a huge pickup truck and driving away. He had yet to see anyone at the wheel of a Crown Vic.

By the time the shelter opened there was a line to get in. He sauntered upstairs and settled on a camp bed, everyone calling him "Bob" as he opened the city map on his knees. The overnight bag was tucked between his feet. He had already stuffed the bag with the gun into a pocket of his jacket, but not before a peek inside. It was a Glock. He'd heard of them, they were mentioned often on *Homicide*, so he didn't feel so bad anymore about the size.

He ran an index finger along the grid of the map until it rested on the location of Flip's, at Aliceanna and Wolfe. It was a good twenty blocks from here. There was still more than an hour to kill, so he decided to drive into Fells Point for a look. He would take a stroll, loosen his limbs for the kill. His stomach growled. Better have dinner too.

Parking was tougher than he had expected, and he ended up forking over a precious fiver at a small lot near the waterfront, a few blocks east of Broadway.

Fells Point was a puzzle to him. He traversed a block on the upper end that looked dilapidated, yet the next few were downright beautiful, disgustingly so, with gas lamps and flower boxes, and bars that were far too cute and proper for a man in a black leather jacket with too many silver buckles. He passed a few restaurants, but the prices posted on the menus made him weak in the knees.

Just when he thought he had figured the place out, he rounded a corner to see a drunk covered in tattoos and a three-day beard, swaying on a cloud of malt. In the next block, he passed a junk shop. He spotted a Latin dance bar, then a nice boutique. Across the way he saw a ratty-looking bridal shop, and something called the Polish Home Club. He wondered vaguely if there might also be a Bosnian Home Club, which produced a spasm of panic. What if the show had already filmed an idea just like his, and it had yet to air? The possibility had haunted him to some extent ever since prosecutor Ed Danvers had joined the cast. The actor's name had leaped out from the credits: Zeljko Ivanek. Possibly Russian, not Balkan, but he couldn't be positive.

At some point in his wanderings, Branko ended up on Lancaster Street heading west; he was about to cross Broadway when a familiar sight caught his eye. It was the green oval sign for Jimmy's Restaurant. His spirits soared. He'd seen them eating at Jimmy's on *Homicide*. One block further to the right was the waterfront, which meant that somewhere nearby was the locus, the Mecca, the center of his universe—Baltimore Police Headquarters, home of the homicide bureau, the place where they did so much of the filming. His pulse quickened, yet he also felt uneasy. He had an illegal piece in his pocket and murder on his mind. Correction: *homicide* on his mind. This was no time to be bumbling into a policeman.

Jimmy's was another matter, seeing as how he was hungry. What were the terms the Americans used for such places? Diner. Greasy spoon.

It was crowded and Branko settled himself to one side of a partitioned table for four, set apart from two men at the other half by a red slab of wood running down the middle. Everything was familiar—the long counter, the sizzling griddle, the huge urns of coffee—right down to the red-checked tablecloths, although he was disappointed to discover that they were plastic.

The menu baffled him. Too many choices across too many groups of food. He was about to settle for a burger when the word "scrapple" caught his eye. Hadn't someone ordered that once on the show? Bayliss? Meldrick Lewis? Or maybe Crosetti, the one who offed himself? Whoever it was, Branko had to try some. He even liked the name: scrapple, like a piece of food that had been in a fight. He had no idea what it was made of, and was too embarrassed to ask, although he knew enough to say "Over easy" when the waitress asked how he wanted his eggs.

A steaming platter arrived in what seemed like only seconds, and by process of elimination he determined that the scrapple was the crispy brown wedge next to the home fries. It looked like a flattened croquette. He took a bite, and was appalled. Inside was gray mush, liverish and creepy. He wanted to spit it out, but didn't know who might be watching. Besides, if it was good enough for Detective Meldrick Lewis, then Branko could tough it out.

Later, mopping the last of the egg yolk with toast, he got up the nerve to ask the waitress the question that had been on his mind since he came through the door.

"Tell me, please," he said, painfully conscious of his heavy accent. "The *Homicide* TV show. They come here still for the filming?"

The two men on the other side of the table smiled and shook their heads.

"Oh, hon, that's dead and gone," the waitress said.

"Dead?"

"Years ago. Packed up and left."

Then she disappeared, off in a flash with her order pad, oblivious to the desolation in her wake.

"Got canceled," said one of the men, perhaps sensing Branko's disappointment. "Long time ago."

Canceled. Dead. Fatal words, leaving him as shattered as if a gunshot had just torn through his chest. He had never expected to hear such words associated with his favorite show, not even one called *Homicide*. No wonder the city had looked so wrong from the air. He should have taken it as a sign, an omen.

His feelings of utter defeat must have showed, even through the icy film of those eyes, because the guy next to him spoke up again, in a tone that suggested the man was trying to cheer him up.

"They did make a movie, though, a few years back."

"Yeah," his companion offered, finding the Samaritan spirit contagious. "A good one. And now they got this other show, *The Wire*."

"*The Wire?*" Branko could barely speak. Worse, he still tasted scrapple on his breath.

"It's another crime show."

"Here?" A glimmer of hope. "Filmed in Baltimore?" In his accent it came out as "Balty-more."

"Sure. Gotta have HBO, though. And shit, cable's forty-five a month as it is."

The two men began griping about cable service, and Branko quickly lost the thread, so he rose, still too stunned to even say goodbye. But by the time he was out the door he was trying to take hope in a new possibility. Somewhere in town, he supposed, men and women were yet huddled over cigarettes and beer, dreaming up plots for made-up cops and killers, even if it was a different show with a different name. With luck he would still be able to offer a winner for their consideration. It wasn't what he had planned on, it wasn't *the dream*, but it was a chance.

There was still a job to do, however, and now it was after dark, and after 7. Dusko Jevic awaited him at Flip's.

It was only five blocks away, and he was there in a few minutes. A banner outside advertised something called *"Natty Bohs in a can"* for a dollar apiece. The way his budget was dwindling, that sounded like a smart choice, even if it involved one of those sweet drinks that came with a paper umbrella.

It turned out to be a beer—weak and watery lager, but beer nonetheless—and Branko downed his in a flash while wondering where Dusko might be. Maybe it was the fellow's day off, or he had quit. If he didn't show up in the next hour, Branko would ask for him, risky or not. In two days he'd be out of the country, so what would it matter?

Then he got lucky. Just after the barmaid took his order for a second Natty Boh, she turned and shouted into the back, "Hey, Douche, how 'bout bringin' up a new case?"

And just like that, there he was in the doorway behind

the bar, an apparition in black, grim and nodding, then grunting as he slammed not just one but two cases of beer into a big fridge.

"Thanks, Douche."

Dusko said nothing. Just nodded again and set off for the back. To get to it you had to be behind the bar. Branko wondered how he was going to do that. He fingered the gun in his jacket, just to make sure it was ready.

A few minutes later he got another break. The barmaid hailed some friends as they came through the front door. Then, perhaps because it wasn't yet crowded, she delivered Branko's second beer and walked out from behind the bar to chat with them, at a table next to an automatic bowling machine across the room. Now was his chance. He dropped from the stool and slipped through the opening, which she hadn't closed behind her, then darted through the back doorway. There were no shouts in his wake, so apparently no one had noticed. He opened a second door down a small hallway, and Dusko looked up suddenly from a small crate where he sat watching a baseball game on a black-and-white television.

"You are a baseball fan?" Dusko asked, a quizzical look on his face. "You wish to know the score?" Then a change came over his face, as if Dusko had recognized something from home in Branko's eyes, or perhaps in the black leather jacket with too many silver buckles. He stood slowly, and his next words were in their native tongue.

"Who are you? What do you want?"

Branko pulled out the Glock.

"Marko Krulic sent me." He nodded toward the rear door. "Let's go."

Dusko backed toward the exit, not taking his eyes off Branko as he fumbled with the dead bolt and chain. The door creaked open to the night. Still no pursuit or noise from behind, although Branko didn't dare risk a glance in that direction.

"Outside," he said.

Dusko stepped into a tiny alley, barely lit, but kept a hand on the door frame.

"Let go of that. Move it."

Then something stirred in the darkness, startling Branko. It was a rat, he saw now, a huge one scuttling toward a hole in the concrete. But it provided just enough of a distraction for Dusko to lunge for the Glock, his hand striking Branko's just as Branko squeezed the trigger. In the tight space of the alley the shot sounded like a small, sharp explosion. The gun clattered to the pavement. Branko reached quickly to pick it up, but Dusko kicked it with a huge grunt, then shouldered past him as Branko lunged across the alley to retrieve it. Got it. But by the time he turned, Dusko was slamming home the dead bolt, safely back inside.

Branko felt like an idiot and began to worry as he heard shouts inside, a real commotion. He looked around for an escape, but just ahead the narrow alley was blocked by a small fence running from ground to rooftop. He went the opposite direction, and the alley turned one way, then the other, before reaching a cinderblock wall topped by chain link and two strips of barbed wire. Branko climbed to the top of the blocks, then jumped, catching a sleeve on the wire, tearing leather and feeling something rake his hand on the way across. He landed awkwardly in a parking lot filled with forklifts, then had to climb a second fence, more carefully this time, before he was back onto Aliceanna, about half a block east of Flip's. He didn't dare head in that direction, so he ran east, then turned left on Washington Street before slowing to a brisk walk. No sense attracting unnecessary attention. His heart drummed. He couldn't believe he'd let Dusko slip away, and so easily. Now he'd have to replan everything, and the man would be on his guard.

Branko needed to get back to his car, so he headed west on Fleet Street, averting his face as he crossed Wolfe in case anyone was on the lookout down at Flip's. Once safely across he felt better. Then he began wishing he had the rest of that second Natty Boh. Watery or not, he needed a beer in the worst way.

A few blocks later he was calmer, perhaps because he had yet to hear a police siren. What Branko didn't know was that the police were the last people Dusko would have called. For one thing, his green card was expired. For another, he too had old friends from the old country who would be happy to lend a hand.

In any case, Branko's wandering as he tried to get his bearings—it was too dark to get out his map—had put him within sight of a bar on Ann Street. It was called the Wharf Rat, a promising name even if it briefly reminded him of his embarrassment back at Flip's. A second beer would be all he needed to settle down. Then he would check the map and make his way back to the car.

The beer here was better, but it was $4 a pop. Another major dent in his stash.

"You should get that looked at," the waitress said, and for the first time Branko noticed an ugly cut on his left hand, already crusting over with darkened blood.

"Yes," he said, "you are right. I caught it in my car door."

No sooner had he drained his glass than he had company—two rangy fellows, also in black leather jackets. Branko experienced a moment of recognition, much as

Dusko had earlier, before one of them said in their native tongue, "Come with us."

He reached for his jacket pocket, but a huge hand stopped him, while a second hand reached inside to retrieve the Glock. So much for self-defense. He figured he had better act quickly, while there were still other people around. So, just as the fellow was pocketing the gun, Branko bolted.

He barely eluded their grasp in his sprint for the door. He bowled over an entering couple, then managed to slip out just as the door was closing, heading left down the cobblestoned street. Glancing over his shoulder, he saw that the two men were only ten yards behind. He expected gunshots at any moment. The waterfront was dead ahead, and he wondered if he was going to have to leap into the harbor. He wasn't a good swimmer, and the water hadn't looked like the sort you'd want to swim in. Footsteps pounded behind him, loud slaps on the stones, but still no shots. Nearing the end of the block, he was relieved to see a cross street going in both directions along the wharf.

But it was the sight to his right that suddenly seemed to make all the difference. He recognized it instantly. In fact, he would have known it anywhere, in any context, but especially here in Balty-more—the hulking brick building with grand arched windows and five fat marble columns aligned across the second-story façade, the blue and white lampposts out front flanking the marble steps of the entrance. And now, as his racing footsteps and rising spirits led him closer, he could make out the black and gold lettering on the plate glass above the door: "*Baltimore City Police.*"

No wonder his pursuers hadn't fired shots. They'd been practically standing in the cops' backyard. Branko ran harder, even as his sense of relief grew. How appropriate that some desk sergeant would now be his salvation. Sure, he had botched the commission, but that too might sell as a script: the hapless hit man, so far from home, saved by the homicide squad, then sent home amid gales of affectionate laughter and promises that he would be a good boy from now on.

He still heard footsteps, but they'd be giving up soon. They wouldn't dare pursue him inside, although it certainly was curious how dark the building seemed. Not at all the vibrant sort of place it was on television. And you would have thought a policeman or two would be in sight by now.

It wasn't until Branko reached the top steps and found the doors locked that he realized his mistake. He shook the handles in vain, peering inside. Empty. Dark. Probably had been since the show left town. Wallpaper peeling in great shards, the floor in ruins. A pigeon strutted into view from the shadows, shitting as it walked.

But even as his assailants reached him, and even as they spun him round by the shoulder and sank a cold barrel into the flesh of his scrapple-filled stomach, Branko couldn't resist a last fleeting vision of what this might all look like on film— camera dollying high for a downward shot of his darkened head and frightened face, the Balkan hit man with the tables turned, yet still with stars in his eyes.

THE HAUNTING OF SLINK RIDGELY

BY TIM COCKEY

Greenspring Valley

I t wasn't simply that the ghost of Slink Ridgely couldn't muster any enthusiasm for Annie Brewster's marriage to the red-haired man. It was more than that. Much more. Slink knew. Of course he did. Ghosts know. Slink watched the ceremony mainly from the area of the empty choir stalls at Saint David's, where he could best see Annie's nervous and hopeful face. He watched the strong freckled fingers take hold of Annie's shaky hand and work the ring onto her finger. Coming in close, he saw the mean truth in the man's eyes. Annie's truth, he already knew. He'd known it for quite a while now.

Doomed, he said to himself. *Doomed, doomed, doomed, doomed . . .*

Slink's real name had been Edward. "Little Eddie," up until he was around five, when he had landed in Johns Hopkins Hospital for a fairly nasty appendectomy and had received not one, not two, but three Slinkies as get-well gifts. Little Eddie was nuts for his Slinkies. *Shing, shing, shing,* he undulated them from hand to hand for hours at a time, one eye trained on the black-and-white television in the corner, for he was nuts about television as well. Hands-down favorite? *The Early Riser.* It was Little Eddie's dream to grow up and get a job like the Early Riser, a janitor in a darkened

TV studio who said, "*Pssst, come over here,*" to the camera first thing in the morning before anyone else had arrived for work, and then put cartoons on for the kids at home to watch.

It didn't work out that way of course. There *was* no such job, except for the one guy who already had it, and of course he wasn't a real janitor, he was the station's weather guy wearing fake dusty clothes and a large fake bottle-brush mustache. Instead, Little Eddie grew up to be a milkman for Cloverland Dairy. Though by then he wasn't Little Eddie anymore, nor Edward, nor Ed, and not even Slinky, which was what the large nurse with the nose mole had taken to calling him during his five days at Hopkins and which Little Eddie's mother had picked up on. By the time he hit his tenth birthday, the diminutive had dropped away and he was Slink Ridgely, right up until his twenty-seventh year and the school bus/milk truck collision at the intersection of Caves Road and Garrison Forest Road. Slink's tombstone read *Edward Charles Ridgely.* The first time Slink saw it he'd scoffed, "Right. Who the hell is *he?*"

Strange day for Slink, that first day of being dead and buried. He logged ten straight hours hovering in one spot— directly in front of his tombstone—and just thinking. Unusual for a guy like Slink Ridgely, who had been a bobber and a weaver, always on the go, go, go.

Slink had loved his job. Four hours sleep was generally all he had needed, so rising and shining at 4 in the morning to start his route had been no big deal. He'd slide behind the wheel of his trusty Olds 98 with a cup of coffee in one hand and a Chesterfield dangling from his lips and be halfway to the dairy before the first light of day cracked the horizon. Skinny as a post, Slink would slip into his white delivery suit in the company locker room, lower his hat carefully over his precious wavy hair, then give a poke to the underside of the brim, easing the cap back on his head just so. Loading the truck took about twenty minutes, then a quick pop into the office to tell pale Sally a racy joke and have her straighten his bow tie for him, then he was ready to roll. The company frowned on its drivers smoking while on their routes, which is why Slink's customers grew to know him as the skinny milkman with the rakish grin and the ever-present toothpick.

Housewives left instructions in the milk box. *Extra gallon of chocolate milk, please. Two dozen eggs next time. When are you getting the sugar donuts in again?* Slink was shown the tooth knocked out in football, the newest edition to the family, he heard vacation plans, the great news about the new job. He caught the sometimes whiff of bourbon on Ellen Matthews's breath, he got the updates on Hal Fenwick's slow cancerous march to the grave. "Christ," he used to say to the boys at the Pimlico clubhouse, "There's this couple on my route. The Burtons? Damn marriage is coming apart right in front of my eyes. Personally, I think the guy is a jerk. Gotta say, I side with wifey on this one."

Slink's luck with the horses wasn't all that great. He had about a half-dozen different systems for picking them, and they all pretty much stank. He ran feverish formulas on his racing form with his No. 2 pencil. You'd have thought he was splitting the atom. "Got it! High Commander to place. Hundred clams." And High Commander would proceed to prance crookedly around the track like a lame Chinaman pulling a rickshaw. Afternoon regulars at Pimlico were accustomed to the sight of the skinny wavy-haired guy with the ripped bits of his losing tickets raining down on him like confetti.

But generally speaking, Slink enjoyed himself. He could never quite get a gal to hang on his arm for very long—which would have been nice—but he knew she was out there somewhere. Just a matter of time. Meanwhile he ran with a pretty fun crowd, had himself a nice collection of swizzle sticks. Holly's Cocktail Lounge. The Chanticleer. The Blue Mirror. True, there were a few "debt sweat" episodes here and there—once he was mildly roughed up out back of the Belvedere, just as a friendly reminder—but on the whole, Slink was considered good people, looking to harm no one. If it's true that he never met a mirror he didn't like, well, there have been far more serious faults in far more flawed people.

Slink never had sex with a regular customer. Not even Ellen Matthews, despite the sometimes sloppy fall of her bathrobe. There *had* been one occasion. Sort of. Ginny Curry's sister visiting from Morgantown. But that hadn't been on the job. Just pure coincidence. The two had struck up a conversation at Sweeney's Bar, sparring good-naturedly over the bitters-to-sugar ratio of old-fashioneds, and ended up on Slink's red plaid blanket in the backseat of his Olds, parked up near Memorial Stadium. It was several mornings later that Slink spied the same woman sitting at the kitchen table with the Curry twins as he was dropping off milk and butter and eggs and cheese. Pure coincidence. Slink grinned and saluted the woman with his toothpick just as she'd turned in her chair and spotted him through the crack of the kitchen door, her red mouth forming a perfect O.

And then Slink died.

Technically, it was the fault of the Brewster's frisky Chesapeake Bay retriever, Sandy. And also a nameless squirrel. Sandy had been accompanying the children on their way to the school bus stop when she suddenly took off after the squirrel that was crossing directly in front of Slink Ridgely's milk truck. Slink spun the wheel, but by mistake he slammed down on the accelerator pedal instead of the brake. The square truck broke through the picket fence of crabby Gus Fulton's place, bounced across a corner of the yard (the perfect pile of raked yellow leaves going up like an explosion), and toppled over sideways at the roadside ditch just as the school bus was coming down that steep part of Caves Road way . . . too . . . damned . . . fast.

The milk truck was lying half on and half off the road. After the collision, it lay completely on the road, twice spun and partially crushed. Bottles of white milk and chocolate milk trundled along the pavement like errant bowling pins. As the crowd gathered, no one noticed the Brewster dog at the edge of Gus Fulton's yard, happily lapping up milk and pebbles.

The kids in the bus were fine. Frightened out of their wits, but fine. The driver of the school bus suffered a bloody nose. But Slink Ridgely was dead. Crushed ribs. Broken neck. His arms were snaked so thoroughly through the spokes of the steering wheel that it was like solving a puzzle trying to get him freed up and out of the truck.

Seven-year-old Annie Brewster felt horrible. She'd been the one holding Sandy's leash on the way to the bus stop, but she hadn't held it tightly enough when the squirrel darted out from the trees. *Now I've killed a man,* she thought. *I don't deserve to live.* Children think this way. She stood saucer-eyed, staring at the dead milkman, while anguish planted itself deep, deep in her belly. He'd been at their house just fifteen minutes ago. He'd brought those sugar donuts. She remembered the toothpick the milkman was always chewing on. She remembered how he always tilted his cap back whenever he talked to her mom. That very morning he had turned to her—to Annie—and winked at her. And now he was *dead*. She felt her tiny heart being slipped into a box and the flaps being folded closed. She spotted something on the road and she reached down and picked it up. It was a toothpick, slightly gnawed on one end. She put it in her pocket and made a vow to keep it forever.

Slink saw all of this from his new vantage point. The dead one. He watched as his body was pulled from the truck and set down on Gus Fulton's grass. He watched as the children were ushered off the bus, and he joined in the sense of relief that they all seemed fine. His eyes rolled as he spotted Ellen Matthews making her way down the street in her robe and worn fluffy slippers. The woman's gait listed somewhat, and Slink worried that when her feet stopped moving she'd topple forward onto the pavement. But she didn't. She came to an unstable stop some ten feet from Slink's body, then folded her hands together and muttered a tearful prayer into the autumn air.

The funeral was held at Druid Ridge Cemetery three days later. Slink's cronies were there. Pale Sally presented the wreath from Cloverland. A few of the drivers banded together to wear their uniforms to the grave site, which Slink thought was pretty classy. It was a beautiful crisp autumn day. Yellow leaves fell from the trees, cascading down like a rain of canaries. Slink watched the proceedings from several dozen angles, one of the many benefits of being dead that he was already catching on to. He was especially touched when little Annie Brewster, who had insisted to her parents in a foot-stomping fit that she be allowed to attend, stepped forward to add a single rose to the flowers already atop the casket. Annie hesitated after carefully placing the rose, then removed her black wool gloves and set them, palms down, next to the flower. She stepped back between her parents and thrust her hands into her coat pockets. There, in the left pocket, she fiddled with Slink's toothpick as the color began to rise into her frowning face.

Her parents were already worried.

Slink took to his new condition like a kid to a sliding board. No problem. Being dead—he discovered—was a lot like dreaming. Or, for that matter, like the feeling that comes from a bellyful of old-fashioneds. The altered state. The affairs of the living were a lot more comical and nonsensical from the perspective of being dead, much the way dreams are freakish and pointless to the living. Tit for tat, figured Slink. And time—he also discovered—was completely irrelevant. The school bus had hit him twenty years ago, the school bus had hit him yesterday. No real difference. The borders between today and yesteryear were completely blurred and he could move back and forth at will. Studebakers and big-finned Chevrolets in the Memorial Stadium parking lot? That would be Jim Gentile on first and the amazing Luis Aparicio filling the hole at short. The Light Rail pulling into the Camden Yards station? That would be the whole new set of over-priced bums.

Other spirits appeared to Slink and he spent time—whatever that was—with them. He still went to Pimlico to watch the races, only now, if he wanted, he could ride with the jockeys as they lumbered into the homestretch. And now, of course, he knew the winners. For what it mattered. He kicked around the long-gone fish market at Market and Pratt, where he had ventured sometimes as a kid. The fish-mongers in their high rubber boots shot their hoses right through him and had no idea. Even dead, the smell of the place was still rank and briny. Slink and another dead crony took in some shows at the Two O'clock Club, but Slink had found Blaze's act a little too agitating, even in his dreamy dead state. That became his joke. "I ain't dead yet." And he'd laugh. But he'd also feel an uncommon warmth in the area of his heart and he discovered that what he was was sad. Being dead brought with it a melancholy streak that was brand new to Slink, something he hadn't experienced much in his living days. It wasn't a *bad* feeling necessarily. The feeling made him thoughtful. Reflective. Gave him something to chew on. Threw a new light on things. Slink meandered into the tiny backstage dressing room at the Two O'clock and watched Blaze playing mother to a tearful dancer, and he was so filled with sadness and joy he didn't know what to do with himself.

"This dead thing," he said to one of his cronies, "it's really something, isn't it? I had no idea."

And he kept his eye on Annie Brewster. That move with the gloves and the flower at his funeral, that stuck with him. He worried about her. A month after his funeral, Slink had watched Annie in her bedroom, jabbing his toothpick against her thighs over and over, just to make it hurt. She was a peculiar kid, cracked odd jokes at odd times, didn't harvest much in the way of close friends. Her teachers called her "artistic" when they weren't calling her "problematic." Annie liked to spend time alone. She read depressing books, she liked to draw, she liked to get into fights with boys. Slink drifted forward to when Annie was sixteen and watched her almost get into some serious trouble with the Burton boy. It was one thing when they were both eleven and pudgy Ted Burton had a loyal puppy crush on her. Then, Annie's little cruelties didn't hit home so much. But later, Annie carelessly plucked a ripe nerve in the hulking boy and he nearly pinched her arms off shaking her the way he did.

Slink worried.

"I feel responsible," Slink told another dead person as they were looking in on the incredible 1958 Colts-Giants game. "She blames herself for my death. You can see it, it's really screwed her up. That's not a healthy girl there. It's like I'm haunting her or something."

Slink checked things out in Annie's sophomore year at Bennington. It was none of his business, he knew, if she was sleeping with her roommate's boyfriend. But he also knew— he'd seen—how she would willfully misplay the affair when it came to light in the spring and earn herself a half-dozen solid enemies. Or the following year, when she would nearly cause her faculty adviser to be tossed out of the school.

And he knew what was coming. He'd been there over and over again already.

"She's got no self-regard, you know what I mean? Poor crazy kid. You just open yourself up for big-time trouble. She's a sitting duck. I feel rotten about it."

Slink attended Annie's graduation. The day was steamy and thick. Everyone, the guests, the students, the faculty, were fanning themselves with their programs. The commencement speaker—a famous actor with an equally famous wife— urged the new graduates to "seize the day" and "to march to their own drum." Annie squirmed in her folding chair and laughed derisively. She contorted the advice, and when she met the actor at a reception following the ceremony, she held firmly to his hand and leaned forward to whisper into his ear, "Seize the drum."

Slink watched sadly as the two refreshed their drinks

and sought a quiet corner to chat. Slink moved forward two months to watch the end of the affair, the famous wife arriving unexpectedly at their Manhattan apartment.

"Who the hell is *this* little thing?"

Annie was out on the sidewalk in under five minutes, still fumbling with the buttons on her blouse. Slink knew that her next three months would go poorly. She'd get no traction in Manhattan. The city spooked her. Her veneer of insular confidence shattered like a sheet of sugar candy. She never found her stride, and in early autumn she left her rent unpaid and took the subway to Penn Station and bought a one-way ticket back to Baltimore. She was crying quietly as she boarded the train. Slink also took the ride. He took it over and over and over again. Each time he knew there was no way to keep Annie from taking the seat next to the red-haired man but each time he tried anyway to will her to keep moving on to the next car.

The man's name was Paul. The toothpick in his mouth wiggled as he turned and smiled at the pretty young woman. Each time she was slow to react, but each time, when she finally did, it was as if her face might crack into a hundred bits. Such a smile.

"Hi." And she slid her small hand into his. Just handed it right over. Slink could've killed her.

No!

Paul Jacobs had blood on his hands. Slink went back a few years to Loch Raven Reservoir on a half-moon night in May, and there he was. Slink couldn't stand to see the act—not after that first time—so he always arrived just when it was over. Clouds drifted swiftly past the moon, giving the scene a pulsing, blue-strobe effect. The trees, the rocks, the flat black water, the shovel. She was a Maryvale girl. Cindi Blake. Car broken down. Help from a passing stranger. The doors on auto-lock, controlled by the driver.

The grave wasn't terribly deep. But deep enough to let a week go by before a couple of teenagers would happen on it. Cindi Blake's photograph had led all the local newscasts the entire week. Her parents pleading for their daughter's safe return. The police asking "for any information." One of those ugly weeks, ending on an even uglier Thursday, when the newscasters looked balefully into the cameras and paused before announcing, "It's over."

He had charm, this Jacobs character. He had the gift of gab, the twinkle in the eye. Slink knew this type. The rough diamond.

And that was the thing. *Rough.* Annie got a little taste of it even before she married him. A backhand at the breakfast table, so fast it was a blur. No marks, and followed that time with apologies, then brooding, then calculated sheepishness, and finally the unchecked fawning. It had worked. She hadn't broken off the engagement. The honeymoon in Bermuda was pretty nice, except for the few minor incidents. Paul charmed his way out of the misunderstanding with that one couple from Charlottesville, though his temper back in the hotel room wasn't a pretty sight. Annie had never learned to swim very well, so she spent her beach time sitting on the pink sand trying not to compare herself to the others. She ran across a short piece in a magazine about the famous actor she'd spent time with in Manhattan. He was divorcing his famous wife. Annie felt like all that was a thousand lifetimes ago. She was amazed now to recall that she had done such a thing. She felt that those crazy brave days were over. Forever. She looked up from the magazine and stared out at the surf. Her voice was barely audible.

"Take me."

And that evening, in the hotel bar, she watched her husband flirting with a systems analyst from London. She watched as the woman laughed and plucked the ubiquitous toothpick from Paul's lips. Back in her room, Annie pulled Slink's toothpick from her travel jewelry case and studied it for several long minutes. Slink was there, in the room. It broke his heart when Annie began to cry in great heaving sobs. It broke his heart even more when she stuck the tip of the old toothpick against her arm and pressed it hard against her skin, until the pucker point was bone white.

Slink shot himself forward to the 1984 Hunt Cup, right up to the fifth jump, as Bewley's Hill cleared the fence with balletic grace. Such a horse. Slink thought he was one of the really great ones. He drifted over to the hill, the irony there that always tore him up. Cindi Blake's parents and their friends enjoying their big picnic while not two blankets away, in low menacing tones, Paul Jacobs was reading his nervous wife the riot act for the unspeakable crime of spilling a smidgen of white wine on his shoe.

Slink hated it. If he'd had hands, he'd have wrapped them around that no good murderous neck.

But Jacobs would die soon enough.

By the time Annie hit twenty-seven, the same age as Slink had been when he'd been broadsided by the school bus, she felt as if she was already dead. She knew that Paul was making time with that realtor who had found them their small brick house just off Lake Avenue. The realtor was a big blonde, with the kind of perverse preppy allure that had always spoken to Paul. Annie picked the long white strands off Paul's sweater as she folded it and stowed it in the dresser.

Personally, she didn't know how the realtor could stand him. There wasn't much charm left as far as Annie could see and what little remained was increasingly edgy. Half the nights, Annie slept on the couch. Though maybe half of those half, he'd come out and pull her roughly by the arm back into the bedroom.

Leave him, Slink would plead wordlessly. *Go. Scram. You don't need to be doing this.*

He revisited seven-year-old Annie. He watched himself leaning against the Brewster's kitchen door, pushing his cap back on his head and chatting with Annie's mother. He watched Annie sitting at the kitchen table in front of a cereal bowl, her legs dangling above the floor. He watched as he winked at her and as she giggled, the legs swinging faster, back and forth and back and forth . . .

Leave him. C'mon, kid. For Christ's sake, I forgive you already, okay?

And finally, she did just that. She left him. Dead on the living room floor on a crisp October morning. He was wearing one of those sweaters with the blond hairs on it. And he was wearing a lump the size of a lacrosse ball on the back of his head. Annie had worried that the bottle would break, but it didn't. He'd been down on one knee, tying his shoelace. She had no idea where the strength came from to swing the bottle with such force. At breakfast that morning, he had pointed out an article in the *Sun*. It had to do with the tenth anniversary of the unsolved murder of Cindi Blake. Annie remembered the photograph of the girl from back when the murder had occurred. She'd been a senior herself. Same age as Cindi Blake.

"I did that," Paul had said casually, poking his finger into the photograph. "I picked her up, beat her with a shovel, and

buried her. Stupid-ass cops. It's a piece of cake to kill someone in this country."

Then he stuffed a toothpick into his mouth and gave her
a big uncharming smile.

The bottle didn't break. It landed with a satisfying *crack*,
and Paul slumped to the floor. Annie stood over him and
watched to see if he moved. He didn't. But to be sure, she
went into the kitchen and returned with the largest knife she
could find and planted it directly between his shoulder
blades. The strength in her arms weakened and she ended up
placing her foot against the handle and shoving the knife the
rest of the way in with her foot.

She went back into the kitchen and fetched the newspaper. She circled the article with a marker, then returned to
the living room and dropped the paper on her dead husband.
It fluttered down onto him like a sheet.

"I did that," she said.

She left the house, wearing only a thin sweater for
warmth. She picked her way through the woods to Lake
Roland and down to the edge of the water. Finally, she
stepped out of her shoes, then hugged herself tightly, watching a pair of mallards as they scuttled across the water. She
felt enormously calm. Tranquil. *It was a stupid little life*, she
thought. *It didn't really work.*

Annie dove awkwardly into the water and began pad-
dling toward the middle of the lake. Slink was watching. As
always, he could see that she was a lousy swimmer. In fact,
she was no swimmer at all. It was a dog paddle, and a lousy
dog paddle at that. Her arms lost their strength well before
she even reached the middle of the lake. As always.

She paused. Her arms slapped the surface of the water a
few times, and then she went under. Silence, and then one

final splash as an arm groped from the water. It looked almost like she was waving. The arm disappeared and concentric circles grew from the spot, wider and wider, until they too were gone.

Slink bowed his head. A wind blew and the trees around the lake released their leaves. They cascaded down like a rain of canaries.

THE HOMECOMING

BY JIM FUSILLI

Camden Yards

He felt his stomach clench as he approached the Fort McHenry Tunnel, and already he had a pounding headache, a growing tightness in his throat. But then Tess spotted the towering cranes in the harbor, said, "Giraffe skeletons," and laughed aloud as flatbed containers swung across the graying sky. He saw her smile through the rearview mirror; sitting back there among the empty seats, she pointed east with the eraser end, amusing herself again, and then made a note in her diary, shaking her head, beaming.

As he packed the van, she asked if he'd show her where he grew up, where he went to school, where he took his trumpet lessons.

"Sure, sweetheart," he said, wishing she hadn't.

Six hours later, crossing the Delaware Memorial Bridge, he could feel the red brick closing around him, the dry dust of the bocce courts at St. Leo's scratch-scratching his shoes, and he heard the murky water slapping Pier 5 at 4 a.m. as the Domino Sugars sign flickered across the harbor: a fourteen-year-old boy with his horn, Little Italy over his shoulder, and his father telling him there was nowhere to go, that he would never change.

Cars were backed up at the tunnel mouth.

Tess swung her bare feet in rhythm as she hummed and

sketched, and he remembered her mother would do the same as she read a script, straddling the arm of their red love seat, iced tea on the table, a mint leaf.

He didn't know if Tess thought her mother the ice-eyed murderer on TV's *Spencer: For Hire* or the playful strawberry blonde in the photo he placed in a floral frame in her bedroom.

The photo was taken in Harvard Square the day he quit Berklee to follow her down. He wasn't ready to play the New York clubs, and he'd already been shunned by Julliard, but she wanted Broadway and there was nothing he could do.

And then came the news, and Margaret Mary turned to fury, a relentless blame spout. Seven months later, only five pounds, six ounces, but otherwise fine. She insisted on Therese Ann, bitterly and without explanation. He shrugged, thinking Tess. Short for *tesoro*, his treasure.

Her figure returned in less than a year, and Margaret Mary bolted west. Her two-word exit line: "Keep her."

He got the furniture too. Needing sanctuary, he loaded the van and went back to Boston, buoyed by his love for little Tess but certain one day she would leave too. A promise: For as long as he had her, they'd be together and he'd give her something they could always share. He couldn't chance it'd only be music—Margaret Mary hated jazz, snickering at his tears when Miles played "Summer Nights"—so he brought his *tesoro* to Fenway Park. Baseball, and fathers and daughters, sprinkled throughout the stadium. Tess holding his hand, little steps, mustard on her dimpled chin.

At the end of each summer, they traveled south: Yankee Stadium, Shea, Veterans Stadium in Philadelphia, and now they were going to see the Orioles at Memorial Stadium, Cal Ripken Jr. on his toes where Mark Belanger once roamed.

Tess liked the O's logo, the blackbird with the orange beak, the sly grin.

By the time they finished the new ballpark at Camden Yards, it'd be too late. She'd be a teenager, gone.

On went the dome light so Tess could keep sketching. He was going to mention he'd never been in the tunnel before, since it was built after he fled. But knowing Tess, she'd ask why he left and he couldn't lie to her.

They beat the Brewers, but it'd started to rain in the fifth and the sparse crowd filed out early. He saw Tess yawn, and she was drawing in her diary, no longer keeping score. When Ripken popped to third to end the seventh, they packed up to go. A cold August night now, Tess in his denim jacket, O's cap on the back of her head, her auburn ponytail draped over the black plastic band. Smiling, but she was dragging.

By the time he warmed up the van and headed south on Ellerslie, she was asleep, stretched across the seats, hands folded under the side of her head.

Mind wandering, listening to Chuck Thompson call the ninth, he missed Lombard, and then he was lost on the way back to a Holiday Inn standing less than two miles from his childhood home. A detour sign pulled him into the construction site for a ballpark where the B&O train yard once stood: orange cones and wooden horses pressing him toward the long, narrow warehouse looking ghostly, hovering above a hole in the ground where the freight shed had been. Eutaw Street blocked off like they were going to make it disappear, and he muttered, "Where the hell . . . ?"

Tess mumbled, brought her legs close to her chest, using his jacket now as a blanket.

He didn't know where he was, the rain a thick mist. Lost

in his old hometown, streets gone. Yellow bulldozers parked haphazardly, oily balls of light, flames flapping in the wind, and he decided he'd go east, away from the warehouse and toward the harbor. Find Lombard and get Tess to bed. The Aquarium tomorrow, a drive over to the Peabody, and then Obrycki's for lunch on the way home.

He stopped, using the sideview to see if he could turn around without winding up in the muck.

A man shouted loud, harsh, and he snapped back, startled.

Bursting from the darkness, a girl scrambled as she raced away, terror in her eyes. Naked above the waist, her blouse torn, she tried to hold her heavy breasts in her arms as she ran, her skirt ripped too, her olive skin glistening in the van's harsh headlights.

And the shouting man drew toward the high beams. Pockmarked and stern, short-cropped curly hair and vacant, wide-set eyes, he tugged angrily at his slacks as he splashed through a puddle and another.

The girl hurried toward the old roundhouse, her face gripped by fear.

The man stopped, his shoes catching in the mire, and he looked directly into the van, raising his hand to block the beams.

Two fists clutching the wheel, his daughter asleep behind him, and he recognized the man.

Bigelow was his name, and he could tell Bigelow didn't know whether to chase the girl into shadows or to come over to tell whoever was in the driver's seat to go the fuck home, sealing his mouth forever along the way.

Walking relentlessly toward the van, Bigelow tucked in his shirt and did up his zipper.

He saw Bigelow eye the Massachusetts license plate.

"Dad?" Tess said, sitting now, rubbing off the sleep.

Reverse, a K-turn, and he roared away from the construction site, then said, "Let's get out of the rain, *tesoro*." Juggled in the seat, she watched as he drove onto 395, exiting to use the pay phone at an Amoco station. Rape at the Camden Yards construction site, he reported. Look for the girl at the roundhouse.

Arthur Bigelow, he added, mimicking his father's thick accent.

Half a mind to drive to 95 and head north, but their clothes were at the hotel, and Tess's Barbies. His Jerwyn mouthpiece in a velvet pouch.

Bigelow saw him despite the blinding lights, and Bigelow had the letters and numbers on his rear plates.

He came back around on 395 and he was near the B&O warehouse again, and there was the green Holiday Inn sign, where it had been all along.

Parked underground, and as he hoisted his drowsy daughter onto his shoulder, damp jacket and her diary tucked under his arm, he tried to remember when Bigelow went from the Baltimore City Jail to the Maryland State Pen. Figured maybe Bigelow was twenty years old by then, a man, since he was entering his junior year at Mount St. Joe's High.

Even as a kid, Bigelow was a thug, a moron, and he had a mouth on him too, and he ran down the son of the fruit-stand man, a quiet boy who wasn't quick to fight, the boy who now clutched his daughter, the elevator rattling as it rose.

His classmates, a loud, swaggering bunch, encouraged him to smash a two-by-four across the back of Bigelow's head. But he found it easier to withdraw, spending late afternoons and early evenings alone in the tumbledown three-room flat off Slemmers Alley.

He took a job at age thirteen as a bus boy at Sabatino's, offered as charity to his father who held off the Arabers from his shoebox store, doing his sums on the backs of brown paper bags, totaling the cost of a half-pound of this, a quarter-pound of that, knowing not a word of English save greetings and numbers. "*Grazie, mille grazie,*" his father would say, bowing his head, his brown chin dotted with prickly gray stubble, his vest pocket torn, his pencil a nub.

While his father worked seven days from dawn to dusk, he put in forty hours a week, and with his own money he bought a trumpet and paid for lessons. His father didn't approve, and telling him his teacher studied at the Peabody Conservatory of Music meant nothing. "*Stupido corno,*" his father muttered, his suspenders hanging loops at his sides.

"My teacher said I—"

"You can't be like everybody else. No, not you, eh? With the goddamn trumpet. What's wrong with you?" he spit, flinging his hand in the air. "And let me tell you, quiet boy, as for this teacher making miracles: *non ci sono angeli.*"

No angels? "Pop, I'm saying—"

Having made his point, the old man suddenly fell into his thoughts. He headed for his bedroom and, as if talking to himself, said, "Or maybe it's too much, too rough. This kid, he don't fight for nobody." Patting his pockets for a tobacco plug, he added, "Trumpet. Bah."

In his mind, there was a red-brick wall around Little Italy, high as the warehouse at Camden Yards, high as the moon. He felt it even when he was out on Pier 5, blowing flawless scales until dawn, the cops letting him be. Blue notes disappearing in the early morning haze, and he wished he could too.

Meanwhile, Bigelow: his face a sudden riot of pimples and pustules, and now the neighborhood girls found him repulsive too. He turned to cold stone, hooked up with a gang, worked his way up to armed robbery.

The elevator stopped hard, and the man flinched, remembering Bigelow had tried to rob the Colombo Bank with a face like that and no mask. Pistol-whipping plump Mrs. Ghiardini, who had two sons at St. Leo's and a baby girl at home, their father a fireman killed tumbling off the back of the truck one snowy night. Fifteen, twenty years ago, said the guys at Sabatino's, nodding knowingly, they would've taken care of it; the cops would've found Bigelow floating in the harbor, hands missing, his skull a jigsaw puzzle. But out of respect for his mother, born Ana Riccardi over on Eden Street . . .

"We home, Daddy?" Tess whispered as he opened the door.

"Close enough, *tesoro*," he replied.

He set her on the bed, knelt to remove her sneakers. Her pajamas were in the drawer under the TV.

"I can brush my teeth better than you," he said, trying to smile.

Waving off the nightly challenge, she offered her baby-soft cheek, then slithered under the covers, clothes and all.

Tess slept as if exhausted, unaware he was sitting on the bed across from hers, staring at her, reaching over now and then to stroke her hair. Tess, who resembled his mother as much as her own: olive hue, the round chin, deep brown eyes. His mother in the photo, him too. Easter Sunday, he's five and she'll be dead in three months.

"Your mother, she was some firecracker," said one of the

guys at Sabatino's. "A temper? *Madonna mio* . . ."

Left unsaid: How did she wind up with a slug like that?

Out of earshot, in the coffee shops off Broadway, actors, writers, producers said the same about Margaret Mary.

"Tess," he cooed in the dark room, and he was thinking as his heart began to pound, and the headache again.

Bigelow could find him—a witness who could confirm the girl's story of assault, of rape. And maybe Bigelow saw beyond the high beams and recognized the man behind the wheel, as the man had recognized him. The fruit-stand man's son down from Massachusetts, the boy with the horn.

On his heels, running his hand across his forehead, he tried to envision the limits of Bigelow's imagination, as if he could fathom a criminal mind.

He figured Bigelow, though full of bad intent, would do what was easiest first: return to Little Italy and see if the fruit-stand man still lived in the crumbling, graffiti-stained wood frame off Slemmers Alley.

He went to a chair by the window, and in the hotel room's darkness a cold shiver swept over him, his stomach leaping to his throat.

Finding no satisfaction behind the rusted bars on the building's windows, Bigelow would calculate: The fruit-stand man's son had been lost in the construction site; his father dead, no doubt; a hotel near the yards, it being too late to drive home to Massachusetts.

Bigelow would find the van.

Tess slept serenely, a wry smile on her face.

He pulled back the heavy drapes. Looking through the rain, he saw the warehouse, pile drivers, excavators, remnants of the old roundhouse, and in his mind, the girl Bigelow had attacked, the panic in her eyes, desperation.

He stood and, as the drapes swung shut, he recalled a restaurant, its back to Slemmers Alley: Mo's Fisherman's Wharf, and maybe the staff was gone by 2 o'clock. The restaurants throughout Little Italy shutting down, Stiles Street empty, the alley also.

Bigelow would wait until then.

Looking at Tess.

Bigelow saw the little girl in the backseat, and she's a witness too.

He parked the van over on Aliceanna a block from the harbor, and he took out the old baseball bat he kept with a couple of tattered mitts under the rear seat. He headed north in the rain, fist wrapped around sullied tape above the crack in the handle.

When he turned the final corner, ready to enter the litter-strewn alley from the south end, he saw a figure.

Darting, he avoided a puddle and pressed himself into the shadows of a garage door and watched as Bigelow looked at the side of the tilted wood frame, stepping back, peering up, down.

He held back as Bigelow, frustrated, turned in the direction of Stiles.

Coming off the door, he shifted the cracked bat to his right hand.

Bigelow was maybe twenty feet away, easing toward a streetlight's halo.

On Stiles Street now, Bigelow went wide eyed suddenly, retreating, raising his hands.

Three men marched at him, scowling, shoulders hunched, and Bigelow protested. "Hold on, fellas," he said. "Hey, hold—"

With startling quickness, one of the dark-haired men brought a tire iron onto Bigelow's head.

Bigelow mewed, staggered, and then issued a sickening gurgle as he fell to his knees.

Another blow, equally efficient, and he heard Bigelow groan.

Bat in hand, he ran forward and, bursting among the men, he slammed Bigelow, cracking him hard across the back of his head, sending him face first onto the wet sidewalk.

The men stomped Bigelow, swearing in Italian.

"My sister," said the heavyset one, "my kid sister. Son of a bitch."

Bigelow tried to roll into a ball.

Tess's father raised the bat and smashed him again, and then again.

And again. And again.

Panting hard, his chest heaving, he looked down, tears mingling with the rain on his face.

Bigelow's blood spread across the concrete.

He heard the thin, beak-nosed man to his left grunt as he drove his foot into the beaten man's ribs.

"Lisa. Lisa Ghiardini," the thin man said. "First the mother, then you rape the daughter!"

The girl he'd seen running through the yards was the daughter of the woman Bigelow had pistol-whipped at the Colombo Bank. A girl from the neighborhood.

He staggered back, the bloody bat dangling from his fingers.

As two thin men continued to pound Bigelow, the stout Ghiardini looked up.

"Pete?" he said, gulping air, steam rising from the top of his head. "Pete Sangiovese?"

The two other men stopped for a moment, and Bigelow let out a low groan.

"Pete," Ghiardini said, gesturing with a meaty hand, "over here. You want another shot? Come on. Take another shot."

He turned, trotting along the alley. Running. Eager to disappear.

The bat went in the river at Fell's Point, sinking beneath Styrofoam cups, condoms, and bobbing pop bottles. Before returning to the van, he ran his hands through a puddle, washing away Bigelow's blood.

He drove quickly back to the hotel, knowing he'd done what he'd had to.

Tess was sleeping, purring gently, and the bathroom light was still on.

The note he'd attached to the mirror above the sink was still there: *I'll be right back. Brush your beautiful teeth!*

Her pink toothbrush was dry.

He showered, and planned to wash his shirt and jeans in the hotel's basement laundry room. He'd have to get new running shoes: Bigelow's blood soaked through the gray laces, clung to the soles.

Putting on his pajama bottoms, he sat on the bed next to his daughter and he stared at her.

For as long as he had her, they'd be together. He would not let her feel alone.

His eyes moistened as he studied her sweet smile, heart-shaped lips, long eyelashes; contentment . . .

No angels?

How could his father have been so wrong?

FROG CYCLE

BY BEN NEIHART

Inner Harbor

Cell Scope is a science education park that sits like some new blown-up nanotech herpes sore on the lip of Baltimore's Inner Harbor. It's a massive glass-and-steel base topped with a billowing white roof. Tonight it's all lit up: holograms, fireworks, lasers, an immense smoke-pot that puffs DNA helixes into the air. Just off Pratt, on the torch-lit front esplanade, a four-girl Cirque du Soleil spinoff band plays whale-call jazz, and it actually sounds haunting, not phony. CEOs from New York and California, Maryland biotech investors, Japanese boys, a couple dozen news cameras, and, lucky me, fifty or sixty print reporters swarm through the mammoth glass doors for tonight's big opening of Frog Cycle, the demented new exhibit I'm supposed to be promoting.

Or, I should say, Frog Cycle in the Kel-Shor Virtual Pond. Seriously, if Kel-Shor's paying $4.5 million, I can spew the full name.

And to be truthful, I should state for the record that I am promoting the frogs, no mordant "supposed to be" bullshit.

But you know what? Pushing through the crowd, angling my way inside the main hall, circulating, I'm a redundant publicist. The frogs sell themselves. They're not just a perfect example of Cell Scope's mission, the translation of bone-dry sci-tech jargon into lip-smacking juicy lovely-bones show biz;

no, they're wicked, they're wrong, they're the end of the world as far as I'm concerned. And this morning, on the test run, they malfunctioned.

The problem is the virtual frogs, the ones featured on the poster. They're big, they're ugly, they're mean. And they slobber. There are a half-dozen of them; they've been re-engineered by geneticists who've broken off from UMBC. They look fine, just like Florida gopher frogs, except they're three times as big. Part of Frog Cycle's appeal is designed to be the interaction between the virtual frogs and Florida tree frogs and green tree frogs and several other scarce tropical frogs and toads. The virtual frogs are supposed to be dominant, but in the misfire this morning the virtuals attacked the naturals, killed them all, ate most of them.

The Kel-Shor people have no idea.

I pop a mint into my mouth and smile past the badges and lapels. There's a lot of dialogue in the air, a lot of bragging and favor-making. I snag a cup of white wine from a waiter, slurp it in two swallows, and duck into the alcove where a smallish crowd ponders a glass-encased model of Frog Cycle that sits on a silver pedestal. I stand on tiptoe and look over the shoulders of some gruff Japanese guys; it's a bit Disney, the model, and before I know it I say, "Ah, kawai!" That means *super-cute*.

The taller of the Japanese guys looks sideways at me and nods grimly. "Very very kawai."

Laurie Hauver's the money girl. She's my boss. I usually have a problem with all three categories—girls, money, and bosses—so it's a pleasure to report that I'm a slave for Laurie, and when I see her disentangle herself from a dilapidated, rouge-unto-death Gilman girl, circa 1990, I kind of plow through the atrium, dodging a Sony robot, an ax-man from used-to-be-Legg-Mason, and a martinet from the *Sun's* biz page. I almost bounce against Laurie, but her force field does its work, and I stand a few inches back, giving her the once over. She looks like someone who is written into a number of substantial wills. A couple of them death-bed, chicken-scratch revisions, screw the notary. She's just had her hair cut short and dyed goldenrod; she's wearing a black backless slip dress, black Laboutin stiletto provocations.

"You don't look too bad," I tell her, almost taking her arm. "How was it—Lovely Lane? How was the funeral?"

"It's something else," she whispers. "It's the first time I've heard the minister refer to the subsequent amputation of the widow's arms during a proper kind of ceremony. I mean, I know the story, but I don't care. It made the minister seem a little bit *inside*. Like he had his own blog or whatever. I took two propranolol—I'm not coming across numb, am I?"

"The opposite."

"Thank you."

I check my watch. "Seven-thirty."

Laurie looks past me. "When the band finishes, we should go in. Oh, I think they may have just stopped. On cue."

A sweetly modulated voice urges us to head into the Kel-Shor Virtual Pond. I've got to say, I feel sick to my stomach, but some of the people rushing past me, they look like they're heading into a medieval tribunal. Someone has defaced one of the Frog Cycle posters; now, a drop of blood hangs from the gopher frog's bottom lip.

"So the Kel-Shor people seem happy," I say. "Naïve."

"They know," she says. "We had to tell them about the misfire. The scientists, um, I think they were persuasive."

"So I'm the naïve one, actually."

Laurie nods.

"You ready?"

"Let's go."

The Kel-Shor Virtual Pond is a five-thousand-square-foot body of water encased in glass with about twenty yards of open air above it. The scientists have really, really messed with nature and speeded up the virtual frogs' metabolisms. They've rigged the weather in the pond so the frogs go through one year in about three hours. What happens is, you sit there looking at the pond in winter, and the frogs are frozen and the pond is frozen and all of the plants are either dead or frozen and the air looks forbidding. So you watch, and the artificial sun gets brighter and the plants bud and start to grow and the ice on top of the pond breaks and the water totally sparkles and it's fresh-looking and the frogs start to come to life.

The pond is ringed by a metallic mesh barrier, and it's covered with a frosted white plastic dome. Beneath the dome, green and brown blobs move like blips on a cardiac monitor.

Movie theater seats run in tiers at a steep stadium pitch away from the pond. The capacity is 312. The first three rows are reserved for staff, VIPs, and the differently abled.

I'm in the front row, at a bad angle, getting settled into my seat, when a taut woman in a forest-green sheath, pearls, and sparkling silver flip-flops gives me her hand and introduces herself as Rie. I've already been briefed on her; she's a potential "problem," so I've got to baby-sit.

"My brother runs Kel-Shor," she says, and plops into the seat beside me.

Without warning, the dangling halogen chandeliers begin to dim and the Frog Cycle soundtrack—cellos, moogs, crickets, a faux-Enya—swells over the sound system.

The modulated voice, this time slightly perturbed, says, *"Welcome to the Kel-Shor Corporation's Virtual Pond, home to Frog Cycle."*

Applause. Applause. Standing O. Someone says *hush.* *Ssshhh.* The cowfolk settle themselves.

Rie sort of winces at me, and then the funniest thing happens: She takes my hand.

"Are you okay?" I ask.

"I'm *scared.*"

"It's fine. I've seen it twenty-seven times. It's astonishing."

The voice is back: *"The development of a successful farming industry—for any amphibious species—depends on the regular and predictable supply of eggs. To harness efficient, safe technologies, to spawn domesticated amphibious species, is the goal. We look to Frog Cycle in the Kel-Shor Virtual Pond. We look. We see."*

"That doesn't make sense," Rie whispers.

"The company thinks it's subliminal," I say. "Believe me."

"I hate my brother."

"Oh."

The frosted dome cover begins to gently lift from the Virtual Pond. It hovers for a moment before it snaps into a lattice harness on the ceiling, pulling with it, like so many spider webs, the clinking clear-filament netting that encloses the pond and its environment.

Rie whispers, "Whoa."

Uncovered, the Virtual Pond looks like a cel from a Pixar movie. The blues are so wet and the greens are so crisp. The plantlife is gnarled but it's accented with, um, "cute" touches, such as tawny freckled trunks and smile-pattern leaves. The water itself is clear as a spring. Silver fish dive and spiral to the surface. You can see the pebbled bottom—ferns, tricks of light, the blipping brown creatures.

At first, you don't think that the showpiece frogs, the engineered virtuals, are in the pond. You think they're waiting for the air to warm up, for the sun to blaze a little bit more brilliantly.

I look down the aisle, trying to catch Laurie's eyes, when it happens. The gasps—all at once, like the whoosh of a roller coaster twisting its first descent. Rie's got a strong grip, the muscles in my arm are tense where her fingers poke me.

"It's them," she says.

"Yeah," I say.

Them. Three chunky brown rocks covered with moss at the edge of the water. The three sit side by side like little lords, grinning insouciantly. Like boulders that grin—broad, immovable.

Until it moves.

The smallest—it's the size of a small fat cat—opens its mouth and lets out a low rumble. It lifts its head and takes an astonishing leap and lands with a moist thud, eight yards to its left, scattering a group of small navy-green pygmy frogs, who let out high-pitched shrieks.

The voice purrs: *"In spring, the frogs come out of hibernation. To mate."*

"You've got to be kidding," Rie says. She lets go of my arm and makes a pucker-face at me.

The voice goes on: *"The male frog embraces the female, holding her tight with his arms. This is the act of oviposition. It may last several days."*

"Oh, come on!" Rie snorts.

The second of the three virtual frogs flies into the air and leaps the entire long length of the pond, like a hurdler show-ing off. It lands on the opposite shore, bellowing in the direc-tion of a tiny albino toad. Its glistening haunches tremble in the light.

Suddenly, lights mounted in the pond increase in bright-ness so the water's utterly translucent. There are hundreds of tadpoles in the water, zipping in circles.

The voice says, *"Cell Scope scientists have patented a gene technique that speeds up the frog's internal clock."*

"That's enough," Rie says. She looks out at the audience, in tiers behind us and in a high, quivering voice shouts, "Somebody stop the music!"

There's some laughter, a lot of *shhs* and *"be quiets."* I'm relieved. The audience is loving Frog Cycle. The way you love a hunt, a dog fight. You're supposed to yell, *Stop!* Maybe you're supposed to yell, *Somebody stop the music!*

I take Rie's hand. "This is real," I tell her. "This is really happening."

Suddenly I feel warmth. I smell algaeic warm wet air. Breath. Venting on my cheek and down my neck. I look over at Rie, and she shakes her head at me. "It's not me, asshole," she says.

I turn and meet its eye. The biggest frog. We're talking twenty pounds. It's less than a yard from me, its big bull head pushing against the mesh barrier, wheezing and looking right at me. A string of drool hangs from its lower lip.

I let out a little cry, my feet scrabbling along the floor. The frog roars. The mesh is chinking and clanging and groaning with its weight.

"You're making it happen," Rie says. "My brother's mak-ing it happen." But she lets me hold her hand, so I know we're safe. I look up the tier; Laurie gives me a quick nod.

* * *

We're in a helicopter out of Martin State. There's an after-party in Talbot County. I am completely smashed, nearly falling asleep, head bouncing against a window. Over the roar of the engine, I can hear Rie behind me, slurring, giggling. "All I could think of was reproduction," she's saying. "I kept looking, against my will, at those hips moving like a piston, spewing that filthy clotted cream. Wasn't it so terrible? Wasn't it? That was so disgusting. Every time I close my eyes, I just see it—and I think it should be outlawed. Oh, but maybe I want to see it just one more time."

For a while, no one speaks. I'm kind of staring out at the purple night clouds and the sparkle of the shoreline in the distance.

Rie makes a little purring noise. I can hear her lips. I guess she's kissing the guy in the seat next to hers.

"My God, honey," she says all throat, "my brother made that happen."

GOODWOOD GARDENS

BY SUJATA MASSEY

Roland Park

J eannie always made it a point to say that the house on Goodwood Gardens had never been her choice. Charlie, however, clung to his belief that their first home in Baltimore had been a marital compromise. It was an argument without an ending—like their family, and like the house itself.

Goodwood Gardens was not actually a park, as the name suggested, but a short residential road in Plat Four, the fourth portion of land developed in the early twentieth century in Roland Park, a magical neighborhood of curving, tree-shaded streets that boasted grand, century-old houses of stone, stucco, and shingle.

The omission of a word such as "street" or "road" or "avenue" in the Gardens' address was something Jeannie found maddeningly pretentious, but Goodwood Gardens had been established as the city's millionaire's row back at the dawning of the twentieth century, and its identity had held. It didn't seem like a place that anyone, least of all a girl who'd grown up in a ranch house in San Mateo, should have disliked so heartily.

Jeannie and Charlie's house had been built in the 1920s, making it one of the newer houses on the street. The residence was huge—ten bedrooms, ten baths, and two powder rooms—more than enough room for a family of three. The place reminded one of an embassy, perhaps located in Salzburg or some other romantic Teutonic locale. The exterior was beautifully half-timbered white stucco, and was ornamented with two battlements from which hung, respectively, the flags of the United States and Maryland.

Jeannie had wanted to remove the flags—the previous owners had left in a hurry, not bothering to take them along—but Charlie thought the neighbors would wonder why. So the flags remained, respectfully illuminated through the night by the klieg-like spotlights that nestled around the house: an excellent security feature, but also another way of showing off the structure, making it look more like a State Department residence than the home of a computer game designer, his three-year-old heir, and the heir's out-of-work, out-of-sorts mother. The only solace, Jeannie thought, was that the house had experienced a succession of seven active owners during the last ten years, so it was completely updated and there were almost no home improvements to be done.

"Just needs a little Restylane," Hodder Reeves, the real estate broker, had said with an airy wave of his hand the first time he'd walked them through. The house was for sale, but without a sign in front. The house had never needed any signage; the real estate agents knew when it was on the market, and brought select clients registered with their own firm who'd been pre-authorized as having sufficient buying power, and who clearly understood that only offers in the range of two million would be considered.

"A little patch-up on the plaster, here and there, to make things perfect. You're from California. You know how that stuff's done," Hodder had said, winking at Jeannie, who was lingering on the first floor while Charlie was leading their son, Ivanhoe, through the second floor's maze of interconnecting bedrooms and baths.

Charlie and Jeannie had offered that day, and six months later, as Jeannie weeded the grass underneath the ancient boxwood hedges that now belonged to her, she thought more about Hodder Reeves. He knew the house well, having managed, for the last five go-rounds, to be both the listing and selling agent for it. Six percent of a house like theirs—that appreciated between twenty or thirty percent each time it sold—was practically enough to live on, although Hodder had plenty of other listings in the charmed North Baltimore trifecta of Roland Park, Guilford, and Homeland. Having grown up on Ridgewood Road in a handsome eight-bedroom Greek revival house that backed up to the one next door to Charlie and Jeannie's, Hodder was a Roland Park boy through and through. His father had founded the region's largest party services company, which Hodder's older brother, Stuart, had taken over; Hodder had also mentioned that all the Reeves men had graduated from Gilman, which would be the perfect school for Ivanhoe.

Jeannie couldn't imagine what a school full of boys would make of a new student called Ivanhoe. Charlie had wanted his firstborn to have a unique name with a historic pedigree. He had suggested Ivanhoe right after birth, when Jeannie was still delirious from mood-altering drugs. When she came to full consciousness and saw the name Charlie had ordered inscribed on the baby's crib chart, she was upset at first, but once again her husband got what he wanted.

Jeannie had gotten over the name brouhaha, but what continued to bother her, she thought as she yanked at some stubborn clover, was that Ivanhoe was one of the heroic personalities in the educational computer game that Charlie had made his fortune designing. Although Charlie would point out that the game's success was Jeannie's doing because of how she, an English major temping at Charlie's fledgling games company, had suggested Charlie read Sir Walter Scott and Mary Shelley for ideas—after all, these were stories old enough not to be copyrighted.

The game was a language-building tool, packed with sharp swords and SAT vocabulary. The American Library Association had called Charlie a hero; and once public libraries and elementary schools started buying the program—well, Charlie could either let himself be bought out, which he thought he was too young to do, or do something creative, like take a wrecked old factory in inner-city Baltimore and remake it into a manufacturing plant for the game.

It was like Goodwood Gardens' past come to life, Jeannie mused, as she continued pulling up weeds from between the bricks. Charlie was the lord of an old factory in East Baltimore; he even went to work in a three-piece suit, wanting to seem like anything but an ordinary computer game programmer. He lunched with people like the mayor, and the lawyer who owned the Baltimore Orioles.

"You know, you could hire someone to do that—but aren't you cute doing it yourself." Hodder Reeves's private-school drawl cut through Jeannie's gardening trance.

The real estate agent was standing a few feet away from her, hands splayed on the hips of his creaseless khakis, which broke crisply on the tops of his cordovan Gucci loafers. He had no socks on, as usual, and was wearing a turquoise Lacoste shirt that made his eyes look even bluer, and the longish hair that curled around the shirt's upturned collar seem youthfully thick and blond, though Jeannie knew for a fact he was over forty and got his highlights at the same salon that she frequented.

"Hi, Hodder. Actually, one of my neighbors offered to share her gardener. It's just that I don't have that much to do anymore, now that Ivan's at St. David's Day School three mornings a week. He's going into his second week there—I can hardly believe it! He loves school." Jeannie didn't mention how it tugged at her heart that her son went so cheerfully, without a second glance back.

"Ivan. Is that a new nickname?" Hodder's voice sounded teasing.

"His teacher suggested it. Ivanhoe's a bit . . . wordy . . . for three-year-olds, don't you think?"

Reeves crouched down beside her, his breath smelling of Altoids. "I think it's charming. As are you. Let me take you to lunch."

"But why?" Jeannie blurted, feeling self-conscious about the dirt on the knees of her Levi's.

"I stopped by to see if you'd come for a quick lunch at Petit Louis. After all, it's our anniversary." At Jeannie's blank stare, he added, "We closed on your house six months ago to this day. Don't you remember, I took you and Charlie out for champagne at the bar there?"

A loud honk came from a black Lexus. Jeannie looked over and realized that Hodder had left his Porsche, with its driver's-side door hanging open, smack in the middle of the street. The more successful a man was in Baltimore, the smaller his car—and conversely, the larger his wife's. Charlie had given Jeannie a Humvee as a Christmas present, and it devoured two-thirds of their garage.

"All right, all right." Reeves gave an apologetic wave to the driver who, after all, could be his next client. "Is it okay if I pull into your driveway? Charlie coming home anytime soon?"

"No, he isn't coming home till late tonight, but I still don't think I can have lunch with you. Look at the state I'm in, and I have to pick Ivan up at 11:45—"

The driver honked again.

"Go in and change, and I'll get over to St. David's and wait with Ivanhoe for you." Hodder grinned. "Then we'll all walk to the restaurant. It's never too early for a boy to learn the fish fork from the salad."

The small, smiling maître d' at the French bistro three blocks away welcomed Ivanhoe without the slightest show of dismay, and Hodder with a great deal of enthusiasm. Immediately, they were seated at a fine table with a booster seat for Ivanhoe, who was delivered a mountain of golden-brown *pommes frites*.

"So, tell me you're happy ever after," Reeves said, after they'd clinked glasses of the Côtes du Rhône the sommelier had suggested.

"What do you mean?" Jeannie unwillingly put down the menu, which looked fabulous.

"It's a great house for a family, right? Almost everyone who's lived there had a litter of little ones."

"If it's such a good house for children, why did everyone leave? Seven families in ten years, right?"

Hodder frowned. "Oh, they all have their reasons. Some divorce, some overstretch financially . . . some change jobs. Most of them choose to sell because, well, the Roland Park market being as hot as it is . . ." he paused. "The house is worth ten percent more now than it was when you bought it in April. If you sold next spring—twenty-five percent more."

Jeannie picked up the menu again, because the last thing

she wanted to contemplate was the hassle of moving house with a toddler. It was time to change the subject. "I wonder if I should bother with this three-course menu. It seems like a lot—"

"You have the kind of body where three courses is not a crime, and the cost should not be a factor, Jeannie," Hodder purred. "If you want something light, go for the grilled salmon on greens. But don't miss the chocolate roulade. You know what they say about chocolate!"

"Ivan will like the chocolate if I can't finish it." Jeannie blushed again, as Hodder was wont to make her do. Chocolate was a substitute for love, or, specifically, sex. Charlie was still interested, but Jeannie found herself so tired after a long day with Ivan that she'd rather have a cup of cocoa than anything.

They put their orders in, and more wine came. Ivan seemed to be growing smaller and quieter, and Hodder larger and louder, as the hour went on. He talked about how it was easy to make inroads in Baltimore society because all native Baltimoreans had inferiority complexes when it came to California and New York—and how he'd come back, after his years at Washington & Lee, and a brief stint on Wall Street, because he wanted to be with real people. He told her about his other clients, one a baseball player who had just signed with the Orioles, whose wife might be a nice friend for Jeannie. The baseball couple had driven down Goodwood Gardens during their tour of Roland Park and would have bought in a flash, except nothing was on the market. So now Hodder was shepherding them through Ruxton, though that was technically out of the city, less convenient . . .

"Are those houses old, too?" Jeannie asked. She'd heard

of Ruxton because, for some reason, a lot of the teachers at Ivan's school lived there.

"Yes. Nineteen-twenties, mostly. Yours is a good ten years older than that." He smiled. "If the walls in your house could talk, I wonder what they'd say."

Was Hodder talking about the past or the present? Jeannie wondered, as she picked at her salad, which had seemed delicious at first but had become suddenly acidic. She felt chilly, too, as if the scoop-necked cashmere sweater and tweed pants she'd changed into weren't warm enough, even on a sixty-degree day. Well, the sweater had a low neck. Possibly too low a neck, from the way both the waiter and Hodder seemed to be smiling at something below the dia-mond-tipped choker she was wearing. Blame it on the Wonderbras Charlie insisted she wear.

"I wonder what the walls in Ivan's room would say." Hodder changed his voice to a sly, light chirp. "*Welcome, lit-tle big man! We'd like to teach you how to bowl!*"

Jeannie put down her fork, because the truth was, she'd sometimes thought she heard a rolling sound when she was in the kitchen. "Why did you mention bowling?"

"Didn't I ever tell you? That series of rooms in the base-ment—the au pair suite, if you ever get one—used to be a bowling alley. The first family had it installed for their entertainment."

"You mean underneath the kitchen?"

Hodder cocked his head to one side, as if he was tracing the house's floor plan in his mind. "Yes. Right underneath."

Jeannie nodded and went back to eating. "Interesting."

"Will you put it back to its original use?" Hodder's eyes gleamed. "You might be able to get a tax credit for that, through the Maryland Historic Trust."

"No, the last thing I need in my life is a bowling alley." Jeannie laughed weakly. The whole thing seemed preposterous, given that she'd grown up in a working class town where the bowling alley was where you went on dates as a teenager. To think that the people in Goodwood Gardens bowled in private—it made her mind spin.

"Hmm. It seems that you do have the energy to go after minute weeds that nobody would ever notice under all that old boxwood."

"Come on, little weeds grow into trees! How do you think the boxwood got that big?" Jeannie felt suddenly defensive.

"Is everything okay?" Hodder's voice softened. "I recall how, when you were looking at the house with Charlie, he was a little more gung ho than you were. But I honestly thought you *loved* the house. I would never have agreed to sell it to you if I thought anything different."

Emboldened by the champagne, Jeannie sputtered, "Come on, do you mean to make me believe that you would turn down two million in cash because you thought one of the partners wasn't quite there?"

"Touché! I didn't know you had such fire in you." Hodder sighed. "You're right. Who am I to say I didn't want to make the deal? But now you're making me feel like a bastard."

"I know it's a great house." Jeannie looked at Ivan, who was pulling at the tablecloth as if he was having as bad a time as his mother. "Still, my gut says that it's just a bit too . . . over-the-top. For me, anyway."

"Just like you, my dear, are over-the-top," Hodder said, taking an undisguised, lingering glance at Jeannie's bosom before sliding his hand over hers. "But in the words of the Romantics song—that's what I like about you."

* * *

Was this how he did it? Jeannie wondered wretchedly, hours later, as she rinsed the dinner dishes while Charlie tucked Ivanhoe into bed in the nursery on the floor above. Was this why all those people moved out within a year or two of buying—because Hodder preyed on the sexual insecurity of the wives and made them want to leave their husbands? Jeannie didn't want to leave Charlie. Her husband was devoted to Ivanhoe, an excellent provider, a considerate lover—so what if he never read books? He knew lots of SAT words, a definite sign of intelligence. And though Hodder was certainly handsome, Jeannie believed from his manner and dress that he was gay, or at the very least bisexual, and what girl wanted to deal with that in this day and age?

What had really given Jeannie chills, she decided, hadn't been Hodder's fingers lightly stroking the back of her hand before she'd belatedly pulled it away. It was what he'd said a few minutes earlier about the bowling alley. She'd heard the rolling sound, usually late, when she'd come downstairs to put her cocoa cup in the dishwasher.

During those times, Jeannie had never opened the basement door. She'd always loathed the actresses in horror movies who heard the omens of their upcoming death, yet still went down to investigate. Jeannie wasn't going into that basement no matter how many track lights were on.

On Saturday evening, Jeannie arranged for Fernanda, her neighbor's housekeeper, to stay with Ivan, because Charlie had bought a table at a gala for the Maryland Historical Society, and he needed her there. Charlie had summoned a salesclerk from Octavia over to Goodwood Gardens with an armload of potential evening dresses, so Jeannie would have no excuse about not having the right kind of dress for an

October function in Baltimore. The perfect dress proved to be a floor-length hunter-green silk charmeuse, cut on the bias and decorated with elaborate crystal beading. It had a high halter neckline and Jeannie hadn't thought the gown was that provocative, but knew she was wrong when Hodder Reeves passed the two of them and ran his fingers down her bare back while he greeted the couple.

"What was he doing to your back?" Charlie demanded, sotto voce, after Hodder was gone.

"I didn't ask for it," Jeannie said under her breath, as they were mercifully interrupted by an elegant white-haired dowager already sitting at the table.

"What a pretty dress. I see everyone's admiring it, including that crazy Hodder Reeves. I'm Hortense Underwood, by the way."

"Charles and Jeannie Connelly," Charlie said, reaching out a hand to her and slipping back into his happy, social personality. "We're new in town, and this is our first time at the Historical Society gala. How about you?"

"Oh, I've been coming for about a million years. Can't you tell?" Hortense said dryly.

"We just moved here," Jeannie said. "Hodder is our real estate agent. That's why he stopped to say hello."

"Oh, so you moved here to buy a house! How exciting. Where is it?"

"Roland Park. On Goodwood Gardens," Charlie added.

"Not the German Embassy? I heard sometime back that a young family had bought it."

"I can't believe anyone really calls it the German Embassy, because my own private name for it is the Austrian Embassy." Jeannie smiled at the woman, who was turning out to be a rescuer.

"The house was built for a furniture tycoon whose lineage was German. In those days, houses went to children, so there were two generations there, and I knew all the Erdmanns. During the war, you can imagine how hard it was for them. They spent all their time at home; nobody would receive them."

Jeannie knew the name: Erdmann & Sons was a company famous for building reproduction furniture from 1900 through the 1960s that cost almost as much as eighteenth-century Maryland antiques. Charlie had seen a picture of an Erdmann sideboard in an auction catalog and been on the hunt for one ever since. Maybe it was fated that they were in the house. But still, Jeannie was unsettled. She said, "I heard they had a bowling alley in the basement."

"Oh yes! I grew up on Edgevale Road and I played with the daughter while we were at Roland Park School—the public primary school," she added. "I was invited to bowl at her home a few times during the '30s. I heard the alley was taken out by some of the later owners. Heaven knows what's there now."

"An au pair suite. As if there aren't enough bedrooms in the house already."

"Yes, but that goes with the territory, my dear." A wry smile cut new creases in Hortense's worn, intelligent face. "So, how is the embassy changing under your command?"

Jeannie glanced at Charlie, who, from his spot across the table, was watching her. It was a loaded issue, because he'd asked her to hire a decorator and she hadn't done so yet.

"Not much," Jeannie admitted. "I'm doing a little bit of weeding, trying to keep up appearances—"

"You do your own gardening?" Hortense Underwood raised her almost nonexistent white eyebrows.

"Yes. I'm from California, originally. I like to be outside."

"There are a lot of others in the neighborhood who garden, too. Once you meet them, you'll feel at home." Hortense smiled, as if Jeannie had been doing the right thing all along. "I'll stop by one day next week. Now's a good time of year to cut back your hydrangea. I want to show you a personal trick that I bet they don't know about in California."

Jeannie didn't know why the visit of an eighty-year-old neighbor should throw her into such a tizzy, but it did. She declined Hodder when he called, inviting her for lunch again, and she practically bit Charlie's head off when he wanted her to organize a dinner party for his friends the night after. Everything, Jeannie felt, had to be just so for Hortense. Their furniture—a motley mix of Pottery Barn, Maurice Villency, and Gaines McHale—was minimal, but at least it could be free of the litter of toys and newspapers and food. The parquet floors were to be swept, the marble ones mopped. Charlie was useless at cleaning—what millionaire would be otherwise?—so Jeannie finally broke down and begged Fernanda to come by in her off hours to give the place a quick dusting, which quickly turned into an all-out cleaning, a two-night marathon of vacuuming that drowned out the sound of bowling that Jeannie seemed to be hearing more often over the past few days.

The prospect of serving a cocktail was also an unending worry. Jeannie usually had a few bottles of wine stashed somewhere, but she sensed an eighty-year-old woman would probably take a mixed drink, or some kind of spirit straight up. She wished the walls would talk, in this case, tell her something like, *Sherry, neat!* Or, *Old-fashioned!* Jeannie could mix a margarita, but that was about all.

Charlie thought she should hire a bartender to come with his own stash, and thus be perfectly assured of making the drinks right, but Jeannie figured this would be pretentious. In the end, Jeannie ran into the liquor section at Eddie's, where a nice young man helped her spend $200 in fifteen minutes, and had someone drive it back to the house and actually unpack it in the butler's pantry. Too bad everything in Baltimore wasn't that easy. She had to drive to Hecht's in Towson to buy Waterford glasses of every shape and size, and was just unpacking them when the doorbell chimed.

Hortense was an hour early. Jeannie hadn't time to change from her shopping clothes to her gardening ones, let alone get all the sticky labels off the bottom of the glasses. The doorbell awoke Ivanhoe from his nap so he was screaming from above, and Jeannie now felt the picture was complete; she was a totally decadent, uncaring trophy wife who knew nothing about caring for children or gardens.

"Oh dear," said Hortense, immediately ascending the stairs. "May I?"

Ivanhoe was terrified when he saw Hortense peeping round the edge of the door, and had to be mollified with a sippy cup of warm soy milk. Then the three of them went outside and Hortense started snipping away, much lower than Jeannie would ever have cut.

"Are you sure I'll get them all back next year?" she asked, looking at the stumps where outstretched boughs holding faded blue blooms had been.

"It's good wood. It will survive. Just like this house." She paused. "Just like you, my dear."

"You can tell I'm out of my element, can't you?" Jeannie said, starting to collect the flowers and branches in a trash bag. She knew that a more organized woman would save the hydrangeas to dry them and then spray-paint gold for the holidays. The holidays. She found herself flinching at the thought of putting on the kind of Christmas Charlie would expect in the house.

"I don't think that's the case." Hortense looked levelly at Jeannie. "If there's a problem, you'll be the only one in this house to solve it. That's all I meant."

The problem. Over drinks—it turned out that Hortense drank whiskey, straight up—Jeannie tried to fish around and find out exactly which of her many discomforts was the problem Hortense had gleaned. But for a straight talker, she was surprisingly evasive—as curvy, in fact, as Edgevale Road.

That night, Jeannie awoke at 2 a.m. and couldn't get back to sleep. The whiskey she'd had with Hortense and Charlie, who came home early, true to his word, had thrown her sleep-wake cycle out of whack. She'd be a mess when Ivanhoe woke up at 6—although he seemed to be awake now.

As the whimpering continued, Jeannie slipped out of bed and padded down the hallway to his room. Ivanhoe was sitting bolt upright in bed, and when he saw her, his whimpers turned to an outright scream. Jeannie pressed him against her breast, and gradually the cries lessened.

"Did Ivan have a bad dream? Everything's okay now—"

"Bad boy," said Ivanhoe. "Bad, bad boy in room!"

"Nobody's here, Ivan. You just had a bad dream."

"No, Mama, he real." Ivan pointed toward the closet. "He shine like, like moon." Ivan pushed the curtain over his window aside, pointing with emphasis at the full moon outside. "He have bib on. He roll a big ball."

Jeannie felt herself shudder. She reached back and

switched on the light. No bowling balls anywhere, and all the windows were latched shut.

"Come on, Ivan, let's get you some milk." She stood up, still holding him close, and started down the stairs and the hallway, snapping lights on as she went. The alarm panel downstairs still said *ARMED*; the doors were all locked. Nobody had penetrated the embassy. She settled Ivan in his booster seat while she microwaved his cup of milk. But when the hum of the microwave finished sixty seconds later, she heard it. Rolling, then a crash. Rolling, rolling, another hit.

"What that, Mommy?" Ivan demanded. "What that sound?"

So her son had heard the rolling sound, too. It was time to get Charlie involved.

Charlie took a logical approach to the whole thing. After Jeannie had woken him, he pulled on a bathrobe and plodded downstairs, cordless telephone in hand. When they'd entered the kitchen, it was silent at first, so Jeannie was frustrated; but then the long rolling sound began again.

"Do you hear it?"

Charlie listened a minute, then said, "It sounds like something's rolling around on the lower level."

"Yes, yes! Exactly. And Hortense Underwood said it used to be a bowling alley."

"Now a nanny suite." Charlie looked thoughtful. "I can't remember what the house inspector said about the foundation being level."

"What does that matter?" The house inspector had been one Reeves had recommended; he'd said the house was perfect, of course.

"I do have my tennis things stored down there. Last time

I was getting ready, I took Ivanhoe downstairs with me and gave him a ball to play with. It's probably just rolling around."

"The basement is carpeted. And the sound is too loud to be a tennis ball."

"What else could it be?"

"Let's go downstairs and look," Jeannie said.

Charlie paused. "Well, if it makes you feel any better, I'll call the police."

That wasn't what Jeannie had expected. She thought Charlie would have gone down with the unregistered Beretta he'd received from a client in L.A., years ago, who couldn't come up with a cash payment; the gun that he kept fully loaded, but locked up in a safe in the bedroom. Jeannie thought Charlie would bear arms because so many of the superheroes in his games did; but then again, why should she expect heroics from her husband, eighteen years her senior and already with a slight predisposition for heart trouble?

Since the call for help had come from Goodwood Gardens, three squad cars arrived within two minutes. Six cops trooped downstairs. By then, of course, the sound had stopped. And they found nothing.

"You have reached Hodder Reeves's answering service. Leave a message, and I will personally return your call as soon as possible. Have a super day."

Jeannie had been calling Reeves every day for a week, but she kept getting the same recorded message; and he hadn't called her back, not once, which seemed peculiar given all the special attention he'd lavished on her so recently. Maybe he was closing a deal with other clients. Or maybe he was worried that Jeannie had figured out he'd sold her a haunted house.

Now Jeannie understood why seven people had owned

the house in ten years. Nobody could stand to keep living with the sound of German-American bowlers, night after night. Ivanhoe had dreamt about the boy in the bib again. He wanted to sleep in their room, which Charlie sternly forbade. Adding to the stress in the house, Charlie's sexual appetite had increased—something Jeannie felt sure was connected to his witnessing Hodder touch her at the gala.

Jeannie's men were exhausting her. If she wasn't servicing Charlie at night, she was spending extra hours at nursery school because Ivanhoe had started to have separation anxiety. During the afternoons, when he was home, he tucked himself into the cabinet next to the stove, hugging himself while Jeannie cooked massive starchy meals she hoped would send everyone to sleep after bed.

In the few hours she had to herself, Jeannie read: three books about the paranormal and a history of Maryland furniture makers that mentioned the decline of Erdmann & Sons due to the death of the heir apparent, Martin Erdmann, after a bout of tuberculosis. The only surviving siblings were girls; and girls, in those days, did not become furniture builders.

Jeannie thought things over during the night, when she would customarily make one trip downstairs to check for the rolling sound, which seemed to be happening sometimes, but sometimes not. After too many sleepless nights, she finally opened her copy of the *Blue Book* and discovered the phone number for Hortense Underwood, who was not listed in the regular telephone directory. When she said she needed to talk, Hortense promptly invited her to come for a visit to Edgevale Road with Ivan.

"I'll come when he's in school," Jeannie said. She was trying to help him forget what had happened in his room, not engrain it any further on his troubled mind. "I do have one favor to ask, if it isn't too much trouble. Do you still have photo albums and school yearbooks, anything with pictures of the Erdmanns? I'm interested in Martin Erdmann, in particular."

There was a long pause. "Martin was a few classes ahead of me at school, but there's a chance. I'll see what I can find for you."

Over strong cups of Eddie's Breakfast Blend served in bone-thin Limoge cups, Jeannie and Hortense examined an ancient, falling-apart literary anthology of student work. There was no yearbook per se, but mixed in with childish poetry were a few cloudy black-and-white photographs of boys and girls lined up on a step, wearing sailor suits.

"This is my class," Hortense said, pointing to a small girl with braids, who looked into the camera with a slightly accusatory gaze. "And yours truly. The girl on the far end is Agatha Erdmann."

"You said Martin was a few years older?" Jeannie stared at Agatha, as if her appearance might spark some recognition.

"Yes. I thought there might be photos of him here, but . . . he must have already died. It was very sad." Hortense shook her head.

"What did he look like? Can you remember?"

"Red hair, freckles, skinny. Oh, and I guess the thing I remember is how the Erdmanns dressed. They were always dressed like diplomatic children, even at a neighborhood public school."

"Do you mean in fancy clothes?" Jeannie pictured a Fauntleroy suit, the kind of costume Charlie had suggested Ivanhoe wear for the family portrait.

"No, I mean a sailor suit, like Agatha's wearing in the

photograph. The children always wore sailor suits, had to wear them well into their teens, much to their chagrin."

A sailor suit. What Ivan had talked about—a boy with a bib —sounded like it could have been a boy wearing a sailor suit. A chill settled over Jeannie, and she told Hortense she hadn't realized how time had flown, that it was time to get Ivanhoe from St. David's and take him home for lunch. Lunch, fol- lowed by a pre-nap story, which, for that afternoon, she chose Babar, the Elephant Emperor whose children all wore sailor suits. And as Jeannie had expected, when Ivan saw the illus- tration of Pom, Flora, and Alexander, he squealed and point- ed, "That one like boy at night-night time!"

Jeannie had no more questions.

That night, she told Charlie she'd be waiting for him in the bedroom after he put Ivanhoe to sleep. Charlie did the bed- time routine in record time—thirty-five minutes—and was halfway undressed by the time he got in the room.

"So, you must be feeling better today," he said happily, grabbing her around her hips and pressing her tightly against him. "What did you do, get some advice on how to relax from that wonderful woman of a certain age?"

"Actually, Charlie, I brought up some of the whiskey." She removed his hands from her body, then pointed to the cut-glass decanter she'd set on the table by the window. "I think we could both use a drink, because there's something serious I have to discuss."

She told him everything. About the sailor suit, the bowling sounds, the long gone household of German-American chil- dren shunned by the neighborhood. He listened carefully, and to her amazement, his first words were, "It's incredible. But believable."

"I don't believe in haunted houses," Jeannie said, surprised that there was no fight. "I never did, and I don't *want* to. But something's going on. No wonder all the young families buy and quickly leave, and Hodder Reeves keeps on reselling the house."

"You keep calling Hodder." Charlie sipped the whiskey, keeping his eyes on her.

"What do you mean?" Jeannie flushed.

"I saw the record of your outgoing cell phone calls."

"It's because—it's because I'm trying to find out about the house! I've called him repeatedly this week, but he hasn't gotten back to me. In the meantime, I've researched more about the family that owned the house." Jeannie told Charlie what she'd learned from Hortense Underwood and saw the jealousy in his eyes slowly replaced by a look she remembered from long ago—the dreaming, about-to-imagine-a-brilliant-idea look.

"It's creepy all right," Charlie said slowly. "If we tweaked the story a little, it'd make a great computer game, maybe one that involves learning the German language."

"Charlie! Is everything a game to you?" Jeannie was distracted, because she could hear Ivanhoe whimpering in his sleep.

"No, it's not," Charlie said sharply. "And don't go to him. If you keep running to Ivanhoe, he'll never sleep through the night."

"I don't know what to do." Jeannie put her face in her hands, hiding her tears.

"Do you think we should do what the others have done—just cut our losses and run?"

"Our gains," Jeannie said. "Hodder said we'll make at

least ten percent profit if we sell. But how can we sell a haunted house?"

"Others have done it," Charlie said. "And before we make any big decisions, let's see if anything else happens. The best games have their roots in reality. Let's learn the untold story of this boy in a sailor suit."

"And how do you propose we do that?"

Charlie thought a moment, then said, "Let's hold a séance. See if you can line up that neighborhood woman and Hodder Reeves. And I'll bring in our new games concept guy, Walter, to record the whole thing."

A séance! Jeannie felt she was living in The Twilight Zone. Charlie left work early the next morning, but not before telling her he expected her to bring him at least three estimates by the end of the week. Jeannie gritted her teeth and agreed. If anything, a psychic hack would buoy her case for getting out.

There weren't many psychics left in the new Baltimore, but Jeannie did find a listing in the phone book that wasn't too far away, for a Sister Natalie's House of Spirits, located on Reisterstown Road near Northern Parkway. Sister Natalie was just the psychic Charlie deserved. Sister Natalie, with her hands decked in heavy rings, her head covered in a zebra-patterned turban, and wearing a mumu, was exactly the stereotype of a woman who communicated with other worlds. And the things she asked of Jeannie—background on everything that had happened so far in the house, four hours to set up before the séance, undisturbed, and a $600 deposit to cover expenses—made Jeannie certain the whole thing was going to be an utter fraud. But that was okay. Jeannie wanted no chance of the sailor-suited boy actually materializing. Let Sister Natalie go off on her own tangent, giving Charlie the kind of glamorous ghosts he needed.

Jeannie spent a good hour with the psychic, telling her everything she could think of relating to the house and its history. Suddenly she realized it was 11:30, and she was going to have to race over to St. David's to pick up Ivan. She wrote out the deposit check and handed it to Sister Natalie.

As their hands touched, Sister Natalie drew back sharply. The check fluttered to the floor.

"I'm sorry," Jeannie said automatically, and bent to pick it up. Sister Natalie appeared frozen when Jeannie tried to give her the check again.

"Is everything okay?" Jeannie could barely hide her impatience. "I made it out to the name you told me, Natalie Black—"

"Your family is in danger," Sister Natalie said, her voice leaden.

"What?"

"Your family is in danger. We were talking about the house before, but there's something else you need to worry about—something very serious—"

Aha! Angling for a return engagement, Jeannie thought. An extra consultation—extra money. "I'm really sorry, Sister, but I am going to have *major* worries if I don't pick up my son from school on time. I'll see you this Friday, okay? Call me if you need directions."

As Jeannie's Humvee joined a stalled line of vehicles a quarter-mile prior to her turnoff from Northern to Roland Avenue, she felt her anxiety quicken. If only she could see ahead to whether or not it was an accident. Blocking her line of vision was a truck: a big white one with red lettering on the back that said, "*REEVES ENTERTAINMENT. FOL-*

LOW ME TO MARYLAND'S GREATEST PARTIES AND MAGIC SHOWS!"

Five minutes later, when she'd managed to make the right turn and proceed toward Ivan's school, she turned over the connection in her mind. Hodder had mentioned that his father's family owned a large party services company. She'd thought that the company dealt solely in tents and chairs and champagne fountains. But obviously there was something more.

There was a message blinking on the answering machine when Jeannie returned home with Ivan in tow.

"*It's Hodder,*" the voice on the recording said. "*I was in Dewey and Rehoboth for a couple of weeks getting a jump on my spring listings, but I just returned this morning. Glad you want to get together! Can we do lunch?*"

Had he heard, somehow, from Sister Natalie about the upcoming séance? As Jeannie was deliberating what to do, the phone rang. She listened to it ring, and when her answering machine picked up, she heard Hodder speak into the machine.

"Jeannie? You there?"

Jeannie picked up the phone. "I'm here."

"Hey, did you hear my message about lunch? I called both your cell and the home, but nobody picked up."

"Actually, Charlie and I want to invite you to join us at home Friday evening." She had to force herself to sound normal.

"Ooh, dinner in my favorite house on Goodwood Gardens, with my favorite clients. It just so happens I am free. Let me bring some wine—would you prefer red or white?"

"Neither. It's not exactly a dinner party, it's a kind of—

games night. There will be a couple of other people there. Could you come at 8, after Ivan's in bed?"

"I'll knock very quietly," Hodder said in a low purr. "And how did you know I love games—grown-up games, especially?"

The séance was going to be a nightmare, Jeannie thought, as she spread out the skirts of her black silk taffeta gown so they wouldn't crease while she sat reading Ivanhoe his favorite Dr. Seuss stories, even after his eyes had closed. Ivan's tiny little hand was tucked in hers, making her sweat in the room that was already too hot. Sister Natalie had insisted on raising the temperature in the house, rather than dropping it, as if to prove how genuine her psychic feats would be.

Finally, Ivan's hand relaxed in Jeannie's and she carefully disengaged herself and arranged his coverings lightly over him. He was already covered in a faint sheen of perspiration, so she cracked open the window across the room.

Ivanhoe's bedroom door was slightly ajar, and she could hear voices below. Hortense Underwood had come early, of course, and she was talking with Charlie about something, until a knock came at the door. It was Hodder, who after listening to Charlie's booming description of the evening's agenda, exclaimed loudly about what a great surprise the séance was. Jeannie suspected this was one instance where Hodder was genuinely surprised, and not up to his usual tricks.

It had been just a few hours earlier, when late afternoon sunshine had flooded Ivanhoe's room, and the two of them had been putting away his laundry in the closet, when she'd found the trick: the quarter-inch nail hole in the closet door. She'd seen something flash in it, and realized, under closer inspection, that there was a very thin lens embedded in the hole that reflected its presence clearly under the glow of a flashlight.

"Ivan," she'd asked gently, "that boy with the bib you see. Where does he stand when you see him?"

Ivanhoe pointed at a spot on the wall directly across from the closet door. "Over there."

So the show took place after dark. When the hologram, or whatever it was, would show up most frighteningly. Hodder wouldn't even need to be in the house to pull off the stunt; he could use a remote control, like people used for their cars, and like Hodder had done when he'd illustrated the features of the house's state of the art security system.

Grimly, Jeannie took care of the hole in the quickest way she could—stuffing toilet paper into it. Then she'd taken Ivan with her down to the basement, where, using an icing spatula, she pried up a dozen floorboards before finding the tape recorder. She'd removed the microcassette to play on the living room stereo. Sure enough, the sounds of a bowling alley, but with added clarity from the high-quality speaker system.

She was angry; blindingly angry. Her rage seemed uncontainable, rushing out in a great wave she wished would sweep over the person who had decided to intentionally frighten her little boy, had turned him into a child who was scared of the dark and hid in kitchen cupboards. And as Ivan's mother, it was her duty to make the amoral monster pay.

Now Ivan was asleep and Jeannie stood in the hallway, listening to the sounds of the guests below and thinking about where to go. She found herself stopping in the bedroom, opening up Charlie's safe, and tucking the Beretta into one of the deep pockets camouflaged in the side seams of her dress. Now her dress was slightly weighed down on the right, but nobody would notice, given that downstairs was dimly lit by candles. She was going to give Hodder the scare of his life, frighten him so badly that he'd ruin his Ralph Lauren khakis for good—

"Jeannie, aren't you done yet?" Charlie's voice came up from the landing.

"Sorry, darling," Jeannie said as she descended the curving stairway.

"Your dress is lovely. It reminds me of the New Look," Hortense said, fingering the black silk-satin. Jeannie thanked her for the compliment, and peeked her head into the front parlor. Sister Natalie sat before a round table draped in red silk. The psychic's deeply wrinkled face appeared solemn, illuminated by candlelight. Her troubled eyes locked with Jeannie's.

"How are you, Sister Natalie?" Jeannie asked with false cheer, looking away from the psychic's hooded stare.

"I don't like this," Sister Natalie said in a rumble that sounded like a bad storm coming in.

"You mean the table's not right, or—" Jeannie cut herself off when she heard the sound of Ivanhoe's voice. She had closed his door, but even through the wood she could hear that he was crying.

"He sounds scared," Hodder said. "Why don't you bring him down to join us?"

"No can do," Charlie said. "Little guy probably had a bad dream. He's got to learn to settle himself down again."

"Children need discipline," Hortense agreed. "Only people can't say that word anymore. What's the word that you young parents favor—limits? Come, let's limit the time that's ticking and seat ourselves in the parlor. Sister Natalie has been waiting so patiently for the spirits to come, I'm sure they're all present and ready to show us a very good time."

"Hmm. Maybe Jeannie wants to go upstairs to see what's going on." Hodder's eyes gleamed, and Jeannie knew, all of a sudden, what her agent wanted. He wanted her to be the one to see the hologram of the boy, to be spooked enough to beg Charlie to sell the house immediately.

"I think Charlie's right," Jeannie said, going against every instinct in her body. "I'll wait a couple of minutes to see if he settles down. Now, does anybody need a second drink or—"

The sound of breaking glass cut through her last words, followed by a thud.

"You bastard!" Jeannie looked straight at Hodder. He'd pulled a new trick out of his hat, just for the evening.

She looked at Charlie for support, but her husband was loping up the stairs, two at a time. The door to Ivanhoe's room banged open and then she heard Charlie cry: "My God, Ivanhoe—the window!"

Thank heaven for the battlements, everyone said later. The big, pretentious, sturdy stucco battlement which supported the Maryland flag was the spot where Ivanhoe had landed a mere eighteen inches under his bedroom window. The boy had enough cuts to require thirty stitches at GBMC, but the plastic surgeon assured them that scarring was unlikely.

Other scars were a different matter. Even though Hodder began burbling out apologies, rapidly, when faced with the long end of the Beretta, Jeannie had been on the verge of doing something unthinkable, but Hortense had managed to gently detangle her shaking fingers from the weapon. Hodder fled the house without so much as a goodbye. Hortense made Jeannie sit down and drink whiskey, and Walter, the new guy at Charlie's company, paid off the rest of Sister Natalie's fee plus a thousand in keep-quiet money. All the while, Charlie cradled his small bloody son in his arms, crying softly alongside him as they all waited for the ambulance to arrive.

Charlie wanted to have Hodder arrested on charges of attempted manslaughter, but their lawyers said the best they could do was charge him with trespassing and possibly wiretapping. It took a good year for the case to come to trial in Baltimore's beleaguered courts. Hodder ultimately received a three-month sentence that his lawyer managed to have converted into community service.

While Hodder picked up discarded soda cans along the Stony Run, Hortense Underwood used the phones to ensure his name was even muddier than the creek's bottom. The preppy real estate agent no longer had a job at the Mount Company, nor would Coldwell Banker, the Hill Company, Long and Foster, nor any of the other big firms in the city, hire him. In fact, the agent who ultimately sold 100 Goodwood Gardens that winter was Hortense's daughter-in-law, the only one who agreed to the couple's desired asking price—ten percent below what they'd paid the earlier year.

ABOUT THE CONTRIBUTORS:

RAFAEL ALVAREZ is the son of a Baltimore tugboat engineer. The author of numerous "Orlo & Leini" tales, Alvarez published a people's history of the Archdiocese of Baltimore in 2005.

JACK BLUDIS is a lifetime resident of the Baltimore area who lived his early years in Pigtown. He was a finalist for both the Shamus and Anthony Awards for Best Short Story in 2004, His novel *Shadow of the Dahlia* was a Shamus Award finalist in 2005.

Kathryn Gudger Bludis

TIM COCKEY spent his wonder years in Baltimore, living in the Cockeysville, Garrison Forest, and Roland Park neighborhoods. He has published five novels featuring Fell's Point undertaker Hitchcock Sewell—the infamous "Hearse" books. He now lives in New York City.

Laurent Cosset

DAN FESPERMAN has lived in Baltimore for more than twenty years, with detours to Berlin and other points abroad as a foreign correspondent for the *Baltimore Sun*. He is the author of *The Warlord's Son* and three other novels, two of which have won Dagger Awards from the British Crime Writers Association.

Liz Bowie

LISA RESPERS FRANCE is a native "Baltimoron" who owes her love of the written word to her parents, Gary and Patricia, for tirelessly shuttling her back and forth to the Enoch Pratt and Baltimore County public libraries during her early years. A former reporter at the *Los Angeles Times* and the *Baltimore Sun,* she is currently a writer and editor in New York City and can often be found hauling a cooler filled with Maryland crab meat up Interstate 95.

Stephen Bryant

Andrei Jackamets

JIM FUSILLI is the author of the award-winning Terry Orr series, which includes *Hard, Hard City*, winner of the Gumshoe Award for Best Novel of 2004, as well as *Closing Time, A Well-Known Secret,* and *Tribeca Blues.* He also writes for the *Wall Street Journal* and is a contributor to National Public Radio's *All Things Considered.*

Jerry Jackson

ROB HIAASEN is a native Floridian who moved to Baltimore in 1993 to become a staff writer for the *Sun.* When hungry for stories or mussel chowder, Hiaasen drifts into Fell's Point, which may or may not have an apostrophe.

Jim Burger

LAURA LIPPMAN has lived in Baltimore most of her life and she would have spent even more time here if the editors of the *Sun* had agreed to hire her earlier. She attended public schools and has lived in several of the city's distinctive neighborhoods, including Dickeyville, Tuscany-Canterbury, Evergreen, and South Federal Hill. She is the author of ten books, including the Baltimore-centric Tess Monaghan novels.

Jim Burger

SUJATA MASSEY graduated from Johns Hopkins University and worked as a reporter at the late but great *Baltimore Evening Sun* before turning to a life of crime fiction. She is the author of nine novels, most recently *The Typhoon Lover.* She enjoys living in Roland Park, though she has pledged never to take up gardening or drive a Humvee.

Frank Ockenfels

BEN NEIHART lived in the "landmark" Marylander apartment building in the Charles Village neighborhood of Baltimore for three years during the mid-1990s. He is the author of the books *Hey Joe, Burning Girl,* and *Rough Amusements,* and his work has appeared in the *New York Times Magazine,* the *New Yorker, Travel & Leisure,* and the *Baltimore Sun.* He currently lives in New York.

Douglas Sonders

DAVID SIMON is a former crime reporter with the *Baltimore Sun*, and the author of *Homicide* and *The Corner*, two works of narrative nonfiction. He is also a writer and executive producer of HBO's *The Wire*.

Denise Kordalski

CHARLIE STELLA played Strat-O-Matic baseball as a kid, until his father put him on a twelve-step program to rein in his addiction. In Stella's world (Strat-O-Matic), the Orioles beat his Mets in seven back in '69 (when he was thirteen).

Ron Belanger

MARCIA TALLEY is the Agatha and Anthony Award–winning author of six novels featuring amateur sleuth Hannah Ives, set in Annapolis, Baltimore, and other locales around Maryland's scenic Chesapeake Bay. She is author/editor of two star-studded collaborative serial novels, *Naked Came the Phoenix* and *I'd Kill For That*, and her short stories have appeared in more than a dozen collections.

Sharon AvRutick

JOSEPH WALLACE has written more than fifteen books and dozens of articles on topics as diverse as baseball, natural history, medicine, and the invention of the light bulb. "Liminal" is his first piece of published noir. He's grateful to Laura Lippman for requesting it, especially since he's a lifelong New York Mets fan with vivid memories of the 1969 World Series.

ROBERT WARD was born and raised in Baltimore and now lives in Los Angeles, where he writes fiction, screenplays, and television dramas. He is the author of six novels, including *Red Baker*, winner of the Pen West Award for Best Novel. "Fat Chance" is about the pull of Charm City, with its neighborhoods and personal history, versus "success" in Los Angeles.

Mary Reagan

SARAH WEINMAN is the crime-fiction columnist for the *Baltimore Sun* and the proprietor of the literary blog "Confessions of an Idiosyncratic Mind" (at www.sarahweinman.com). Her stories have appeared in several print and online publications, including *Dublin Noir*. She lives in Manhattan, only a Metroliner away from Baltimore.

Also available from the Akashic Books Noir Series

D.C. NOIR
edited by George Pelecanos
304 pages, a trade paperback original, $14.95

Brand new stories by: George Pelecanos, Laura Lippman, James Grady, Kenji Jasper, Jim Beane, Ruben Castaneda, Robert Wisdom, James Patton, Norman Kelley, Jennifer Howard, Jim Fusilli, Richard Currey, Lester Irby, Quintin Peterson, Robert Andrews, and David Slater.

GEORGE PELECANOS is a screenwriter, independent-film producer, award-winning journalist, and the author of the bestselling series of Derek Strange novels set in and around Washington, D.C., where he lives with his wife and children.

BROOKLYN NOIR
edited by Tim McLoughlin
350 pages, a trade paperback original, $15.95
*Winner of SHAMUS AWARD, ANTHONY AWARD, ROBERT L. FISH MEMORIAL AWARD; Finalist for EDGAR AWARD, PUSHCART PRIZE

Twenty brand new crime stories from New York's punchiest borough. Contributors include: Pete Hamill, Arthur Nersesian, Maggie Estep, Nelson George, Neal Pollack, Sidney Offit, Ken Bruen, and others.

"*Brooklyn Noir* is such a stunningly perfect combination that you can't believe you haven't read an anthology like this before. But trust me—you haven't. Story after story is a revelation, filled with the requisite sense of place, but also the perfect twists that crime stories demand. The writing is flat-out superb, filled with lines that will sing in your head for a long time to come."
—Laura Lippman, winner of the Edgar, Agatha, and Shamus awards

DUBLIN NOIR: *The Celtic Tiger vs. The Ugly American*
edited by Ken Bruen
228 pages, trade paperback, $14.95

Brand new stories by: Ken Bruen, Eoin Colfer, Jason Starr, Laura Lippman, Olen Steinhauer, Peter Spiegelman, Kevin Wignall, Jim Fusilli, John Rickards, Patrick J. Lambe, Charlie Stella, Ray Banks, James O. Born, Sarah Weinman, Pat Mullan, Reed Farrel Coleman, Gary Phillips, Duane Swierczynski, and Craig McDonald.